T0146454

Fraser Springs

The Infamous Miss Ilsa

LAINE FERNDALE

Crimson Romance
New York London Toronto Sydney New Delhi

CRIMSON
ROMANCE
Crimson Romance
An Imprint of Simon & Schuster, Inc.
1230 Avenue of the Americas
New York, NY 10020

First Crimson Romance ebook edition NOVEMBER 2017.

CRIMSON ROMANCE and colophon are trademarks of Simon and Schuster.

For information about special discounts for bulk purchases, please contact Simon & Schuster Special Sales at 1-866-506-1949 or business@simonandschuster.com.

The Simon & Schuster Speakers Bureau can bring authors to your live event. For more information or to book an event contact the Simon & Schuster Speakers Bureau at 1-866-248-3049 or visit our website at www.simonspeakers.com.

ISBN 978-1-5072-0808-3
ISBN 978-1-5072-0613-3 (ebook)

Praise for Laine Ferndale

The Scandalous Mrs. Wilson

"Ferndale's debut introduces a character that has faced challenges and learned to overcome. Readers will want to continue reading more by this author and about Fraser Springs. A quick, light read that historical romance fans will enjoy."
—Library Journal

"The author gives us a strong woman in Jo ... [and] a fast-paced story with characters that show their true colors. Jo was a character that didn't throw up her hands and say, woe is me ... She stood her ground and fought for what she felt was right. You had to love her, strong, brave, stubborn, beautiful, and if there was a scandalous nature to her, then all the better."
—Night Owl Reviews

Prologue

Vancouver, British Columbia

November 1906

As she stepped into her employer's parlour, Ilsa Pedersen wished that a wildfire would destroy the entire West End, this awful house, and every last person in it. Or maybe an earthquake: that would be even better. Something to shake the petit point and paintings and gilded clocks off the walls, and rattle that expression off Mrs. Whitacre's smug face.

All three members of the Whitacre family were waiting for her arrival. Theodore Whitacre sat to one side of the room, looking as if he wished he could disappear into the depths of the wingback chair. His thin, pale face was frozen in a vacant mask; his green eyes were fixed on a point somewhere to the far left of Ilsa's shoulder. He'd clearly moved beyond mortification and into a sort of stunned mental absence.

The two adult Whitacres in the room were more engaged. Mr. Whitacre, grey and bent, had propped himself up against the heavy oak mantelpiece, where he fumed a steady billow of pipe smoke in the direction of the chimney. He seemed to be more bored than angry. He was probably simply annoyed to have been pried out of his study over a domestic squabble. Mrs. Whitacre, however, positively vibrated: the sea of ruffles and furbelows and lace on her elaborate day gown rustled like a tree in a high wind.

Mrs. Whitacre had been a famous beauty in her day and devoted a great deal of time and money to rejecting the inevitability of becoming "a woman of a certain age." Ilsa, as the household's only housemaid, had spent hours tending the ranked army of powders, potions, paints, and perfumes crowding Mrs. Whitacre's marble-topped vanity. Her chestnut hair was kept meticulously dyed, styled, and piled high atop her head, and her stoutening figure was corseted so dramatically that her posture resembled that of a belligerent pigeon.

In the previous households where Ilsa had been employed, it had been the men of the house she'd had to watch out for. Here, though, Mr. Whitacre had treated her like a ghost who conveniently appeared with supper dishes or tea at the appointed hours, and Theo had been ... She risked a quick glance at Theo, who continued to ignore her. There was no point thinking about what Theo had been to her. No, in this house, it had been *Mrs.* Whitacre who had done her best to make Ilsa's life miserable. And now there she sat, perched on the edge of a settee, her eyes bright with malice.

Mr. Whitacre continued puffing away for another excruciating minute, until his wife cleared her throat in his direction. The entire room waited as he exhaled a final stream of white smoke before knocking his pipe out into the hearth and placing it carefully atop the mantel. Mr. Whitacre never rushed. Ilsa wished to God he would, just this once, and get this over with.

"So. This is the girl?" The question was addressed to Theo, who had found something of deep interest in his lap blanket's pattern. He managed a quick nod.

"Speak up, boy. You're a cripple, not a mute."

Ilsa's fists clenched at the barked command, but Theo didn't even flinch.

"Yes, sir."

"She's a pretty little thing, I'll give you that. How old are you, girl?"

"Sixteen, sir."

"Hmph. Well. You can't go chasing after the help, boy. Vulgar, you know. Lowering."

"Teddy wasn't 'chasing after' anything," Mrs. Whitacre purred. "He's a good boy, Papa, you know that." Mrs. Whitacre's affectedly girlish habit of calling her husband "Papa" had always made Ilsa's skin crawl. "That little piece of street trash practically forced herself on him. Tell him, Teddy."

Ilsa's fingernails were digging red crescents into her palms now. She risked another glance at Theo—surely now he'd speak up for her, explain how things were between them. His parents were making everything sound so ugly.

He met her eyes this time. Their gaze held for a heartbeat, and then ... his slid away. She could almost feel the little threads that had grown between them snapping, one by one, like a spider web in a storm. He remained silent.

Mr. Whitacre made a disgusted snort. "For God's sake, Olivia. You can't expect the boy to admit he hasn't got the gumption to get up a skirt without being pushed under it." Theo did flinch at that, just a little. "Enough melodrama. This is what comes of your soft heart, dear. When you employ a charity case, you get what you pay for. The whole situation was practically courting disaster. Pack your things, girl, and see yourself out."

Mrs. Whitacre preened. Theo remained silent. Over the past few months, Ilsa had heard Theo talk about so many things: the history of complex words, the purpose of the tiny bones in the human ear, how when he turned eighteen and left this place, they were going to ... He opened his mouth as if to speak, but closed it once more and looked downwards. Ilsa's heart clenched. That's how it was going to be, then. She'd have to look out for herself.

"And my wages? I'm still owed from last month, and ..."

Mrs. Whitacre laughed, a short little chirping noise with no humour in it at all. "Your wages? You should have thought about that before you wormed your way into my son's bedroom."

And that was all it took for years of training—keep quiet, be a good girl, be grateful, remember your place—to disappear in a single, enraged instant.

"Mrs. Whitacre, you are a nasty, heartless *bitch*." She tore the stupid little frilly cap from her pale curls and hurled it on the floor.

The resulting chaos resembled something out of the pantomime comedies she loved to watch at the vaudeville on Sundays. Mrs. Whitacre declared she had never *in her life* been spoken to in such a way, and sailed towards Ilsa with bloody murder in her eyes. Mr. Whitacre attempted to bellow at her but almost immediately began coughing, which distracted Mrs. Whitacre long enough for Ilsa to scurry out of the parlour and down the service stairs to her little closet of a room.

She stripped off the rest of the ridiculously old-fashioned work costume, changed into her one good dress, and crammed the uniform into her carpetbag. The wretched things had come out of her pay, after all, and maybe she could pawn them. Her only possession that held any real value was a small tin horse that had once belonged to the cavalry of a toy soldiers set. Even though her instinct was to snap its head off and leave the broken pieces on Theo's bed, she could probably pawn it, too.

When she emerged into the kitchen, Cook was nowhere to be found. At least one thing was going her way today; there wasn't exactly any love lost between herself and the flint-souled old lady who kept the Whitacres fed. Ilsa pushed two loaves of bread and a half-dozen apples into her bag and popped open the enamelled tin canister where she knew Cook kept the petty cash for deliveries. She counted out six dollars and fifty cents, exactly what she was owed and not a penny more.

And so she found herself in the barren alley behind the Whitacre house, with snow beginning to fall, no hat on her head, and nowhere to go. She couldn't go back to the girls' home; the matron there had been very clear that this placement was Ilsa's final chance. The home considered its obligations to her ended. Her only friends—acquaintances, really—were other orphans and domestic servants. She'd have to find more work, and soon.

Squaring her shoulders, she settled her grip on her bag and set off down the alleyway in a direction that hopefully would cross a trolley line sooner or later. She could do this. Even if she had to burn that itchy wool uniform for warmth and sleep under the Granville Bridge, she would be okay. At least she would be clear of that wretched house and its wretched inhabitants.

Even Theo.

Especially Theo.

Chapter 1

October 1912

It was dusk when Theodore Whitacre arrived in Fraser Springs, and even the brilliant sunset couldn't hide that the town was exactly as dull as he expected. From the deck of the SS *Minto*, he could see a few brick structures and cramped wooden houses crammed tight against the placid lake. Past the huddle of buildings, there was nothing but wilderness as far as the eye could see: dark shadows of trees and rocky bluffs for miles and miles.

A dozen or so electrified streetlamps flickered to life at the edge of the dock and down along the boardwalk. Within an hour of his setting foot in the town, someone would brag to him about the modern streetlamps. He guaranteed it.

Somewhere, his colleague, Marcus Simpson, was experimenting with the latest silver nitrate cures for gangrene. James Doolan, his study partner, had taken a post with the provincial government and would be working to improve sanitation efforts in shantytowns. Theo would be treating babies with runny noses and prescribing sugar pills to old ladies with hypochondria. Maybe, if he were very lucky, he'd get to bandage up a hunter who'd shot off a finger.

Theo suppressed the urge to run through the whole miserable story again—his mother's tantrum when he'd mentioned Paris, the posting he should have had, the endless fights, his final worn-out submission—to see if there had been any way out of this farce of an "apprenticeship." Dwelling on it didn't do him any

9

good. He was here for the foreseeable future, and he might as well resign himself to it. The boat's horn sounded three times to signal its arrival. The ship's porter came by to make arrangements to transport Theo's baggage to the St. Alice Hotel, where he would be living and working.

"You okay to carry that bag, sir?" the porter asked.

"Of course," Theo said, gripping the black leather satchel like a lifeline. Any self-respecting doctor should at least carry his own kit.

The dock was fairly empty, only a few men shifting crates about according to some unknowable logic of their own. He was the only passenger disembarking at Fraser Springs.

He recognized Dr. Edward Greyson immediately, even though he had aged since Theo had last seen him. Same round and cheerful face, same vest straining to contain his large belly, but now he wore little round spectacles, and his hair seemed have migrated down entirely to his muttonchops. Only a few wispy strands remained on his head.

"Teddy, my lad!" Dr. Greyson called, waving his hat.

"Hello!" Theo awkwardly gripped his cane and bag together in one hand and the guardrail in the other as he made his way down the gangplank. Dr. Greyson watched intently. The journey had stiffened Theo's weakened leg, exaggerating his limp. Damn.

The two men shook hands on the dock. Dr. Greyson continued evaluating him, lips pursed.

"Well, well, Little Teddy, that limp of yours is almost dignified. You look like you've been through the wars." He chortled to himself.

Theo nodded. "You look well." Lord, he hoped Greyson would remember to call him Dr. Whitacre in front of patients. This Little Teddy business certainly wasn't professional.

"It's the hot springs that do me good, son." He swung his arm in a wide circle, gesturing vaguely to their surroundings. "Might take care of that limp. You never know."

Actually, modern medicine did know. A little hot water might soothe some aches, but there was no such thing as a healing spring. The old man probably believed in balancing humours and bloodletting, too.

Dr. Greyson should have retired before the turn of the century, but instead he'd set up in Fraser Springs, practicing medicine as more of a hobby than a profession. He'd been the Whitacre family physician during the terrible year of Theo's battle with infantile paralysis, and his mother remained convinced that the good doctor's brilliance was the sole reason her son remained in the world.

"You will be doing Dr. Greyson such a service," his mother had assured him. "He's getting on in years, you know. And he's so pleased to take you under his wing now that all that boring schoolwork is done. Really, it's the least you could do after everything he's done for us."

Theo had bitten his tongue to keep from pointing out that if it were up to Dr. Greyson, he would still be stuck in bed, unable to walk. Or that Dr. Greyson would hardly be much of a mentor. Based on the letters and editorials Greyson had submitted to the professional journals, his views and practices were at least forty years out of date. Theo wanted a career as a clinician, not as a minder for a doddering old man.

He sighed. Perhaps he was being unfair. There was something to be said for doing a bit of journeyman work as part of one's medical training, and more than one of his professors had remarked on his lack of bedside manner. It might well be better to practice here than under the watchful eyes of British Columbia's finest medical men.

He was grasping for silver linings, and he knew it.

"I look forward to getting to work," Theo said. "Perhaps we could meet tomorrow to speak about the caseload?"

Dr. Greyson waved his hand dismissively. "Tomorrow's Friday, and I don't fancy working so close to the weekend. Anyhow, we've got to get you settled. Lovely hotel, the St. Alice. I think you'll find that Fraser Springs is not the backwater you might think it is. Why, we've got these electrical lamps! A lovely modern touch, don't you think?"

Theo stifled a sigh. "I'm sure I'll be very happy here."

"Of course you will. You won't have to expose yourself to tuberculosis and cholera and all those foul urban diseases, for one thing. Say what you will about some of the locals' manners, but they're a hardy bunch. And quite friendly, quite welcoming. Speaking of which, there's a reception tonight. In your honour."

"A reception. That's …"

"It'll give you a chance to meet the best and brightest of the town, shake a few hands and whatnot."

"I thought I would be treating only the hotel guests, not the entire town."

Dr. Greyson smirked. "Fraser Springs doesn't get graced with the presence of a Whitacre every day. And curiosity is a force of nature in a small town, you know. Some people will grab at any excuse to meet a new face." He sighed as if he was giving Theo only a small part of a very long story.

So that was it: his last name and social position had followed him even here. "I see."

"Anyhow, it's all in good fun. Clean yourself up a bit, make small talk. Make a good impression right away, and they'll forget all about that limp of yours. Speaking of which, can I carry your bag for you?"

The idea of this stooped old man acting as his porter was too much. "No, thank you. I'm quite capable."

Dr. Greyson looked sceptical of that but simply nodded. "Of course, dear boy. Of course. Well, I'll show you to your room. You'll want to tidy up before your big debut."

No one else seemed to notice him as he and Dr. Greyson walked along the boardwalk, the tip of his cane clacking along the planks. Thank goodness for that. His kit was knocking against his weak leg, throwing him off his balance. It took all his willpower to maintain his stride until he reached the hotel.

The St. Alice Hotel was a tall brick building with plaster columns flanking its front porch. Although it was small by Vancouver standards, the hotel looked stately and imposing compared to the more modest structures around it. He entered into a high-ceilinged lobby whose pink marble floor was inlaid with a compass-rose mosaic, as if Fraser Springs were the centre of the universe, not a far-flung outpost.

A short time later, he stood in front of the mirror in his small suite, adding the finishing touches to his evening dress. It wasn't a bad effort, he had to say. Theo knew he could cut an impressive figure at first glance. He was careful to keep his hair perfectly trimmed, his collar and cuffs well starched, and his suits beautifully tailored. A man had to work with what he had.

Already, he could hear music coming from the ballroom below, where the reception was to be held. He hated these to-dos, but it was nice that the town was making an effort to welcome him. And you never knew. Maybe the woman from the photograph would be here. Fraser Springs had been in the papers a few years back after an act of arson, and Theo had been strangely drawn to the newspaper article's grainy image of a young woman posing near the ruins of some building or other. She looked so very much like … Well, dredging up the past didn't do anyone any good, but it hadn't stopped Theo from cutting out the photo and keeping it.

He picked up his cane. It was, honestly, too ornate for good taste. The handle was a golden eagle's head—which meant that Theo had to curve his grip uncomfortably around its pointy, hooked beak—and the shaft was inlaid with mother of pearl, ebony, and rosewood, ending in an embossed golden ferrule. He knew it was gaudy, but that meant he could pass the thing off as an affectation rather than a necessity.

The runner on the grand staircase that led to the lobby was made of slippery red plush carpet, and he gripped the bannister tightly to keep his footing secure. Falling on his face in front of all these people probably wasn't the kind of first impression Dr. Greyson was expecting of him.

The ballroom was filled with a surprisingly large crowd of people in their Sunday best. A banner proclaiming "WELCOME DOCTOR" hung across the far end of the space. As one, they all began clapping, and a five-piece brass band broke into a rendition of "For He's a Jolly Good Fellow" played with more enthusiasm than skill.

Being the centre of attention made his heart pound and his palms sweat. He'd loathed his birthday as a child, because it'd meant awkward stares and lectures from his mother if he failed to make the correct facial expression when receiving a gift. But everyone here obviously meant well, and it wouldn't do to seem anything less than gracious and professional. "Hello?" he said over the sound of the tuba, waving with his free hand and trying to smile warmly.

One middle-aged woman in an enormous, extravagantly plumed hat separated herself from the general mass and began to sail towards him. Theo's smile faltered as he realized that she was clutching small notecards in her gloved hands. Oh good God, would he be expected to give a speech? The only thing worse than being the centre of attention was being the subject of introductory remarks.

He stepped forwards without devoting his full attention to the movement of his legs or the precise placement of his feet. His gait hitched and he lurched sharply. It took him two more steps to recover his stride, and by then the damage had been done. The music stopped. The enormous room with its tray ceilings and inlaid mosaic floor fell silent. The woman in the ridiculous hat was staring at him.

He knew that stare. It started at his cane, then it moved to his leg, and before it reached his face, the starer's mind was made up. That was the maddening thing about his condition. When people looked at him, they didn't see that he'd graduated at the top of his class at Victoria College. They didn't see that he could stitch a wound in a way that would leave no scarring, that he could recite Tennyson from memory. No, the only first impression anyone ever seemed to have of him was that he was a cripple. Well dressed and expensively educated, yes, but a cripple all the same.

In the excruciating silence, a few people had begun whispering behind their fans and cups of punch.

The Hat Woman had managed to snap her eyes back to his face, but her own round face was now very red. Theo extended his hand, but instead, she placed her arm gingerly on his shoulder, as one would do with the very young or the very old.

"You must be Dr. Whitacre!" She mispronounced the name— "White-ay-kur," rather than "Wit-ucker"—but he nodded without correcting her. "Welcome, welcome, welcome!" Her voice was high-pitched and cloyingly sweet. "I am Mrs. Robert McSheen, madame president of The Society for the Advancement of Moral Temperance, chairwoman of the Women's Charitable Brigade and Civic Life Contingent and head of the Convalescence and Spiritual Uplift Brigade. We are just so delighted to have you in our town!"

"Thank you, ma'am," Theo said. "It is a pleasure to be here."

Her smile had a bit of a panicked glitter to it. "Yes! Well. That is ... yes! It's so very good to have you here, of course. We had planned a small ... gathering ... to allow you to meet the town. No dancing, of course!" She tilted her head at his cane, and her hat magnified the motion so that her subtlety was painfully clear to everyone in the room.

At this, a disappointed murmur went through the crowd, and the band traded uneasy glances before loudly shuffling through the sheet music on their stands. Everyone was dressed for a dance, Theo realized. He was the only one in formal evening wear —even Dr. Greyson had on a short coat and practical-looking shoes. He had only arrived two hours ago, and Theo was already ruining their fun.

"That's entirely unnecessary, I assure you," he said in an undertone, hoping to keep any further embarrassment to a minimum. "There's no reason not to continue with your dance." He tapped his cane on the ground, a nervous habit that was especially ill-timed just now. "I do enjoy listening to popular music." Popular music? He sounded like an old man. Pathetic.

"Oh, but we hadn't planned a dance at all! Just a quiet social reception," Mrs. Robert McSheen replied, her voice still overloud for the hushed room. "These gentlemen here," she motioned to the uncomfortable looking band, "were just leaving, and then we'll have cake and punch—non-alcoholic, of course—and then wrap up before too long, because you must be terribly tired from your journey."

"I feel quite well, ma'am. And I look forward to meeting everyone."

It was no good. Within fifteen minutes, the band had been shuffled off and the citizens of Fraser Springs were standing in clusters around the edges of the room, whispering. Theo made polite conversation with Mrs. McSheen, although her idea of conversation was mostly a loud monologue that spanned topics as diverse as her secret for a moist coffee cake (applesauce) to the rash that plagued her younger daughter (eczema) to the streetlamps (so modern) and her thoughts on the future glories of Fraser Springs. She uttered the phrase "our beloved Fraser Springs" so often that the town began to seem like a Catholic saint: Our Lady of Perpetual Dullness.

Theo suggested she might introduce him to some of the people in the room, so Mrs. McSheen led him on a whirlwind tour of a collection of the Finest People in Our Beloved Fraser Springs. He couldn't remember any of their names, but they all had one thing in common: a smile that did not extend to their eyes. It was the expression one would address to an outsider and ruiner of dances. They all tried to assure him they had a brother or great uncle or aunt once removed who had been crippled, and they knew exactly how Theo felt.

He could say with complete certainty that they had no idea how he felt.

Still, he shook hands. He tried his best with small talk. He sipped the punch and praised its flavour, though the sugar left a film on the roof of his mouth. Within half an hour, the gathering had mostly petered out, and one side of the banner had slumped onto the floor. Empty of people, the ballroom looked cavernous, dwarfing the attendees who remained.

It wasn't long before even the Finest People in Our Beloved Fraser Springs melted away, and Mrs. McSheen declared that the reception had been a great success and it was time for Theo to get some much-needed rest. He said his good-nights.

Upstairs, he undressed and performed a series of stretches, followed by strengthening exercises. Someone had left a complimentary bottle of Restorative Vitality Water, which, according to its label, was brewed from the hot springs water and promised to "restore Good Health and Youth" and cure everything from skin conditions to extreme nervousness. Theo uncapped the bottle and took a drink, then spat it out all over a silk potted fern. It tasted like the devil's bathwater. He looked around for something to rid the taste from his mouth.

Finding nothing, he walked over to the window, which brought in more foul-smelling air. It was dark now, and the streetlamps could only manage small pools of light. Despite the mugginess, he closed the window and lay down on the bed. Fraser Springs was shaping up to be a disaster: not just boring, but actively unpleasant. How would anyone trust him to treat them if he couldn't even manage a welcome dance?

Well, at least he hadn't had to give a speech. Thank God for small blessings.

• • •

Ilsa arrived home to Wilson's Bathhouse just before nine o'clock. She took her time opening the creaky porch door. Sometimes the hinges made a shrieking, grinding noise that set her teeth on edge, and she didn't want to wake anyone.

She managed to ease the door open and shut without a peep, but when she made her way into the dimly lit kitchen, she discovered that she needn't have bothered keeping so quiet. Josephine Sterling was still up and about in the kitchen, crushing sharp-smelling herbs into huge bowls of oil for the next week's massages.

"You're home early," her employer—and best friend—noted. "Did something happen?" Jo may have gotten married two years ago and now was expecting her first child, but she hadn't slowed down in the slightest.

Ilsa sighed and began unlacing her dancing shoes. Her dancing shoes were, in fact, also her church shoes; she only owned two pairs. But tonight they should have been her dancing shoes. "The whole thing was cancelled."

Jo stepped back from the scarred wooden table and collapsed into a kitchen chair next to where Ilsa wobbled on one foot, tugging angrily at her laces. "Cancelled? Mrs. McSheen's been planning that reception for weeks."

Ilsa chucked a shoe across the kitchen. Jo's eyebrows rose at this petulant display, but damn it felt good to throw something. "Apparently the new doctor disapproves of dancing."

"Why? Is he religious?"

"It doesn't matter. He complained as soon as he stepped into the room, and Mrs. McSheen cancelled everything. We just stood around drinking watered down punch." She lobbed her other shoe to join its mate next to the potato bin. Stupid punch. Stupid shoes. Stupid potato bins and stupid doctors with their stupid opinions on stupid dances.

"It's not fair. Those high-society women finally relaxed enough to let us have a little respectable fun in the St. Alice, and now they're going to be ten times as bad. I definitely heard Mrs. McSheen saying that Fraser Springs 'abhors' dancing."

Jo groaned. It didn't take much to send Mrs. McSheen on a moral purity crusade, and the last time that happened, the entire staff of the bathhouse had found themselves on the wrong end of an angry mob. "Oh Lord. Well, was he handsome? It's the least he could do."

Ilsa smiled in spite of her foul mood. "You know, I don't think I should answer that. You're a proper married lady now."

Jo shook her head, smiling. "So he's handsome."

Ilsa shrugged. "Dark hair, overdressed. I didn't get much of a look at him, honestly. I missed his grand entrance, and then Mrs. McSheen backed him into a corner. Her hat blocked every angle." Jo let out a decidedly unladylike snort; Mrs. McSheen's elaborate hats were the stuff of local legend. "I snuck out with Annie as soon as we could."

"Has Annie given up on her charming prince so easily?"

Annie, another of the bathhouse's employees, had been cheerfully declaring her intention to propose marriage to the new doctor, sight unseen, for weeks now. "Annie might still want him—she's that desperate—but she couldn't very well push herself past Mrs. McSheen."

"Well, I'm sorry. I know how much you were looking forward to tonight. The poor man isn't going to make many friends at this rate."

"Yes, we're all terribly sad for him." Ilsa sighed again. "I should go get out of this dress before I manage to spill something on it."

"You look so pretty in it, though. Is it new?"

"New to me. I got it secondhand." And then spent her precious few free hours for two weeks pulling it apart and remaking it into something a little more flattering, a little more modern.

"I'm jealous anyway. It's nothing but shapeless sacks for me." Jo rested her hand on her swelling stomach with a little smile Ilsa tried not to resent. She was happy for her friend, after all. Jo had wanted a baby for so long.

"I'm glad you're jealous. It'd be a shame to waste my dress entirely."

"Ha. You are very clever and I hate you."

Ilsa smiled her most innocent, angelic smile. It worked on almost everyone, with the exceptions of Jo and the bathhouse's dour handyman, Nils. She'd missed this lately, these late evenings in the kitchen, tossing insults and advice back and forth with Jo. That friendship had been slowly changing ever since Jo's marriage. Not necessarily for the worse: Owen Sterling was a good man, and his love had made Jo happier and more relaxed. But he had undeniably taken over some of Ilsa's old role as confidante and partner. That was only natural, but it still stung from time to time. And now, with Jo about to become a mother, Ilsa was subjected to daily scenes of domestic bliss.

"I still think you should have come tonight. Enjoyed one last week of looking like a lady and not a sleepy whale."

"Too late. I already feel like a whale. Owen went, anyway."

"If you'd been there, you could have made him overrule Mrs. McSheen about the music, and we could all be dancing right now. And then everyone would have had a nice new bit of gossip about your outrageous behaviour."

Jo smiled; Owen's authority to "overrule" decisions in Fraser Springs had been a running joke in the bathhouse ever since he'd been elected mayor last year. "You may be right. The Wilson's Bathhouse girls are entirely too respectable these days. Drama at a public dance might have be just the thing to restore our reputation as a den of sin and vice." She yawned.

"All right, Mrs. Whale. It's past your bedtime."

"Bossy. That's what you are," Jo grumbled. "Who's in charge here?" But she rose anyway and pulled Ilsa to her feet with her. "I hereby declare it bedtime."

"Yes, ma'am." Ilsa smiled. They headed towards the stairs together, and she rescued her shoes from their exile among the potatoes. It wasn't the shoes' fault they'd had nothing to do tonight, poor things.

Ilsa slept in a room in the steeply pitched third floor. Usually, the upstairs rooms were filled with girls laughing and whispering, and she would fall asleep to dozens of half-heard conversations and the private dramas of the eight other women who lived and worked at Wilson's Bathhouse. Today, however, all was quiet. Everyone was either already back in bed or had snuck off to enjoy the rest of the holiday evening at Doc's Saloon with beaus and sweethearts.

As the senior attendant, Ilsa had a room all to herself. It barely fit a narrow bed, her sky-blue wash basin, and a little white armoire, but it was home, and she treasured the bit of privacy it provided at the beginning and end of each day. She undressed and hung her pretty frock on its peg in the armoire. Even in the dim light, its leaf-green shimmer stood out in stark contrast to the row of identical white shirtwaists and smocks and her serviceable grey and blue skirts. She ran her hands over the silky, slippery fabric of the dress, so much softer and lovelier than anything she'd ever owned before, and then closed the armoire door with a snap.

Why did she care about some stupid dance anyhow? As if a dance organized by Mrs. McSheen had ever had the possibility of being any fun. Best-case scenario, she would have spent the evening dodging the clumsy feet and even clumsier advances of dozens of married, elderly, or just plain desperate men. The promise of a fresh addition to the limited pickings of a small-town marriage mart had also lured the few unmarried ladies of Fraser Spring's upper class away from their endless tea and crochet. At least she hadn't had to stay long enough to endure their condescending looks.

Ilsa slipped into her nightgown, sat on the edge of her bed, and brushed out her pale hair until it crackled with static electricity. She was just bored. That was all. She'd been working at Wilson's Bathhouse for five years: long enough that her hands could do the work without her brain even attending to it. The same regular clients. The same treatments. The same girls with the same gossip. And Jo had been so distracted and tired lately. Still, Ilsa was lucky to have this work. She knew that.

Hair brushed and braided, she reached under the bed to begin the final ritual of the night. She pulled out a hatbox, a lovely pink-striped thing that had helped to justify the amount she'd spent on her Sunday hat. Lifting its lid, she carefully took out a plain, black-covered photograph album, a stack of fashion plates, a little packet of letters bound in ribbon, a pot of glue, scissors, last Saturday's newspaper, and a pencil: all innocuous items in their own right, but all representing two years of hard work and one very big secret.

She opened the newspaper first and flipped to the advertisement section in the back. Bolts of ribbon were going for ten cents a length, with a discount for "the trade," and scrap lace could be had "at a fetching price." What constituted a fetching price? A sale on feathers offered ostrich plumes from five cents each.

The ribbon could be purchased wholesale for three cents, but the price of lace varied so much depending on the quality. As for ostrich feathers, the fairness of the price probably depended on your proximity to an ostrich. Did ostriches live in Canada? She had never seen one. She circled the ad and underlined "ostrich feathers," then clipped it out neatly and pasted it in the album beside an ad for the price of paste jewels in bulk and one for "Mortimer Hayley, dealer of bulk goods, no order too small." The glue stunk like furniture varnish, so she worked quickly to keep the odour from seeping into the rooms next door.

Most of the stores were on Hastings or Georgia Street; the shopping district for women was probably still concentrated there, around Woodward's Department Store. When she'd lived in Vancouver five years ago, she certainly hadn't had the free time to wander town comparing prices and locations. She flipped to the "Rentals for Commerce" section. It would cost her fifty dollars a month for a storefront no bigger than this room. Hastings Street was more expensive, but if the customers were there … Or maybe there was a side street, a little less pricy. She really needed to go to Vancouver and see it all in person.

Usually, this work made her feel like a character in a detective story. Every scrap of information was a clue, and one day she would find the answer and claim her reward. But tonight, the small print swam in front of her vision, and thoughts about the stupid dance and stupid Mrs. McSheen and stupid, boring Fraser Springs tugged at the edge of her concentration. Even flipping through the fashion plates didn't soothe her restlessness. She should probably call it a night.

By the time Ilsa restored the hatbox to its place under the bed, the rest of the girls were returning from their evening adventures, creeping up the stairs, trying so hard to be quiet but hitting every squeaky plank along the way. Creak. They'd giggle. Creak. They'd giggle louder. Shhh, one would tell the other.

Ilsa had grown up in orphanages, and nothing lulled her to sleep like the sounds of poorly hushed mischief. Yes, Fraser Springs was home. These people were her people. She didn't have any reason to complain. And yet when she closed her eyes, the contents of the hatbox raced through her mind. The price of buttons, where to buy the best bulk fabric, the cost of storefront rental—her future spread out before her like an arithmetic problem she was so very close to solving.

Chapter 2

Theo awoke to a knock on his hotel room door. He sat up, disoriented. When had his bedroom been submerged by a tide of red velvet and waxed fruit? Where was the clock on the wall? It took a moment to realize that he was not at home. He was still in Fraser Springs, and last night's humiliation had not, after all, been a bad dream.

His limp was always worse in the morning, so he sat up and massaged his knee, testing its range. The fall weather wasn't helping either.

The knocking continued.

"Coming," he called.

He swung his legs around to the side of the bed and reached for his dressing gown and cane. The first few steps seemed to take hours. The knocking increased in insistency.

"I said I'm coming."

The hotel's porter stood on the other side of the door, hand frozen mid-knock as Theo jerked it open.

"All right, what is it?" Theo grumbled.

"Good morning, sir." the porter said, admirably professional in the face of Theo's groggy rudeness. "It's a quarter to nine, sir."

"Oh?" Was there anywhere he needed to be?

"Mrs. Robert McSheen is waiting for you downstairs, sir."

Theo paused. The Hat Woman from last night. He didn't remember making any plans to meet her. "Is she ... expecting me? At a particular time?"

The porter's face was blank. "I don't have any information on that. Would you like me to go ask her?"

"No. Tell her I'll be right down."

"Very good, sir."

Damn, damn, damn, damn. Theo shut the door. Dr. Greyson had specifically told him to take the day off, but apparently the Fraser Springs welcoming committee had other plans. He attended to his appearance as quickly as he could, splashing cold water on his face to wake himself up. He found himself stymied, however, by the choices staring him down from his partially unpacked trunks. What passed for appropriate attire in this town?

His dark suits might come across as too formal, but a twenty-three-year-old doctor with a limp needed all the professionalism he could muster. He added a plain linen pocket square, then pomaded and slicked back his hair. There. That wasn't bad, especially not with such short notice.

Mrs. McSheen was waiting in the centre of the compass mosaic downstairs. She wore another enormous hat that was adorned with wine-red plumes and … were those taxidermied sparrows? He suppressed a shudder. Her dress' acres of purple fabric had some kind of striped pattern in the weave that seemed to flash and shift as she moved. The effect was clearly intended to be mesmerizing but in practice inspired seasickness.

"Good morning, Mrs. McSheen," he said. "I'm so sorry to keep you waiting."

She sniffed. "That's quite all right. You are not entirely at fault, Dr. Whitacre. I had not arranged a formal time to call, as I assumed that you would rise around seven, as Dr. Greyson does. I forgot that people from Vancouver tend to keep later hours. Not everyone believes in 'early to bed, early to rise,' I suppose!"

Today seemed to be shaping up to be exactly like yesterday. He assembled what he hoped was a smile. "It isn't like me to oversleep. The fresh air here …"

"Yes!" Mrs. McSheen trilled. "Isn't it marvellous? Well, come along. We have so many calls to make, and we are already late."

Theo tried to ignore the rumbling in his stomach. The thought of facing the Finest People in Our Beloved Fraser Springs without the benefit of breakfast was daunting. Still, this town was his home for the near future, and perhaps this was an opportunity to remedy the poor impression he'd already made. "Lead the way," he said with all the cheerfulness he could muster.

They met the proprietor of the general store; the telegraph operator; the Presbyterian minister, the Episcopalian minister, and the Methodist minister; a flock of ladies with hats to rival Mrs. McSheen's; and a banker and the banker's brood of small children. Theo worked hard to shake hands and smile politely and find something to praise about the town at each stop. His guide continued to confidently mispronounce his name, and he lacked the courage to correct her. He was going to be Dr. White-ay-kurr for the duration of his stay, it appeared.

Dr. Greyson was nowhere to be found.

Eventually, they arrived at a building at the end of the boardwalk whose plate glass front window proclaimed it to be "Wilson's Bathhouse."

"Now, this stop would not normally be on my tour. I must warn you that Mrs. Sterling is in a family way." She paused for effect here, presumably to allow him a chance to absorb the horror of visible pregnancy. "When I was expecting a blessed event, I certainly did not make a spectacle of myself. But of course, you are a physician. I'm sure you would know all about the dangers of overexertion during pregnancy, so I would consider it a kindness if you can talk some sense into the lady." He wasn't sure if that was a request or an order. "And her husband, Mr. Owen Sterling, is the mayor." Mrs. McSheen added this last in a pinched, grudging way, as though it pained her to admit that the town had a mayor at all.

Theo didn't know what to say to any of this. In truth, he'd only absorbed a rough outline of the entire morning. Something about services and pregnant spectacles and the mayor? The sun was high overhead, and the morning chill had burned off into a warm humidity that was surely unseasonable for autumn. The heat combined with his lack of breakfast was beginning to make him lightheaded.

The interior of Wilson's Bathhouse, however, was blessedly cool. An attractive, auburn-haired woman in her mid-twenties was writing in a ledger at a long counter; she rose to greet them as they entered, revealing a pronounced curve about her midsection.

"My dear Mrs. Sterling. I do hope you're keeping well?" cooed Mrs. McSheen. "I just dropped round to introduce our town's newest addition. Dr. Whitacre, Mrs. Owen Sterling."

"Welcome." Mrs. Sterling extended a hand. "Please, call me Jo." The woman was indeed large with pregnancy. Did Fraser Springs have access to a midwife, or would he be expected to attend the birth? His limited obstetrics training had been damned awkward, since he'd spent at least half the practicum sessions with his eyes averted. How much worse would it be to have to socialize with the lady afterwards?

"It's a pleasure to meet you, Mrs. Sterling," he said, dragging his attention back to the situation at hand. The parlour was abruptly filled with a half-dozen girls in white dresses and smocks. Mrs. McSheen dutifully set about introducing each one, though it quickly became clear she did not know most of their names.

"And this is …" She looked expectantly at the girl.

"Mary," the girl supplied.

"Yes, of course. Mary! And this is …"

"Doris." And on and on. Theo said hello to all of them like a smiling, handshaking automaton. "And I believe that's everyone," Mrs. McSheen finally announced. "Where is Mr. Sterling?"

"Either working in his study or out and about with Nils," Mrs. Sterling said. "Would you like me to send for him?"

"Oh, please don't trouble yourself. I'm sure we'll run across him sooner or later." Mrs. McSheen seemed relieved that she would not have to face being upstaged by so august a personage as the town's mayor. "We'll be on our way, then."

"Oh, wait," Mrs. Sterling interjected. "I'm afraid you have one more hand to shake, Dr. Whitacre. You can't leave without meeting my right-hand woman. Ilsa!" she called cheerfully over her shoulder. "Come and meet the new doctor!"

Theo's attention snapped back to the room so quickly that he physically lurched. He steadied himself with his cane. Ilsa wasn't a common name. But it wasn't uncommon, either. He just hadn't heard it in a long while, that was all. Nothing to be getting worked up over.

The slim, female figure who drifted in through the door was backlit by the sun, and he could only make out a slender silhouette with an aura of messily pinned pale hair. But it was her. Unmistakeably her.

He watched the shock of recognition pass over her face as she stepped closer, saw her step falter. Mrs. McSheen's voice came from somewhere far away: "And, of course, this is Ilsa."

"Ilsa Pedersen," he whispered.

"Yes, that's what I said. Ilsa, may I introduce Dr. Whitacre."

She didn't say a word, just nodded. His mind was racing as quickly as his heartbeat: perhaps it would be better if they pretended not to know each other? He certainly didn't want to explain their personal business to Mrs. McSheen and the assembled staff of Wilson's Bathhouse.

"It's lovely to meet you, Miss ... Pendergast, was it?" he said.

She seemed to have to force herself to meet his gaze, but when she did, he stared at blue eyes fringed by eyelashes so pale they were only visible when the light hit them at an angle. He knew that one eye was just slightly greener than the other and that there was a faint birthmark behind her left ear. He forced himself to adopt what he hoped was a neutral expression and held out his hand for her to shake.

"A pleasure to meet you, Dr. Whitacre," she said at last. She reached across and shook his hand quickly, then stepped back immediately to stand beside Mrs. Sterling.

"Actually, it's White-*ay*-kur," Mrs. McSheen corrected.

Ilsa's lips quirked up at the corners, and Theo's stomach flipped. He knew that look, the one that always meant she was barely holding back a smart-aleck response. "Oh," she said. "I'm sorry, Dr. White-*ay*-kur. I mispronounce things all the time, I'm afraid."

Theo felt his cheeks flush with heat. "Well, there are variations on the name. But, um. Yes, I suppose *Whit*-ucker is the … most common … in my particular branch of the family."

He didn't need to look at Mrs. McSheen to register her displeasure. "So I have introduced you incorrectly all about town this morning?"

Theo knew he should smooth over the situation with Mrs. McSheen, but his attention was currently committed to that little smile on Ilsa's face. She was staring right back at him now, as if daring him to look away first. Mrs. McSheen was saying something. Damn. He had missed it, and now everyone was waiting for his response.

"Not incorrectly, just … an alternative pronunciation." He forced himself to turn and smile at Mrs. McSheen. "Really, the pronunciation doesn't matter."

"Now I'm going to have to go back and correct them! The whole town!"

"That's not … I was merely trying to …" He fought the urge to glance back at Ilsa, who was probably enjoying his discomfort. Which, of course, he richly deserved. Did anyone else in the room know about him, how he'd betrayed her?

"Save it," Mrs. McSheen snapped, storming out of the bathhouse.

Was he supposed to follow her? He glanced at Mrs. Sterling, as if she could remind him of his lines in this farce. Her expression gave him no clues. If anything, she seemed as confused as he was. He sighed and adjusted his cane. "It was lovely to meet you all," he said to the room at large. And, finally, he made eye contact again with Ilsa. "Lovely."

And, without a word, she turned on her heel and left the room.

• • •

As she fled back to the safety of the kitchen, Ilsa exhaled a breath she didn't realize she had been holding. The girls were giggling madly in the room behind her, but that wasn't unusual.

She plunged her hands back into the tub of dishes she had been working her way through before Theo—before Dr. Whitacre had arrived. How on earth was he here? Of all the places in the world where a rich man could be a doctor, he somehow picked Fraser Springs? She yanked out a glass, rubbed it vigorously with the washcloth then slammed it back into the soapy water again.

"Careful!" came Jo's voice behind her. "You're going to break something if you keep that up."

Ilsa placed the glass gently on the drying rack and turned around. "That dog and pony show out there put me behind, and it's not like any of those lot are going to help me, and ..."

"Ilsa."

"What?"

"How did that doctor know your last name? And why did he pretend he didn't know it?" Jo's voice was gentle.

Ilsa sighed. If only she'd seen his face last night, she could have been prepared for this. Seeing him wouldn't have felt like such a blow to the chest. "How should I know?"

"Ilsa."

"What?"

Jo smiled. "You're a terrible liar."

Ilsa looked around. A few of the girls were milling about the kitchen door, most likely trying to eavesdrop. She lowered her voice. "I used to work for his family. As a maid. A long time ago."

"That doesn't sound so terrible. He looked like he was going to faint when you walked in."

"It was years and years ago. And I didn't leave with a nice letter of reference," she admitted. "Probably because I called his mother a heartless bitch the last time I saw her."

Jo, God bless her, didn't laugh. "I'm sure she deserved it. Did he mistreat you? Because if he did, Owen and I will gladly make his life so miserable, he'll be sorry he set foot in Fraser Springs."

The idea of driving Theo from the town with her own personal posse was tempting, but Ilsa shook her head. "No. He … Dr. Whitacre was always kind to me. He's not that bad."

Jo nodded. "Well, I'm sorry he gave you such a shock." She put her hand on Ilsa's shoulder. "And I'll talk to the girls. There won't be any gossip."

After Jo left, Ilsa abandoned the washing and walked out into the kitchen garden. The shrivelled tomato and bean stalks and the crisping leaves made a soothing, rustling sound. She took a deep breath. He was walking now, clearly. He seemed taller, and broader in the shoulders, but the way he had looked at her had been just the same as the first day she'd met him. A startled, curious stare, magnified by wire-rimmed spectacles.

Her first glimpse of Theo, all those years ago, had been a pale face made paler by his dark hair and green eyes. He'd been sitting in bed with a checkers board on his lap, moving the pieces on both sides—playing against himself. He had looked much younger than sixteen.

When she came in with a saucer of beef tea on a tray, he watched her out of the corner of his eye, pretending not to notice her as he moved the pieces, playing both sides of the game.

She'd been on the job for only a day, and she was determined to keep her head down and stay out of trouble this time. Ilsa set down the tea and collected the napkins and dishes left from the morning. The checkers clacked on the board's thin wood, and she risked a glance towards the bed as she turned back for the door.

His board was a complete disaster. If he'd been playing anyone except himself, he'd have been trounced immediately. Pathetic. "You shouldn't break your back row," she blurted.

He looked up. "What?"

Ilsa set the tray down. "Your back row. The other side can't win if your back row is full, so try not to move them."

Theo's instinct had been to shield the checkers board from her view. "I'm quite good at checkers. I've beaten my tutor for years now."

"Either he's not much of a tutor, or he's letting you win."

He flushed, his embarrassment pushing colour to those waxy cheeks. "He wouldn't do that."

She bent over the checkerboard. As she'd suspected, both sides of the game were wide open. "I could beat you in two minutes." As soon as she said it, she regretted it. She just couldn't manage to be respectable. This was her last chance, and she was already insulting the house's sick son.

"No, you couldn't."

In for a dime, in for a dollar. "Yes, I could."

"Prove it."

Ilsa looked back at the cups and saucers waiting to be taken back to the kitchen. "I'm not supposed to dawdle. Cook said to come right back down."

Theo smiled. "If she notices, I'll tell her I made you stay." He took a toy soldier off the bedside table. "And I'll give you this." Even from across the room, she could see it was expensive. It was expertly painted, and it wasn't made of wood. She could trade it for enough pocket money to buy a dozen silk ribbons, or tickets to see the vaudeville. She didn't know many sixteen-year-olds who still played with toy soldiers, but then again, most of the sixteen-year-old boys she knew were working at the dockyards. Things were different for rich boys, and even more so for boys who seemed to spend all their time in bed.

Among the ranks of toy soldiers, Ilsa found her eye drawn to the little tin horse that represented the cavalry brigade. It was the size of her hand, painted gleaming white with grey dapples; its saddle and bridle were shiny gilt, with reins made of tiny strips of real leather. Its neck and front leg were arched so daintily that she ached to stroke the little horse like a kitten. She looked behind her, expecting to see Cook bearing down on her, but the house seemed quiet. It really was a lovely horse. "Five minutes," she said. "And I want the horse, not the soldier."

"Deal," he replied without hesitation. She sat down on the edge of the bed and reset the checker pieces.

Two minutes and eleven seconds later, Ilsa captured his last piece.

"You cheated!" he whined. "They must teach you all sorts of gypsy tricks in that orphanage."

Ilsa shrugged. "I'm not even that good." In the girls' home, they'd played checkers with all manner of boards and pieces: lines of chalk in the barren yard, with leaves and stones, bits of paper stored carefully under someone's bed. A kid who was really good at checkers never went hungry.

"Tell me how you did it," Theo said. "You must have a trick. My tutor has never beaten me."

Ilsa sighed. Theo picked up the little toy horse, clutching it tightly in his fist. Her absence had probably already been noted by Cook. "I have to go."

"Will you come tomorrow?"

"Only if you give me the horse, welsher."

He smiled again, challenge flaring in his big green eyes. "Best two out of three."

A door slammed somewhere in the bathhouse, startling Ilsa out of her reverie. How long had she been standing here, staring at the desiccated rows of peas and wax beans without really seeing them?

Theo had cost her too much then, and he certainly wasn't worth troubling herself over now, especially when she was so close to realizing her plans. The reappearance of someone from her past was a shock, yes, and now that the shock was over, it was time to compose herself. No more blushing. No more pointless regrets. She was too old for that nonsense.

She would give Theo Whitacre a wide berth. And he would probably go on calling her Miss Pendergast and pretending to have never met her. Fraser Springs was small, but not so small that she couldn't avoid a person if she set her mind to it. And besides, the society ladies wouldn't be able to resist a handsome doctor for long, limping or otherwise. The local daughters of privilege would be strolling arm in arm with him along the boardwalk in no time. Ilsa had her world and Theo had his, and that was simply the way it was going to be.

• • •

Theo couldn't get back to the hotel fast enough. He ordered some sandwiches to his room, then stretched out on the bed. Mrs. McSheen was angry with him. The whole of Fraser Springs hated him as a joyless spoilsport. But right now, he didn't care.

He pulled the newspaper clipping out of his wallet and studied it. He had never really believed that Ilsa was the woman in the photo; the caption beneath the image had read "Mrs. Josephine Wilson, Rescued From Fire." But it had looked so much like his memory of Ilsa—the loosely curling fair hair; the large, pale eyes; the proud tilt of her chin—he hadn't been able to resist cutting it out and keeping it.

Yes, of course it was her. It had been her all along. Mrs. Josephine Wilson must be the "call me Jo" of Wilson's Bathhouse. Ilsa worked there. Somehow, the newspaper must have gotten the names mixed up.

He munched on a sandwich. This was bad news, even though it didn't feel like it. He'd spent six years turning what had happened with Ilsa over and over in his mind until he could no longer separate fact from fiction.

They had played checkers together: that was true. And it was true, also, that one day she'd curled up beside him in his bed, rested her head on his shoulder. They'd kissed. That was true. That had happened.

He could remember that moment in crystalline detail. He hadn't meant to spend so much time with Ilsa. But then his mother went away on a three-month visit to her sister's family, and his father wouldn't have cared if his son played checkers with the devil himself. Checkers led to chess. Neither of them knew how to play chess, but they cobbled together the rules using a book that Theo's tutor had brought and their own imaginations. They bickered over every move, each accusing the other of cheating, and sometimes Ilsa would swat him on the arm.

And then it turned out that though Ilsa could read, she only read from grocery lists. So Theo pulled down book after book and taught her the words she didn't know. They would sit together on his bed when Ilsa could sneak away from her work for a half hour, and he'd read to her, and then she'd read to him.

Theo had always hated the adventure novels with which his mother stocked his shelves, because they might as well have been called *Adventures Theo Would Never Have*. Or *It's Very Fun to Be a Young Man If You Can Walk Properly*. But in Ilsa's telling, the stories came alive. Her reactions were half the fun. After a dramatic scene, she'd stop and say, "That didn't happen. That would never happen! Would that ever happen?"

A few days before his mother returned, Ilsa fell asleep with her head against his shoulder as he read to her. He reached down and swept away a curl stuck against her cheek. The gesture sent a shiver down into his stomach, but before he had time to process the sensation, her eyes opened and she blinked at him sleepily. Her mouth was parted, just slightly.

"I fell asleep," she murmured.

"You did," he whispered.

"You must have been boring," she said.

"Very boring," he agreed.

And that was when she tilted her face up and kissed him. Or he kissed her. It was hard to say. Their touch was tentative at first, but his body, which he had been told for years was wrong and feeble, felt completely whole—completely right—when pressed against hers. His hand skimmed her cheek. She placed her palms on his chest and that, too, felt right.

Finally, she pulled away. "I should go."

He tried to pull words out of the fog of his brain. "Yes. Of course. I'm sorry I ..."

Ilsa kissed him again. "This was nice," she whispered.

After she left, he looked around the bedroom that had been his world for so long. He was surrounded by storybooks and games, by distractions of all kinds. His room looked like a nursery, not a place for a man on the brink of adulthood. Even though she beat him at nearly every game they played, he felt powerful around Ilsa. She didn't talk to him in a baby voice. She didn't call him "Teddy." There was no pity in her expression. The way she had looked at him, half asleep, her blond curls all askew ... He wanted to be the type of person who deserved to be looked at like that.

He'd spent six years after that perfect afternoon listening to his mother tell him that Ilsa had been just trying to get a piece of the Whitacre fortune. She'd been the help, not a friend: a little urchin looking out for herself. Maybe Theo had seen what he wanted to see.

He had already interfered too much in Ilsa's life and he needed to focus on his own work.

The sandwiches had improved Theo's mood considerably. The morning may have been a complete loss, but there were plenty of productive ways to spend the rest of the day. He should find Dr. Greyson and start settling into the practice. He should probably also speak to the hotel management to clarify the responsibilities that came with the post. The old doctor might be happy to operate on a handshake and his good word, but getting something in writing would undoubtedly be for the best.

Theo's lower back cramped, so he lay on his side and twisted to try to stretch the tense muscles. His doctors had always expected that his weak left leg would give him all the trouble, but it was his good leg and his lower back that pained him the most, since they took on the additional strain of compensating for his weakness.

He began a checklist in his head as he turned over and stretched the other side. Dr. Greyson, then hotel management, then supper, then finish unpacking. He would not think of Ilsa. Who was a bathhouse attendant now. It might not be the most respectable occupation, but it was better than … No, he needed to get out of this room and talk to someone who didn't have either a ridiculous hat or a mess of blond curls fringing her heart-shaped face and startlingly blue eyes.

He cleared his mind again with great effort. Dr. Greyson, then hotel management, then supper, then finish unpacking. He could do this. The only thing worse than being marooned in Fraser Springs would be crawling back in defeat to the big empty house in the West End, with his tail between his legs, after less than twenty-four hours. He would have to make a success of this.

Chapter 3

Between the return of old ghosts and her racing thoughts, Ilsa had slept terribly. In the morning, she'd turned too quickly in the kitchen and slid an entire batch of raw biscuits from the pan onto the floor and then burned her hand on the oven door for good measure. She'd had to backtrack for forgotten towels, pitchers of water, and bowls of massage oil at least four times already. It was as if her head had been attached to a different body in the night.

By lunchtime, Jo noticed her foul humour, took over her appointments, and sent her out of the bathhouse under the pretence of running errands. Ilsa sighed. The situation must have been truly dire for Jo to rearrange the schedule. It wasn't fair to give her boss an extra burden, but maybe a long walk was just what she needed.

She tried to make the best of the unexpected reprieve as she strolled along the boardwalk. She had even changed into her favourite skirt, whose cornflower blue fabric had been laundered a hundred times until it was buttery soft and draped like silk. People nodded to her and smiled as she passed them, and she smiled back with every appearance of good cheer. The sun was shining, the breeze was brisk and refreshing, the leaves were brilliant reds and oranges, and she was determined to enjoy herself.

And yet, from the moment she'd stepped off the front porch of Wilson's Bathhouse, she'd been flinching at every man who passed her line of sight. When she entered the post office, the sight of a slim, dark-haired man standing with his back to her had made her stomach flop. And yet, when he turned out to be the assistant bank manager, she felt almost…disappointed. Was she avoiding Theodore "I don't believe we've met" Whitacre or was she trying to run into him? And would doing so make her feel better, or so much worse?

Maybe she should give in to the extravagance of taking tea at the St. Alice. Theo was here to work with Dr. Greyson, and Dr. Greyson kept an office and an examining room in the hotel. She'd have to pass by the door twice on her way in and out of the lobby, so it would only be natural to poke her head in to say hello.

And then what? Sit down and have a long heart-to-heart, maybe catch up on all the thrilling events in her life between being his housemaid and running errands for a bathhouse? She could ask after his mother's health. "Doing well, I hope. And are you still wrapped around her bony finger, or have you grown a spine of some sort? Delightful! Yes, the weather is lovely today. I do hope the rain holds off, don't you?"

By the time she arrived back at the bathhouse, the sun was just beginning to set, and the last of the afternoon clients were drifting out the front door. After two more turns up and down the boardwalk, her roiling emotions had settled down to a dull, dissatisfied ache. Theo had no reason to seek her out, and she had nothing to say to him that he'd welcome hearing.

She went straight up the stairs to Jo's office. At this time of day, it was the most likely place to find the Sterlings: Jo would be tallying up the weekly accounts, and she could already hear Jo's husband Owen clattering away on his typewriter. The door stood open, so she simply knocked once on the doorframe on her way in.

"Mail delivery for Wilson's Bathhouse," she announced. Jo looked up from behind the wide oak desk and smiled.

"I'll take everything except the bills and the letters of complaint. Those are all Owen's."

Ilsa tossed most of the bundle down on the blotter in front of Jo, keeping back the two catalogues of notions and ready-to-wear clothing for herself. "Not falling for it. He only gets fan letters on pretty pink stationery." Mr. Sterling wrote popular novels, so he did get a fair number of letters from admirers. And a fair number of those letter writers knew him from his brief reign as Most Eligible Bachelor in Vancouver.

Behind her, Owen snorted and pushed back from his writing table on the other side of the room. "Untrue." She shot him a sceptical look as he strolled over to flip through the pile of envelopes. "I also get fan letters on pretty lavender stationery. From time to time."

"He suffers so much for his art, Ilsa," Jo said. "The poor dear." Owen grinned and leaned over to plant a kiss on his wife's smiling lips.

Ilsa slid her gaze away to the view of the lake beyond the office window. It wasn't that she was uncomfortable with displays of intimacy—she'd walked in on this very couple in a far more compromising position when they'd first been courting, and she hadn't turned a hair. But this casual physical affection between two happily married people was embarrassing, somehow. Her own parents had certainly never kissed and cuddled in front of her on the rare occasions that her pa had been home from the fishing fleet. And every other husband and wife she'd seen had been coolly distant. At least in public: perhaps they were all more like Owen and Jo behind closed doors.

"Did the walk help?" Jo asked, calling her attention back from the window.

"A bit," Ilsa replied. Jo either didn't notice the unusually vague reply or chose not to push at it.

"You missed all the excitement. Mrs. McSheen paid me a call."

"Oh good Lord. What have we done wrong this time?"

"Nothing, yet. It seems that Mrs. McSheen has heard rumours that His Honour the Mayor"—she rolled her eyes towards her husband, who was now half sitting on her desk —"has given his blessing for a dance to be held on the premises of Wilson's, and she required his direct assurance that the event would be properly … I believe the word she used was 'chaste'?"

"Decorous," Owen volunteered. "And I assured her everything would be thoroughly decorous, and she sailed back out of here in high spirits."

"Wait," Ilsa said. "We're hosting a dance? When did that happen?"

Jo shrugged. "I mentioned the possibility of hosting something to make up for that damp squib of a welcome party for the new doctor. And then Owen said something about the idea to Doc at the saloon, and now it seems that the entire town is expecting a dance come next Saturday."

"And I've given the event my blessing, so we can't back out now," Owen said. "That's just bad manners."

"It would be easy enough to clear out the dining room," Ilsa said, thinking out loud. "And there's all the bunting from Victoria Day. But we'd have to order in some of the food, because I don't know when we'd have time to …"

"Slow down, General!" Jo laughed, holding up her hands in a gesture of surrender. "I was going to ask if you'd mind putting something together, but you're clearly three steps ahead of me."

"I have a pretty new dress and dancing shoes that've barely been out of my room. I'll organize everything. You can spend the rest of the week vomiting and making Owen fetch things for you."

"She hasn't vomited at all this week," Owen noted cheerfully.

"Good. And get those ankles un-swollen by next Saturday, ma'am. Because we're going to be doing a lot of dancing."

She could still hear the low murmur of Owen and Jo's banter coming through the grate as she sat on her bed and opened the first of the catalogues. After a quick skim, she began re-reading the pages she'd dog-eared, circling items of interest in red grease pen. There was a sale on cash registers at Woodward's. Now that was something she hadn't considered. Did you really need a cash register to start, or could you make do with an accounts ledger? You wouldn't want a line of customers out the door while you tried to add the numbers by hand, but was it wishful thinking that customers would be beating down her door? And a proper cash register would make the whole shop seem more legitimate. She sighed. *Cash register?* she wrote in the catalogue margin.

She was so close. She'd met her savings goal last month: a full year's wages. In a moment of bravery she had planned a trip down to Vancouver around this time, but, with Jo so heavily pregnant, she'd cancelled it before she'd mailed a letter to a single broker. True, Jo would have given her the time off without hesitating, but the idea of leaving her friend with a newborn and a business to run in order to seek her own fortune made her stomach twist. She loved Jo, and Jo had more than earned her loyalty as both a friend and as an employee, so how could she explain that for the past three years she'd spent every free moment meticulously planning her escape? Would Jo understand that it was nothing personal? That she was a good boss, but she was still a boss, and Ilsa didn't want to take orders from anyone?

And now there was this dance to think about. She flipped to the blank page at the back of the catalogue and began making a list. A good punch could make or break a party. Something with wine and rum. Perhaps some spices would be appropriate: were they out of cinnamon? If they used cinnamon, some floating apple rings or cranberries would make the punch look festive. Food was more difficult, especially on short notice. Perhaps that salted ham hock in the cellar could find its way into some pastry. Would the St. Alice sell their tea menu at a reduced price if she ordered enough? And where had they stored the bunting after the Victoria Day celebrations?

It was always something. Jo's pregnancy. Theo's arrival. This dance. She was never going to see her own name painted in gold on a storefront sign if she didn't focus. She'd already missed getting the store up and running for the Christmas season. Perhaps it was better to aim for a March opening, right as ladies were considering their Easter dresses and their spring and summer wardrobes. At this rate, she'd still be planning dances in Fraser Springs next summer, then next fall, then Christmas again, and the summer after that.

No, she was ready. All her plans were falling into place, and nothing was going to hold her back. Not Jo, not this dance, and especially not Theo Whitacre.

• • •

Dr. Greyson's office in the St. Alice Hotel smelled strangely familiar: the melange of pipe smoke, liniment, and wood polish had been the background to many tedious hours of Theo's youth. In fact, it looked as if someone had chiselled the old office out of the Vancouver medical building and set it back down in Fraser Springs. The same amber apothecary jars lettered with gold script. The same framed anatomical lithographs. The same overstuffed chair and long desk strewn with papers. Even the skeleton, which Dr. Greyson had once used to demonstrate to Theo exactly what parts of his body had gone wrong, still stood in the corner of the room. It was yellowed now, the ribs slightly askew and the pelvis twisted, so that it seemed to have aged along with Dr. Greyson.

"When I took this post, they had movers set my old office up just the way I'd left it," Dr. Greyson said, as if reading Theo's mind.

Maybe it's because he was fully grown now, but the room here seemed smaller than the one in Vancouver. The large furniture had felt distinguished then, but here it made the room seem cramped and airless.

"Yes, I thought it looked familiar," Theo said. He wandered over to one of the medical diagrams that hung on the wall. As a child, he had marvelled at all the complicated parts of the body and how beautifully they all fit together, but now he noticed the errors the diagram contained. That spleen was too large relative to the pancreas, and the diagram of the heart was based on the old understanding of the relative functions of each chamber.

"I have arranged to turn one of the examining rooms into your office. You can furnish it as you see fit. You will meet patients here with me so that I can supervise your consultations." Dr. Greyson sat down in his overstuffed chair and lit a pipe.

"I understand the need for a trial period, but I was brought here to lighten your workload, not increase it." The only other chair was reserved for patients, so he leaned against a bookshelf filled with specimen jars and books. The last thing he wanted was to remind Dr. Greyson of when he was Little Teddy, Infant Paralysis Patient and Pitiable Invalid.

Dr. Greyson made a dismissive gesture with his pipe and leaned forwards in his chair. "It's important that we don't misunderstand one another, young man," he said, making eye contact. "While your dear mother might have sent you up here with the idea that I'm an old man needing help, you'll find that this is not the case. I am the one doing you a favour. There are not many physicians who practice medicine in the traditional fashion, so I am your last chance to get a real education in the profession."

The glass front cabinet near the door prominently displayed examples of what he meant by traditional medicine: Fatoff Obesity Creams, Lydia E. Pinkham's Vegetable Compound, Mrs. Winslow's Soothing Syrup. Snake oil and nostrums, all of them. Soothing syrups had been out of favour for a decade at least, given the controversies about dosing teething babies with morphine. One entire shelf was filled by neat rows of Restorative Vitality Water in gleaming green bottles; Dr. Greyson was encouraging that nonsense as well.

Theo cleared his throat. "I am grateful for the opportunity to work with you, but I assure you that my education has been quite robust and—"

Dr. Greyson's cheeks pinked. "Oh, I'm sure you got a robust education from those charlatans at Victoria College." His expression implied that the word *robust* was a euphemism for something vulgar. "We don't need to get into my opinions on that diploma factory. In my day, you apprenticed under a respected doctor, you learned your trade, and you respected the medical traditions. None of this folderol of ether and carbolic, either. A doctor never used to be afraid of getting a little blood and bile on his coat. And now we're pretending that a speck of dirt under the nails will kill a body dead." His face was red now, and the only thing that stopped his rant was a coughing fit that sent bursts of pipe smoke to join the general haze around the ceiling of the room.

It was clear that he thought Theo was here for a kind of re-education: a return to the time where bloodletting was sound practice and germ theory was heretical nonsense. Hell, maybe he could whip up some arsenic paste to poison old women in the pursuit of a clear complexion.

Well, he would have to lead by example. Even someone as set in his ways as Dr. Greyson couldn't object to treatments once they'd been proven effective. Once he'd earned the old man's trust, they could reach some common ground. Theo put on his most deferential expression. "Quite so. One's education is never truly finished."

"Yes," said Dr. Greyson, recovering his breath. "Of course. Starting with lesson one, which will take place this Saturday. People want a doctor who's a pillar of the community, someone they can respect, someone they like. People have been talking about you, Teddy. And it's not just the citizens of Fraser Springs. Word gets around, you know."

Theo knew exactly what was coming. The cancelled welcome dance. The graceless social rounds with Mrs. McSheen. The horrifically awkward scene at Wilson's Bathhouse.

"In fairness, no one informed me about the, erm, social expectations of the position."

"My boy, that is the wrong outlook entirely. You should have been up and about at seven, ready to accept visitors. When you entered the ballroom, you should have immediately requested a song from the band and asked Mrs. McSheen for the first dance. You should have certainly corrected the pronunciation of your name right away. How do you think that dear lady, who was doing her best to help you, felt?"

"I was trying to spare her feelings." Theo could hear the whining tone creeping into his voice, and he hated it. Dr. Greyson might be a relic, medically speaking, but Theo had made a decidedly bad start, and there was no getting around that.

"Well, you didn't spare anyone's feelings. Not a bit. For a boy who was brought up around the best and brightest of society, you have proven yourself remarkably impervious to charm and good grace. But luckily for you, there's a second chance. Since that first evening was …"—the words "a disaster" hung unspoken between them for a moment—"cut short, Wilson's Bathhouse will be hosting a dance of its own this Saturday. You will come as my guest, you will summon up all the manners your dear mother taught you, and you will hope to hell that the citizens of Fraser Springs are as gracious as I know them to be."

Theo sighed. Dr. Greyson was right. "Yes, sir," he said.

"Very good. I will pick you up at eight o'clock tomorrow evening. And for God's sake, lose the top hat and tails."

"Understood."

Dr. Greyson's expression softened. "Cheer up, young man. If a country dance is the most uncomfortable part of your medical career, you won't have much to complain about. Learn to handle this bunch, and you'll be well positioned for your own practice."

If Theo had his way, he wouldn't be a practicing physician at all, but he knew better than to say that to Dr. Greyson. A man who clearly did not believe in germ theory or laboratories would not take kindly to Theo's pursuit of a career in epidemiology. Still, academia was its own small town. The same byzantine rumour mills and petty gossip. The same intricate protocol that always seemed to elude him. If he ever wanted to discuss bacterial mutations with Dr. Stottert in Germany or trace milk-borne scarlet fever in France with Dr. DuBois, he might as well practice by talking boils and bunions with the Finest People in our Beloved Fraser Springs.

"Yes sir," Theo said.

Standing for so long had brought an ache to his hip and knee. Now was probably not the best time to tell Dr. Greyson that he could not dance. But he would show up, shake hands, make small talk, and hope to hell that Dr. Greyson was right and that the people of Fraser Springs—and one person in particular—were forgiving.

Chapter 4

By the following Friday, Ilsa was cautiously optimistic that the dance would be a success. Or, if not a complete success, at least not a shambles. Invitations had been delivered to those who would be offended by anything less formal, and word of mouth had taken care of the remainder of the guest list. The members of the town's brass band were still disgruntled after their abrupt dismissal from last week's dance, but Ilsa had begged and borrowed a satisfactory assortment of phonograph records for the evening. The food situation was well in hand and under budget, largely thanks to Doc Stryker's gracious offer to supply the beverages. Given Doc's well-known opinions on the appropriate amount of alcohol in a "festive" punch, the dance was unlikely to be dull.

The planning had effectively been a second job for the past ten days, eating up the few free hours in her evenings. There hadn't been time to even open this week's newspapers, and she hadn't updated her notes since Sunday. It was frustrating; although she knew that she'd done twice as much work as usual, it still felt as if she'd done nothing that mattered.

On the bright side, the rush of preparations had helped keep her from dwelling on the fact that at any given time, Theo Whitacre was working and sleeping and taking tea just a few hundred feet away from her. She'd been up and down the boardwalk dozens of times, and yet their paths hadn't crossed again since that awful introduction at Wilson's. She'd even gone to the St. Alice to personally deliver an invitation to "Drs. Greyson and Whitacre," and Theo had been out of the office.

The familiar early morning routine of setting up the kitchen for breakfast was not, unfortunately, enough to keep her mind occupied. Once she'd run down her mental list of food preparations for the day and for tomorrow's party, she moved on to the guest list. The guest list brought her, inevitably, to Theo. The fact that she hadn't seen him was beginning to seem less like luck and more like he was avoiding her. It was a small town; unless someone was confined to bed, she was going to see them at the dock, or the general store, or the post office. And Theo clearly wasn't confined to his bed these days.

She certainly had nothing to say to him, but didn't he owe her an apology, or at least an explanation, even after all these years? They'd been introduced, after all. He knew where she worked, where she lived. He might be a doctor these days, but he was apparently still a coward.

She banged the big enamelled coffeepot back onto the stovetop, making a satisfying *clang* to punctuate her righteous displeasure with the spoiled young doctors of the world.

The sound was immediately followed by a sudden, awful screeching, and she nearly jumped out of her skin before she realized that it was only the noisy porch hinge opening.

"You scared me half to death with that racket!" she said as the kitchen door pushed open. Nils, the bathhouse's handyman, strode through with two huge pails of water.

"Good morning to you, too," he replied. He set down his load carefully, barely making a sound against the wood floor, before heaving the first pail over his shoulder to pour it into the kitchen cistern. Ilsa wasn't above staring appreciatively at the casual display of strength; it really was a shame that a man as well put together as Nils Barson was more interested in bugs and muskrats than in getting himself a sweetheart.

He put the empty pails out on the porch and came back in, wiping his hands on his denim trousers. "Coffee ready?" he asked.

"Depends. When are you going to fix that devil door?"

He grunted vaguely, which was about the extent of his vocabulary most mornings, and grabbed his usual mug from the shelf. She went to the icebox for the milk and then joined him at the big central table.

"Are you coming to the dance tomorrow?" she asked.

"Not planning to."

"But this is *my* dance. You'd have fun, I promise." Another grunt. Were all men incapable of basic conversation or just the ones she met? Or maybe it was just the young, handsome ones who had so much trouble talking to her.

Which gave her an idea …

"Actually, I need you to be there. As a favour." He narrowed his eyes at her over the top of his mug, considering.

"You're up to something."

She was, in fact, formulating a little bit of a plan, but she didn't care for the way he said it. "I beg your pardon."

"You only make that sweet face when you're up to a scheme."

"I do not scheme! I'm … organizing."

He huffed and drained the rest of his coffee. "Fine. What's the favour?"

"I need you to dance with me and look like you're having fun when you do it."

"There'll be a dozen men at your dance who can do that."

"But they might get the wrong idea if I flirt with them."

"And I won't," he sighed.

"It's a compliment! You're trustworthy."

"So we put on a little show. Who for?"

"Have you met the new doctor?"

"No."

"Well, I have. And he owes me an apology."

That got Nil's attention. He might not be a romantic, but he was as protective as a guard dog when it came to the Wilson's girls.

"Nothing like that!" she rushed to assure him. "I just want to make a point, that's all. He might not even show up, but if he does, I need to make sure he sees me having a wonderful time."

"I still don't understand."

"That's because you know nothing about men," she said, patting him on the arm.

"Canadian men, maybe. Danes are straightforward." He sighed. "One dance."

"Three dances and flirting."

"Two. And next time you make a pork roast, you save all the crackling for me."

"Deal," she said.

Nils sighed as he stood and brushed himself off. "Flirting. I don't know why people can't just say what they mean," he muttered as he dumped his mug in the sink. "Would save everyone a heap of trouble."

Ah, Nils really didn't understand. The situation with Theo was complicated, and his ignoring her was only causing things to fester. She was actually simplifying things, giving him a little push so that he'd realize the error of his ways. What was that saying about daylight being the best anti-septic? She'd make sure he couldn't take his eyes off of her, then give him an opening to speak to her privately so they could get everything out in the open. Scheming accomplished, she rinsed out the mugs, put the milk in the icebox, and got back to work.

• • •

As he approached Wilson's Bathhouse on Saturday evening, Theo scouted for a back entrance he could sneak through. Mrs. McSheen would be in there. Ilsa would be too. The risks that came with encountering either of them suddenly seemed unacceptably high. He barely attended to Dr. Greyson as they walked along together, Greyson prattling on about the town's great and good.

"Now, Mrs. McSheen has a lovely daughter just your age, but she is currently away at university in Toronto. Quite a tempest in a teapot there, I can assure you." He lowered his voice confidentially. "Myself, I don't hold with educating a female up to that level. Especially not in math and sciences. At any rate," he went on, "the Peters girl and the Bellweathers' daughter will both be in attendence. Both lovely creatures with all the charm and social graces one could hope for. The Bellweathers are the proprietors of the general store here, but they're connected to Lionel Bellweather. I'm sure you've met Lionel, great friend of your father's."

Dr. Greyson paused as if waiting for Theo to reply, but Theo had honestly lost the thread of names and relationships several steps back. He steered into a new subject. "And the owners of the bathhouse are the Wilsons?"

"No, as a matter of fact. Wilson was the original owner, as I understand it. The place is currently run by the Sterlings. Wilson was the name of Mrs. Sterling's first husband, who died many years past."

That name at least seemed familiar. "Isn't the mayor named Sterling?"

"Precisely. Mr. Owen Sterling. Do try to make up to the Sterlings, dear boy. Mr. Sterling's a pleasant fellow. A writer, you know. Novels, adventure stories. I don't go in for that kind of piffle, but they're reviewed quite well, I believe. And he's friends with Mr. Morse, who owns the St. Alice."

Theo could hear music and voices coming from the bathhouse, and the electrical lights blazing in the windows lit the boardwalk festively. Just an hour or two. Shake a few hands, remember a few names, smile. He could do this.

Dr. Greyson didn't bother to knock, opening the establishment's front door directly into a scene of swirling colors and laughter.

There was no servant to take their hats or coats, nor had a host greeted them properly at the door. The whole business struck Theo as hopelessly awkward, although Greyson seemed untroubled by the irregularity. He merely stood on the threshold between the small foyer and the large main room, smiling avuncularly until someone noticed their arrival.

A large Victrola held pride of place, currently playing a raspy recording of "In the Good Old Summer Time." A flock of young men and women clustered around it, giggling and elbowing each other as they argued over the assortment of phonograph cylinders. A slim woman separated from the whirl of dancing and conversation and hurried over to them.

Theo's breath gave a little hitch. Ilsa. Her cheeks were flushed, and she seemed genuinely pleased to see them. Her pale hair was braided and piled high on her head, and her lips glowed with the faintest trace of rouge. She was wearing a confection of a dress, layers and layers of some sheer, shimmering fabric in soft green that rippled and flowed like water as she moved. He forced himself to meet her gaze. Because that was the polite thing to do, and also to avoid admiring how the little spangles of embroidery drew the eye down her body or how the dress nipped in at her waist just so.

"Good evening, Dr. Greyson!" she said. Was she slightly breathless? "And good evening to you as well, Dr. Whitacre." She smiled and held out her hand. Theo froze, years of etiquette drills suddenly clamouring for priority. One might shake hands with a married lady, but a young lady never offered her hand to a gentleman except upon first introductions. But to reject her hand so publicly would be equally rude. Would a nod suffice? Did any of this even apply to a dance held in a bathhouse in the middle of nowhere?

Dr. Greyson seemed untroubled by the intricacies of the situation, taking Ilsa's proffered hand and raising it to his lips with exaggerated courtliness. Ilsa beamed at him. No wonder all the

Vancouver matrons adored the old man. Greyson stood back for Theo to do the same. Well then. The important thing was to carry oneself with confidence.

"Good evening, Miss Pedersen," he said. He took her hand, barely brushing his fingers against hers. Even that mild contact, the sensation of skin against skin, was enough to send a jolt into his abdomen. He wanted to snatch his hand back, and he wanted to linger, to keep touching her. Her hand still had the same rough calluses, not the soft hands of the gently bred girls of his own set. He had always been so fascinated by her hands.

Ilsa stepped back before he had a chance to embarrass them both with his clumsy indecision.

"Ah, so you've met," said Dr. Greyson, oblivious to the memory well Theo had blundered down. "Well, that's one less introduction to make."

"We've met, yes." Ilsa's expression was polite, but her eyes had a spark of mischief: an effect of the punch and dancing, most likely. "The refreshments are on the side table there," she said. "Enjoy yourselves!"

With that, she disappeared into the crowd. Theo relaxed. He had pulled off the most dangerous part of the evening. If he could handle Ilsa, he could handle a dozen eligible daughters and sharp-eyed mamas. This wouldn't be so bad. The room was decked out with red-and-white bunting and sprays of greenery. The gang around the Victrola had clearly reached some accord, and the contraption was now playing a lively waltz. Couples formed and began twirling around the dance floor. At the far side of the room, a long credenza was heaped with serving trays of food and an array of punch bowls. Good thing he had listened to Dr. Greyson and left off his evening wear. Even his waistcoat was pushing him to the edge of formality.

Dr. Greyson ushered him to a group of older women stationed along the edges of the makeshift dance floor, chattering and fanning themselves while keeping watchful eyes on their husbands and daughters. Time to get down to business, then. For half an hour, he put his social skills through their paces. He found it helpful to make up mnemonic devices for every person he met. The strategy had served him well in medical school, and there was no reason why he couldn't learn people the same way he had learned the five steps to sanitarily lance a boil.

The sisters Penelope, Ophelia, and Pauline's initials formed POP, though this had the unfortunate side effect of running the nursery song "Pop Goes the Weasel" through his mind whenever he saw one of the three. He recalled that Mr. Sterling was the mayor because he had a sterling reputation, and that Mr. Bellweather was the general store owner because he sold bells in any weather. Theo was getting the hang of it.

Even more mercifully, the dance had more gentlemen than ladies, so no one called on him to dance. Still, as he made small talk, he couldn't resist scanning the crowd for the flash of a green dress and a blond head. There she was, tending the punch bowl. There she was again, dancing with someone, her head tipped back in laughter.

Finally, he was able to excuse himself and head to the row of chairs along the back wall. His knee and lower back were already throbbing, so he propped his cane against the wall and settled himself gingerly onto a seat. He rubbed his knee as he watched the dancers. Ilsa wasn't hard to spot. She was spinning around the room with a burly blond man in a threadbare coat. Hadn't she already danced with him once this evening? The song ended, and she smiled and laid her hand familiarly on the man's arm. Theo took a long swallow of his drink to chase away the sudden sour feeling in his stomach. She whispered something into her partner's ear, and the man laughed and gathered her back into his arms. The next song started up, and they twirled away across the dance floor.

So Ilsa was spoken for. Not that it mattered, of course. It would have been shocking if she weren't. She was by far the most attractive woman in the room. She had such a lovely smile. And she'd always had the gift of making you feel comfortable around her, as if you were the only person on earth. As if you mattered to her.

"Feeling okay, Dr. Whitacre?" The voice jolted him back to the present. Mrs. Sterling stood just to his left, wearing a blue dress that was lovely but years out of fashion even to his untrained eye, and strained nearly to bursting about her midsection. He hurried to his feet to greet his hostess.

"Oh, I'm quite well, thank you. You've organized a very lively evening."

Mrs. Sterling smiled. "I wish I could take the credit. Ilsa organized it all; I'm only a guest at my own party."

"Then please give my compliments to Miss Pedersen."

Mrs. Sterling raised her eyebrow. Was it the name or the way he said it? He needed to steer the conversation back to safer ground. "Would you like to take a seat?"

"Lord, yes. I feel like I've been on my feet for years." She eased herself down onto the chair beside the one he'd vacated, leaning just a little into the arm he'd offered to assist her.

Theo took his own seat and racked his brain for appropriate small talk. "It's been very nice to make everyone's acquaintance."

But Mrs. Sterling was looking at his leg, which he realized he was rubbing again. "Is your knee giving you trouble?"

Theo shrugged. Everyone loved to talk about aches and pains, especially with a doctor. "I'm just resting it."

"Old injury?" she asked.

Theo braced himself. "No. I had paralytic fever as a child."

The mere mention of paralytic fever was usually enough to send people into at least five minutes of hushed condolences and stories about their mother's friend's niece who had been stricken with the same disease. Instead, Mrs. Sterling seemed to brighten. "That's what I thought. We have a treatment for partial paralysis that I've seen do wonders for correcting asymmetry."

At that moment, Ilsa appeared to press a cup of lemonade into Mrs. Sterling's hands.

Mrs. Sterling smiled. "You really don't have to play nursemaid for me all night."

"Someone has to, and that glad-handing husband of yours is busy telling that story about the bear for the hundredth time."

Mrs. Sterling's laugh was full of affection. "You love that story and you know it." Ilsa responded with an impolite snort, which only made her employer grin broadly. "At any rate. I was just mentioning our paralytic treatments to Dr. Whitacre. What do you think?"

Ilsa's mood became serious all at once. Was she remembering how much he'd loathed the "treatments" he'd been subjected to all those years ago? Scalding hot flannel wrappings. Ice baths. Electrical shocks. "I think he should try," she said after a long moment. "You can't come to Fraser Springs and not try the hot springs."

The very last thing in the world that Theo wanted to try was another quack cure. It was a waste of time, at best. "I've heard nothing but glowing reports of your services," he said neutrally.

"All the more reason to visit," Mrs. Sterling said. "I think we could even arrange for the first treatment to be complimentary."

"Oh, but I would insist on paying," he stammered.

"Then it's settled," Mrs. Sterling said, clearly delighted. "We have men's hours on Tuesday afternoons."

"Well, I'm still figuring out my schedule. I'll have to …"

"When do you do your rounds?" Ilsa asked.

"Every morning from nine to twelve thirty. Then I'm in the office at the hotel from three to six. But I'd have to check my …"

"Perfect. One o'clock on Tuesday, then," Mrs. Sterling said. Theo glanced desperately at Ilsa. Surely she wouldn't want him underfoot? It was hard to read her expression. He had expected irritation, but she seemed … thoughtful?

"Does your leg still hurt when you bend it?"

"And when I don't bend it. I'm used to it by now. It doesn't matter."

Her pale eyebrows drew together and her lips twisted to one side; her recognized the expression instantly, even after all these years. It was the face she made when she disapproved of something and was trying very hard not to offend you by pointing it out. He sighed. "Oh, just say what you want to say."

"It's only that you shouldn't be in pain just because you're too stubborn to try something new. If there's a chance we can help, you should try."

"I don't want to waste your time trying to fix something that can't be fixed."

"It's not about fixing you!" Ilsa clearly spoke more forcefully than she'd meant to, because her next words were much softer. "It's about making you hurt less. You don't even know what the treatments are."

Mrs. Sterling was staring at them as if they were a tennis match, volleying back and forth, and he was suddenly aware that he was in danger of causing exactly the kind of scene that Greyson would lecture him about for weeks.

"Fine. On a trial basis."

"Of course," Mrs. Sterling said. "I'll be sure to have Ilsa see to your visit personally, since you're already acquainted." Ilsa directed a glare at her that would have melted stone, but she blithely ignored it.

"Thank you, Mrs. Sterling." He stood. Better get out of this conversation fast before he got hustled into anything else. "I should let you ladies get back to your beaus." At the mention of beaus, Theo swore that he could see a little smirk light up Ilsa's face, just briefly. "If you'll excuse me, ladies, I believe Dr. Greyson has a few more people he wants me to meet."

He nodded politely and pushed out along the edge of the swirl of dancers. He risked a glance back over his shoulder; Ilsa and Mrs. Sterling had their heads together.

Dr. Greyson did indeed have several more people for him to meet, primarily men and women of middle age who wanted to take the opportunity of a very public dance to discuss their puzzling skin conditions and irregular bowels. Theo caught himself stealing glances at the dancing couples and the knots of roughly dressed men collected around the refreshment tables. He wouldn't know what to say to any of them, but at least they probably wouldn't ask his opinion of their suspiciously shaped moles.

"Isn't that true, Doctor?" piped a reedy voice some two feet below his line of vision. He wrenched his attention back to the ancient Mrs. Parks.

"It's not impossible, I suppose," he hedged, having lost the thread of their conversation. Mrs. Parks bobbed her head with enthusiasm and turned to her companion, whose name was either Miss Westman or Miss Eastman. "You see!" she said. "I knew that specialist didn't know his business." Damn. Whose orders had he countermanded now? Greyson and Mrs. Sterling were nowhere to be seen, which meant that the only other person who might conceivably rescue him from this conversation was …

"Miss Pedersen!" Ilsa heard her name and stopped in her tracks.

"Hello, Dr. Whitacre. Is there something I can get for you?" She smiled sweetly, and his two elderly conversation partners narrowed their eyes, ready to defend their claim on his attention.

"Yes. Thank you," he agreed immediately.

Ilsa waited a moment, her smile fixed in place, before surreptitiously nudging the tip of his cane with her foot.

"Oh! The thing is, I need, um … your opinion," he finished lamely.

"Exactly. About the liniment." Mrs. Parks and Miss Eastman/Westman visibly relaxed—liniments were, indeed, a perfectly respectable topic for a private consultation. "We have some already made up, if you'd like to come to the kitchen with me." Theo nodded gratefully and trailed after her like a rescued duckling.

In the relative quiet of the kitchen, the thumping of his cane on the floor seemed excruciatingly loud. He sank down into a chair with a sigh.

"Don't be melodramatic. Mrs. Parks isn't that bad." Ilsa joined him at the table, sliding a glass of cold water over to him.

"Thank you. But if you'd been answering questions about bunions all night, you'd be melodramatic as anything."

"I work here, remember? Bunions pay the bills."

"New topic, please," he said. She laughed, and he found himself smiling foolishly back at her. This was all so much easier without a roomful of people staring at him. "I've been meaning to talk to you, actually." Ilsa's smile tugged away into a flat line. He swirled his index finger in the condensation ring that his water glass had left on the table, giving himself a moment to measure out the words he'd been turning around in his mind all week. "I didn't handle myself very well when I saw you here."

"No. You didn't." Her voice was level, and her face gave nothing away.

"I understand if you're angry with me for pretending to not know you."

"I was angry at you. And then you disappeared."

"I didn't mean to disappear. I was ... busy."

"I see."

"Are you still angry with me?" he ventured into the long pause that followed.

"I don't think so. Not really." Theo let out the breath he hadn't realized he'd been holding. "We were both surprised, and it was awkward with everyone right there watching. And you're apologizing now." There was a hint of a question in that last sentence, and he leapt into the breach, dignity be damned.

"Yes. Absolutely. I am apologizing. Sackcloth, ashes, the whole bit." That teased her smile back out.

"Good. Bygones, then."

"Pax," he agreed. God, he'd missed this, the way they'd always been able to talk easily and freely with each other. "It wasn't a bad surprise, finding you here. I had no idea."

"And you're a doctor now. How did that happen?"

"The usual way, I suppose. Victoria College has a very good medical program."

"No, I meant how did you talk *her* into letting you get a job?" Ah. His mother. That fight felt like so long ago.

"It's a long story. But the important part is that I won and nobody disinherited me in the process."

"Well, that's good," she said. "It suits you. Do you like being a doctor?"

"I do. Very much."

The smile she gave him then was so bright and sincere, it might as well have been a hug. "Good. I worried about you, Theo."

He was still trying to work through that admission when the swinging door into the kitchen burst open. A wild tumble of skirts and feminine laughter followed, and Ilsa was up and away, marshalling the chaos into an orderly procession of bread slicing and lemonade pouring and tray carrying. Minutes later, Theo found himself alone in at the table, with only a half-full glass of water to keep him company.

Chapter 5

Trying to get a gaggle of sleepy, tipsy girls to clean up after the dance was an exercise in futility. Mary had been sweeping the same patch of floor for what felt like fifteen minutes, Annie was nibbling leftover canapés under the guise of carrying trays back to the kitchen, and Elsie and Norah were giggling in a corner like schoolgirls, not even pretending to work.

The electric lamps cast an orange glow across the now-empty great room; she still missed their old oil lamps sometimes, but the new lights were less work. The odours of punch and cologne lingered in the air, mixing with the pine scent wafting in through the open windows.

"The sooner we get this done, the sooner we can go to bed," Ilsa noted loudly to no one in particular. The girls picked up the pace incrementally.

Jo returned from ushering the last guests out, humming a melody that had played on the Victrola hours before. "Well, I do believe you've pulled it off, Ilsa. I never thought I'd see the day when Mrs. McSheen and our clientele praised the same party. The only way Owen could get Doc and his crew out the door was by promising to host again for New Year's."

Ilsa laughed. "If the punch is strong enough, that lot will praise any party."

Jo wandered over to help her unstring the bunting. "It was a good night, though. That young doctor didn't look like he disapproves of dancing after all."

The giggling from Elsie and Norah grew louder. Jo cut her eyes at them. "Do you ladies need an extra job to do? I see tables that need wiping down and punch glasses that need washing."

"Miz Jo, is it true that new doctor is going to come here for treatment?" Norah asked. "I call dibs."

"No, me!" exclaimed Elsie. "Do you think he got shot? I wouldn't mind a bit of a limp as long as ... you know ... nothing else is limp." A storm of giggles greeted this witticism.

"I hear he's rich," said Annie, instantly animated.

"Ilsa will be treating Dr. Whitacre, and if you all don't stop gossiping and start cleaning, you're going to be on latrine duty for a week," Jo said. She didn't sound entirely serious, but it was more than enough to motivate the girls to put in a more sustained effort.

Soon, Ilsa and Jo were alone in the great room, putting away the last of the washed and dried glassware. "I don't care if Norah or Elsie takes on Dr. Whitacre," Ilsa said.

"I know. But I already told him you'd do it. Unless something happened tonight to change your mind?"

"No. We had a chance to talk a little, actually. I think ... I think everything will be okay." She stacked the last punch glass into its place in the hutch, and they began to circle the room, switching off lights and snuffing candles. At last, everything was orderly and quiet, the room lit only by the faint glow from the stairs that led up to the second floor hallway. Jo paused on the first landing, touching Ilsa's elbow to stay her before she could continue on upstairs to her own bedroom.

"All right. I am dying of curiosity, and I need you to put me out of my misery." And her very pregnant best friend sat herself firmly on the stair above Ilsa, blocking her way. "You worked for his family once. He was nice." She crossed her arms and waited.

Ilsa sat down in the stairwell, twitching Jo's skirts to one side with a show of more annoyance than she actually felt. "You never used to be this nosy. I was fifteen, almost sixteen. The Whitacres hired me on as a maid of all work. Theo was bedridden then, and his father was a thousand years old, so it was supposed to be a safe house."

"Supposed to be?" Jo prompted.

"It was. The cook was a nightmare and Mrs. Whitacre was worse, but I never had that kind of trouble there. But Theo was close to my age, and we were both so unhappy and so lonely, and—." She indulged in a short sigh. "The short of it is, his mother found us in bed together. We weren't even doing anything ... you know. Not really."

"But bad enough?"

"Bad enough," Ilsa agreed. "His mother dragged us all into some kind of hellish family meeting and sacked me in front of everyone. He just sat there. Never said a word. Wouldn't even look at me. So I left, and then I got work at the dance hall you hired me out of. And you know the rest. I never saw him again until he showed up here."

Jo's expression was soft. "Did you love him?"

"I was sixteen. It wore off." She'd intended it as a joke, but it came out sadder than she'd meant it to.

"Part of me has always felt bad for leaving him alone in that awful house, with those awful parents. Even if he deserved it." Jo nodded loyally. "But I'm not angry anymore. We were both so young. And he really didn't have any control over that situation." She picked at a loose thread on her skirt, near her knee. "I've seen it since then, you know. In some of the girls here and back in Vancouver. They're put so far down for so long that when they finally get a chance to make a choice for themselves, they just freeze up. And they usually end up picking the worst of all their options."

Jo reached across to rest her hand on top of Ilsa's fidgeting fingers. "Not you, though. You always grab for that brass ring."

Ilsa smiled in the darkness, though her stomach sank a bit. If only Jo knew what brass ring Ilsa was grabbing for next. "I'm stubborn like that. But that's not everyone. And I know now that it's not something you can change. Or stay angry about." She turned her hand over to squeeze Jo's hand.

"No wonder he's so awkward. It sounds like he never really had a childhood," Jo mused.

This hadn't occurred to Ilsa. Since she had arrived in Fraser Springs, she'd treated a handful of people with varying degrees of paralysis. While many of them had difficulty walking, all of them still led normal lives: jobs, spouses, families, friends. They were bakers and farmers and loggers. What held Theo apart from other people was his past, not his limp.

"He could also be awkward because he's a spoiled little prince."

"No, I'd say this is definitely a case of inexperience. He just needs to be drawn out of his shell by someone charming. And I think it would help if that person were also pretty and blond."

Ilsa snorted. "Oh you do, do you? This wouldn't be because you love meddling in other people's lives."

"It's not meddling if it works. Didn't I predict that Sally was going to run off with that lumberjack last season? And wasn't I the very first person to notice the spark between Ethel Barker and Mr. Haywood?"

"Two cases. You're a legendary matchmaker."

"It's true, though. I should start selling love potions."

"You'd make a fortune this month alone. Half the mamas in town are already scheming to marry their daughters off to the handsome new doctor."

"I knew it! You think he's handsome. You're desperate to get him alone and rekindle your tragic romance!"

Ilsa pinched her friend's arm. "Hush it. You're making a hen out of a feather with this tragic romance business. I'll treat him, but the minute things get uncomfortable, I'm passing him off to Elsie or Norah."

Jo smiled. "That's all I ask." She struggled to rise, and Ilsa helped pull her to her feet.

"Oof. By the time this baby's ready to be born, I'm going to have more muscles than a stevedore from hauling you up all day long," Ilsa said.

Jo looked down at her swollen belly. "It won't be too much longer, I hope. I'm running out of doorways I can fit through."

"As long as you can still get into bed on your own. Try to not arrange any more marriages in your sleep, please."

"No promises. Good night, Ilsa."

Ilsa extinguished the remaining lights and followed Jo up to bed. It felt good to talk about Theo. Hell, it felt good to have cleared the air with him. Clearly, all the problem needed was a few glasses of rum punch and a private conversation. How silly her worries over the past week seemed now. Theo wasn't the soul mate she had imagined at sixteen, and he wasn't the snivelling coward she'd cast him as either. Tonight he'd shrunk back down to mortal size, just a rich boy turned into a slightly awkward man, no better or worse than any other man.

She shut her bedroom door behind her and began to settle in for the night, sparing a guilty glance under the bed where the hatbox sat neglected.

Chapter 6

When he had agreed to give treatment at Wilson's Bathhouse a try, Theo had only planned as far ahead as the immediate benefit. Namely, that Ilsa and Mrs. Sterling would stop badgering him. Only afterwards, on the walk home, had it struck him that a hot-water soak in one's three-piece suit would be both absurd and bad for the fabric. Of course he would have to wear bathing trunks. In front of strangers. And Ilsa.

Although the changing rooms were private, the baths at Wilson's Bathhouse consisted of a large communal pool. The room was bustling with patrons and staff; it smelled strongly of cedar from the wooden planks along the deck and of pungent minerals in the steaming hot springs water. On the walls, someone had assembled a mosaic that was meant to look like Greco-Roman ruins but depicted no myths Theo was familiar with. Light filtered in from tall, thin windows that ran down the far wall.

Well, it was just one time. He'd give this quackery a fair shake, which would satisfy everyone, and then he'd never have to do it again.

Even fully clothed, he knew he drew stares. Undressed, nothing could hide his left leg, which curved inwards at the knee like a pencil in a glass of water. His thigh and calf muscles were much less developed on that side, which made his knee look oversized and bulbous. He worked hard to maintain muscle mass in his upper body and his right leg, which only added to the lopsided effect.

Presumably, none of the other men would care what he looked like, but that rationalization had never eased his instinctual shame. In medical school, he had busied himself asking the professor questions or volunteering for laboratory chores just so he would not have to change out of his surgical robes in front of the others. He waited until they had left to go to meals or the pub, then dressed alone in the resident changing room, which was always cold and lit by a single gas lamp.

He made his way across the short stretch of open floor from the changing room to the edge of the pool, but no one seemed to pay him any mind. Inside the pool, sitting on planks submerged a few feet below the surface, a dozen men lounged. Many had wet towels draped over their heads and necks, but all wore contented expressions. The staff—dressed in white skirts and blouses with white aprons—moved confidently around the edges of the pool, reapplying the towels and handing along tin cups of cold water as needed. The only noise was the swish of skirts and the drip of water.

Just fifteen minutes. He could do this.

"Shall we get you into the springs, Dr. Whitacre?" came a quiet voice. He would recognize that husky lilt anywhere. He tensed his bare shoulders to keep himself from cringing in embarrassment.

"Sure," Theo said. Anything to get this over with.

He tried not to look at Ilsa, focusing instead on navigating the slippery wooden planks and easing himself down into the pool. Still, the glances he got out of the corner of his eye were distracting: the humidity had loosened her blond curls and caused her white dress to cling to the curves of her body. The hot water seemed to fizz against his skin.

"Comfortable?" she asked.

"Yes," he said.

"We'll start you with fifteen minutes of exposure. I'm going to drape a cold towel over your neck to regulate your temperature."

"Fine." The chill of the towel contrasted with the heat of his lower body was … pleasant, he had to admit. It was an illusion, a classic case of referred sensation, but the fizzing water felt as if it was dissolving the aching gnarls or muscle in his legs and back. Just the effects of applied heat. Nothing magical.

"Leg troubles?" an old man asked.

Theo sighed. The other men had been watching him after all. "Yes. Paralytic fever when I was young." He braced himself, waiting for the pitying looks, the overly cheerful follow-up questions.

Instead, the man just nodded. "Me too. Real bitch, ain't it? Begging your pardon, ladies."

Theo couldn't see the man's body beneath the water, but from the chest up, he looked totally able-bodied. He seemed too well groomed to be a miner, but the scars and ropy muscles on his shoulders and arms suggested a hard life.

"Oh. I've never met another adult with the condition."

The man looked surprised. "Stick around here long enough, you will. It's pretty common. Lots of folks I grew up with had it. Now that I'm older, people assume it's just my age, which suits me fine."

Another man chuckled. "That's the one benefit of being poor. By the time you're forty, everyone you know is banged up in one way or another. Why, just in this room we got a few missing digits, broken bones that didn't set right, and more arthritis than you can shake a stick at. Welcome to the club."

As the man gestured around the room, the details of his fellow bathers came into focus. How had he not noticed the glass eye on that man or the fact that the person sitting beside him was missing his arm at the elbow? He had been too busy worrying about himself.

"You're very frank about it," Theo said.

The man next to him gave a gruff bark of laughter. "Ain't nothing here contagious. And having one hand never held me back from

anything but tying my shoes. Which is why I wear such nice boots."
He chortled and wiggled the toes of one foot above the surface of
the water. "When I asked my Katie to marry me, I says to her, 'I
only got one hand, but, by God, I'm offering it to you in marriage.'"

The entire group groaned, and Theo couldn't help but join
them.

"Said yes, though. And still with me twenty years later."

That unleashed a flurry of anecdotes. One man, missing a
finger on his right hand, told the story of tricking a young mine
geologist into thinking he'd dissolved it in hydrofluoric acid,
which the rest of the group said they'd heard a hundred times. The
other man with paralysis, whose name turned out to be Walter,
told Theo about how, after his initial sickness had worn off, his
father had handed him an axe and said not to come back inside
until he'd chopped a cord of firewood out of a downed oak. He'd
fashioned himself a crutch from some branches, then spent the
entire day panting and puffing and falling over until the wood
was cut. "Best medicine you could ask for," Walter said. "Old dad
knew how to make you bounce back."

Theo was almost disappointed when Ilsa returned. For the first
time, he felt welcome in Fraser Springs.

"That's enough for the day," she said.

"Aww," said one man. "We were just starting to get acquainted."

Ilsa gave them all a suspicious glance. "He's new. You lot better
not be scaring him off."

There were loud protests of innocence as Theo pulled himself
out of the water. He reached for his cane, but his hand was too
wet, and the carved eagle's beak slipped away from him. The noise
of the cane ricocheted off the walls, amplifying the noise. The men
laughed, but it wasn't a derisive laugh. It was the same way they'd
laughed at everyone else's stories.

"You need to get yourself a good hickory cane instead of that
monstrosity," said Walter.

"Walter!" There was a note of warning in Ilsa's voice.

Theo smiled. "No, it's absolutely a monstrosity." He bent over to pick up the cane and hold it to the light so the inlaid mother-of-pearl shone. "It's the stick equivalent to Mrs. McSheen's hats."

At that, the entire room erupted into laughter.

"Dr. Chicken Leg here is okay," Walter said, as Theo wrapped a towel around his waist. "You ladies should let him come back some time," one of the other men called. Theo smiled as he began to limp towards the changing room. He would take "Dr. Chicken Leg" over "Little Teddy" any day.

• • •

When she entered the treatment room, Theo was seated on the enamelled tin table. Most of her male clients stripped to the waist, or further, but Theo was wearing a two-piece union suit that ended at his knees. It was so clean and crisp, she suspected he'd had his launderer iron the thing, which made her smile a little. He looked nervous, his hands gripping the table's edge as if he were afraid he'd topple off if he let go.

"Would you like to get started?" she asked, settling into her professional self. Theo's was just another body, with just another combination of aches and pains to remedy.

Theo nodded and thankfully did not turn to look at her. He didn't need to. She could imagine the expression on his face so clearly based on the tension in his shoulders and back. The mint salve's heat radiated through its glass bowl and its sharp fragrance filled the room. Ilsa set the bowl down and put a hand on Theo's arm. He flinched just slightly.

"All right then. I'm going to have you recline on your back with your legs stretched long," she said.

He nodded again and repositioned himself. "Okay." She moved next to the table, pushing the lower hems of his union suit up a few inches to allow her better access to his knees and thighs. Theo dragged in a harsh breath, and she paused.

"If anything I do hurts, tell me. But for this to do any good, it's going to have to be a little uncomfortable."

Another nod. Up close, he was more muscular than she expected: his back and shoulders were firm and straight, tapering into narrow hips. Even in his legs, there were lean muscles, clear strength—a strength she suspected he worked very hard to maintain. Still, it didn't take an expert to see that he was in pain. Every time he shifted, he radiated tension and discomfort.

She slicked her hands with oil and began at the ankle of his stronger right leg, working her way up the calf with sweeping motions. How strange to be touching him again. How strange to see his body laid out this way in daylight, when she had known it so well in the dark of his childhood bedroom, hidden under heavy blankets. How strange to feel the curve of his lower leg, the tight muscles of the thigh above it, to be able to search out all the places where his pain was hidden.

He was too tense, his entire body held rigid and resisting the pressure of her hands. "This will work better if you can relax," she said into the quiet of the room. "Try to think of something pleasant, if you can. Sometimes humming a piece of music or running your multiplication tables helps take your mind off the discomfort." Dwelling on the past, or on present discomforts, didn't do any good for anyone—it was one of the cardinal truths of her own life.

Theo breathed out in a long sigh that might have been frustration or might have been surrender. Either way, he seemed to lay a little looser. She smoothed her hands over his calves, falling into the rhythm of her work. Soon, she located one knot high on his thigh, near his hip, that seemed to be causing the most problems. When she pressed into it, his breathing quickened.

"This will hurt, but I need to release this. Can you take a deep breath?" Theo did as he was told. "And let it out slowly …" His chest sank as he exhaled.

She pushed her thumb and the knuckle of her index finger hard into the knot, moving it in a circular motion until she felt it give way, then followed its path to another one, setting off a chain of tension and release along his hip and up his torso. Her work must have been very painful, but he didn't flinch or gasp.

"Still good?" she asked.

"Yes," he said, though his breathing seemed a little laboured.

"You should have had this worked on this ages ago," she murmured.

"I know," he said.

"Can you remove your undershirt and turn over on your stomach? I'd like to loosen your back before I work on the other side." He looked sceptical, and she smiled reassuringly. "I'll turn away to protect your modesty." That earned her a glare, but he sat up and did as he was told.

In the awkward silence that followed, she kept her eyes down and then folded his clothing neatly—someone had worked too hard on it for her to wrinkle it, after all. When the sounds of Theo's shifting finished, she turned back. She dipped her fingers into the little bowl of salve and traced a line along the path the tension traveled. "It starts here. Once you get problems here, it radiates outwards like so." She traced her finger in arrows towards his neck and shoulders.

"The rhomboid," he said.

"Hmm?"

"That's the rhomboid muscle," came a muffled reply. "It connects to the deltoids just there."

"Oh." She was glad he couldn't see her flush. Even here, when she was supposed to be completely in control, he showed up spouting Latin. "I don't know the names."

Theo paused. "No, but you know the muscles all the same." He grunted as she dug her thumb into yet another muscle knot. "I learned it in school, but you"—he inhaled sharply as she pushed down harder with the heel of her hand—"you were always better when it came to practical things."

Ilsa was silent. She couldn't tell if he was praising her or criticizing her, so she continued working her way along his back.

"What's this muscle?" she finally asked, moving her hands between his shoulders.

"Trapezius."

"And this one?" Her hands went farther up his neck, into his dark hair.

"Sternocleidomastoid."

"You made that one up."

She could feel the muscles in Theo's neck shift as he laughed. "I know all the names, but I can't do anything to fix it. All the naming in the world doesn't help you if you can't fix the problem. It's like knowing what to call every river and mountain on the map and still getting lost in the wilderness."

She let the silence hang for a long moment, running her hands up and down his neck to stimulate the blood flow. The odour of the mint salve mixed with the scent of his cologne. His back was such an interesting contradiction of strength and weakness.

"Have you found anything that helps yet? Your leg, I mean."

"Morphine," he replied curtly. "But I'd rather live with the pain than start down that road."

She had no ready answer to that. She knew that people could become addicted to laudanum and morphine, but to choose pain when relief was available seemed so grim.

"You can do what you like," she said at last. "I'm going to start working down to your left leg—let me know when it hurts."

Stretching the contracted muscles was torturous for both of them. The heat of the soaking tub had eased some of the tissues, but not nearly enough. She would stretch and straighten the knee as far as Theo could bear, and then hold that position and count aloud to ten with him. After the first count of ten, Theo's voice was ragged with pain.

They went through three more rounds before she stepped back and wiped her hands on her apron. "That's enough for today."

He made something halfway between a groan and a sigh before clumsily turning and twisting to sit upright on the treatment table. His face was flushed, his pupils dilated hugely. She knew it was from the pain and exertion of the stretching, but it reminded her of the last time she'd seen him without his shirt on. She could feel the heat rising in her cheeks as he reached for the undershirt she held out for him. Their hands touched for a moment and that, too, was so familiar.

"Thank you," he said, quietly. "I ..."

She turned away and busied herself by tidying up the towels. Whether it was from his expression, the warmth of his hand, or simply the physical effort of her work, she was feeling uncomfortably overheated. Time to wrap this up like a professional. "I think that went as well as could be expected. But one session on its own won't do much. If you would like to book another appointment, talk to Mary at the front counter. Have a good afternoon."

With that, she gathered the bowls and towels and whisked out of the room, heading straight for the kitchen, where he wouldn't follow. She set them on the table, then sank down into a chair. She was being terribly rude. He certainly wouldn't make another appointment. Which was for the best, but she hated to scare away a paying customer. He was just trying to set things right between them, and now she was the one making a hash of it. Everything felt so tangled up.

After waiting long enough to be fairly sure that Theo was gone, she smoothed the front of her apron and headed to the parlour to meet her next client. Men's hours were ending soon, and Mrs. McSheen's sickly niece would be her final appointment of the day; she was unusually grateful for the change in gender. After that, she'd be finished out front and could take her frustrations out on mashing the potatoes for dinner.

Mrs. McSheen's niece hadn't arrived yet, but Annie was there waiting, grinning broadly. "I think that new doctor is sweet on you," she said. "You should see the tip he left. And he already booked appointments through to next month."

Chapter 7

During their rounds at the St. Alice Hotel over the following week, Theo and Dr. Greyson saw to a dozen gentlemen and old ladies with symptoms ranging from "malaise" to "general irritability" to "a touch of palsy." The latter had excited Theo momentarily— it might be an actual medical case, perhaps the lingering effects of a small stroke—but it turned out that this palsy only came on when the patient hadn't eaten and could be remedied by a scone and a bit of jam. They were all more interested in his calling card than his diagnosis. Many were from Vancouver and were friendly with his "dear mother." A few found him "charming" and "very distinguished."

It wasn't medicine. It was just the same old social calls that his mother made, only with a stethoscope substituted for a cup of tea, and a little good old-fashioned hucksterism thrown in for good measure. To every patient, Dr. Greyson prescribed his "vitality water" to cure their ailments. A bargain at just two cents a bottle, he kept declaring, until he reminded Theo of a carnival barker. They could have enjoyed the same miracle draught from the hotel taps for free, but that wasn't Theo's place to point out. Oh well. Nothing in the hot springs water was likely to do any harm. It was just a waste of money.

During his lunch break on Tuesday, he took a walk to stretch his leg before his appointment at Wilson's. He had to admit that the treatment had helped. This was the first time in recent memory he'd walked and stood for hours at a time without needing to lie down after. It was a shame the deep massage had to be accompanied by Ilsa's hands on his body, and Ilsa's body so close to his own, and her voice counting along with him.

His back and neck had buzzed from mint salve and the massage, and he could imagine so easily the path her hands had taken. It felt as if they were still on him, and he could almost hear the lilt with which she'd pronounced the muscle names in her low voice. It was so easy to let his imagination wander to the moments in his darkened childhood bedroom.

No, those thoughts were dangerous. He had to pretend that she was an entirely different person. In a way, she was. Hopefully, he was nothing like the boy he'd been at sixteen. Ilsa's touch was just another type of medicine now. Her fingertips skimming along the hair at his neckline was no more erotic than when he laid a hand on someone's back to feel the wheeze of their rattling chest, or felt under someone's jawline to palpate their thyroid.

His thoughts were interrupted by the sound of someone running up the boardwalk. He turned to see the hotel's porter, his face flushed and breathing hard. "Excuse me, Dr. Whitacre, sir," he gasped. "Mrs. Deighton's taken sick and I can't find Dr. Greyson."

Theo hustled back in the porter's wake as best he could. He entered Mrs. Deighton's room expecting to see yet another case of too many petit fours at tea. Instead, he was immediately assaulted by a terrible odour, one that reminded him of the Vancouver slums down by the riverfront. The woman in the bed was pale as wax, and her lips were chapped.

He approached the bedside. "I'm sorry you're feeling unwell, Mrs. Deighton. What seems to be the trouble?"

Mrs. Deighton croaked as Theo got out his thermometer.

"She's got vomiting and ... and very loose stool, sir," the porter said in an undertone.

As he waited for the thermometer to finish its reading, Theo pinched the skin on the back of the woman's wrist and watched with increasing alarm as it bounced back far too slowly. She was terribly dehydrated.

"She was healthy at breakfast, sir," said the porter.

A limited number of things could cause such a sudden and severe onset of symptoms, especially since she did not have a fever. This looked, in fact, an awful lot like cholera.

Theo took the porter by the elbow and marched him to the door. "I need you to get the cook to set a pot of water to boil. Bring it to boiling for a few minutes, then let it cool. Stir in six tablespoons of sugar and a half tablespoon of salt, and bring it up as fast as you can."

The porter nodded gravely. "Right away, sir."

Theo returned to his patient's bedside. "We're going to get you feeling right as rain, Mrs. Deighton. We need to replenish your fluids."

The woman's eyes fluttered open, and she managed a nod. "Is it food poisoning?" she croaked. "I'll have their heads if it's food poisoning."

"I don't think so." If it was cholera, water was the most likely source. "You've been with us only a few days, so it could be you picked something up on your journey here. But I'll need to run some tests to know for sure."

As he waited for the porter to return, Theo opened the window to air out the room. Then he removed some test tubes from his bag and carefully took samples from Mrs. Deighton's half-empty water glass and the washbasin by the bed.

He had just put the stoppered test tubes into his bag when Dr. Greyson knocked at the door. He entered without waiting for a response and nodded to Theo as if relieving him from duty.

"My dear Mrs. Deighton," he said as he crossed the room to her bedside. "I'm so terribly sorry. The porter only just notified me of your indisposition." His face darkened as he looked across the room to the open window. "Close that window! Honestly, are they teaching you anything at medical schools these days?"

Theo sighed. If this was cholera, it wouldn't matter if the windows were open, closed, or made of solid gold. Doctors had stopped giving credence to the miasma theory in the '50s. But arguing in front Mrs. Deighton would not ease her mind. Theo did as he was told.

"Sir, may I speak to you privately?" he asked.

Dr. Greyson ignored him. "Sounds like you have a nasty tummy bug. I know it's unpleasant, but these matters run their course in a day or two. I'll stop by later on this evening with a lancet, and we can reduce that fever for you."

"She doesn't have a—" Theo began to say, but thought better of it. "Sir, could I speak to you in private?"

"Not now, boy." He crouched down and patted the old woman's hand. "Never fear, Mrs. Deighton. We'll have you up and about in no time. You rest, and I'll return tonight with a bit of something to help you sleep."

"Thank you, Dr. Greyson," Mrs. Deighton croaked. "You're so very kind."

"I'm sorry if this young man bothered you. He's still in training, but he means well."

Theo gritted his teeth. "I hope you feel better soon," he told the patient.

Just as they were leaving, the porter returned with the mixture Theo had ordered. "Here, sir. I hope it's cooled enough."

"Very good," Theo said. He turned and crouched down by Mrs. Deighton's side. "Now, ma'am, you've lost a great deal of fluid. This mixture is designed to restore your energy. You can sip slowly, but drink as much as possible. Ring the porter, and he can bring you more when you're done. It's vital that you drink as much as possible."

The woman looked to Dr. Greyson, who was scowling. "It can't hurt," he finally muttered. "You drink that, try to get some rest, and I'll be back to see you soon."

The walk back to Greyson's office was a tense one. Clearly, Theo had broken protocol again, but what was he supposed to do? Ignore a desperately sick woman until Greyson finished his three-course lunch and nap? Cast aside science to placate the old man's pride? If this was cholera, they had to act quickly.

Once inside the office, however, Greyson did not leave much room for debate. "I don't know what was in that concoction of yours, but you are not to treat my patients without my permission again. The lady has the stomach flu, pure and simple."

"She doesn't have a fever," Theo said as calmly as he could.

"I held her hand, and her temperature was clearly elevated. You don't need to go jamming thermometers into everyone's mouths to see that. Bedside manner, Teddy."

"It's not the flu."

"Oh? What's your diagnosis, Doctor?" He pronounced *doctor* as if it were an insult. "Some rare tropical pleurisy? A case of the purple-spotted kahoots?"

"Sudden onset, violent diarrhea, and vomiting. No fever. Fishy odour. Extreme dehydration. She's in desperate need of rehydration, not bloodletting or opiates." Theo took the test tubes out of his kit. "I'll have to run some tests, but she presents with all the classic symptoms of cholera. The hotel staff need to start boiling the water."

Dr. Greyson's face had turned from mottled red to purple. "The most reputable hotel this side of the Rocky Mountains most certainly does not harbour cholera. Cholera is a disease transmitted by beggars and streetwalkers, not people like Mrs. Deighton." He snatched the test tubes from Theo's hands.

"If it's not cholera, what's the harm in my running a test to confirm that I'm wrong?"

"Because!" Dr. Greyson sputtered, dropping the tubes into the work sink with a carelessness that made Theo wince. "Because it's a waste of time and energy. A wild goose chase. And I will not permit it! A microscope won't help you if you don't have a doctor's intuition, and you, Little Teddy, don't know the first thing." He practically spat out the words *Little Teddy*.

Doctor's intuition wouldn't help a bit if that doctor were operating on assumptions fifty years out of date. It took all of Theo's self-control to keep his own face calm and impassive. He'd spent his entire childhood being shouted at and belittled; in a good mood, his parents could make an angry Greyson look like a pussycat. Instead, he did what had served him best through his mother's hysterical crying fits. He took a deep breath and nodded. "Yes, sir. Is there not even a small chance it's cholera?"

"There is no ..." Greyson checked himself and lowered his voice to a hiss. "No cholera in this hotel!"

"Yes, sir." Time for a change in tactics. "I'll run the tests just to get some practice, then. I hope to study with Dr. DuBois in Paris after my tenure here. He's the leading expert on communicative disease and has done some very interesting work mapping the sanitary—" The redness of Dr. Greyson's cheeks suggested that he did not care one whit about Dr. DuBois or epidemiology. "Even if it's not cholera, running the tests would be a great help to me."

"There. Is. No. Cholera. In. This. Hotel." Dr. Greyson said, pounding the desk beside Theo to punctuate each word.

Theo sighed. Now was clearly not the time for talks about his future. "Very well, sir. I hope you're right."

"I know I'm right. Go do something useful. Update your charts."

Dismissed, Theo returned to his little cubby of an office and shut the door behind him. He took a deep breath, set his shoulders, and began to unpack his microscope. Dr. Greyson could forbid him from testing Mrs. Deighton, but he couldn't keep him from looking into the hotel's water supply. He would test every well and spring in the province, if that's what he felt was necessary. Maybe this would make a fine paper, something to show Dr. DuBois. He could imagine it already: "A Case Study in Cholera Transmission in a Spa Community."

But first, he needed the samples. Theo didn't know which was worse: not being able to use his medical training or using his medical training and having no one listen to him. When he had proof, they would have to listen, especially if more guests at the St. Alice fell ill.

He was going to be late for his appointment at Wilson's as it was. He would be seeing Ilsa, though. That, at least, would be something that went right today. He didn't bother to change his shirt or his suit—he'd only be stripping out of them in a half hour anyway.

He made it less than halfway down the boardwalk to Wilson's Bathhouse before his nascent good mood was flattened. A tall, yellow-haired man had fallen into step alongside him somewhere around the general store. He looked to be Theo's age or a bit older, but he was built like a bull moose, exuding an aura of disgustingly wholesome athleticism. He was also the man who had danced with Ilsa four times. Which was four times more than Theo had ever danced with her. He didn't even know the man's name, and he loathed him on sight.

They tramped on in silence for a while, Theo's limping gait setting the pace. He wished to God the fellow would simply lengthen his stride and pass him, but he must have been determined to be polite and not show up the poor cripple. Nevertheless, manners were manners.

"I don't believe we've met," he offered.

"No," the other man agreed. "Nils Barson. You're the new doctor." Not much of a conversationalist, then.

"I am, yes. You're also headed to Wilson's?"

He nodded. "I do odd jobs there sometimes. Most days, really." He paused, and then added, "Ilsa works there, too."

"Ah." They walked the rest of the way in mutual silence. What on earth could Ilsa possibly see in this man? She was so clever, so light and quick, and this Barson fellow was a clod.

But he was a very handsome clod. The world was a truly unjust place. He glared at Barson's broad back all the way to the front porch of the bathhouse, and kept right on glaring as the man disappeared around the side of the building. Probably headed to chop wood for five straight hours and then lift a series of increasingly heavy rocks. Yes, Theo definitely loathed him.

His second session in the big communal soaking room was more comfortable than his first, and yet he found himself responding to the other men's questions and stories with monosyllables, or simply drifting off into his own distracted thoughts. He couldn't shake the image of Ilsa dancing, light and graceful as thistledown, with that lug of a handyman. His pale, twisted leg seemed more repulsive and useless each time he looked at it, refracted under the surface of the hot springs' fizzing water. By the time Ilsa arrived at the edge of the tub to escort him to the treatment room, his gruff mood was attracting odd, wary glances from his fellow patrons.

They walked down the cedar-panelled hallway to the treatment rooms without saying more than the minimum "Hello" and "How are you feeling today?" Once the door was closed, he stripped down to the waist and settled onto the cold enamel-topped table without waiting to be asked. Ilsa raised one pale eyebrow at this, but she let the moment pass without comment.

Like the communal room earlier, the massage process felt less alien the second time around, the sensations of slippery oil and sure hands on his bare skin less startling. Ilsa's presence, however, remained as distracting as ever. In fact, without her easy small talk and her soothing narration of each new stage of the massage, it was even harder to ignore the fact that Ilsa was treating him in such a clinical, professional way. She didn't flirt. Her touch didn't linger significantly on his body, as she had let her hands linger on Nils Barson's strapping chest and shoulders when she'd danced with him.

It was impossible to tell how much time had passed before she finally broke the silent tension. "Are you okay? It's like your muscles are fighting me here."

"Yes. It's been a hard day, that's all."

"Trouble with a patient?"

"I don't talk about my patients." Ilsa's hands stilled on his lower back, lifted away a fraction. He didn't need to see her face to know that his abrupt answer had offended her. "I'm sorry. It's not your fault that I'm in a bad mood."

He'd been looking forward to this afternoon since the moment he'd left her side last week. Reuniting with Ilsa, having a chance to get to know her again, was the one good thing about this entire, godforsaken town. He might not have it in him to make witty repartee right now, but he could at least stop acting like a lion with a thorn in its paw.

He cleared his throat. "So. How long have you lived here?"

If the abrupt change in topic surprised her, she recovered quickly. "Almost five years."

"And have you worked for Mrs. Sterling all that time?"

"I have. She's the best employer in the world," she said without a moment's hesitation. "And she's my friend."

"Ah. That's good." Would he ever be able to inspire that kind of instant, unconditional loyalty? He rather doubted it.

"It is," she agreed. "Do you think you're ready to try stretching that knee out again?"

"I suppose there's no worming out of it at this point. Do your worst."

The process was just as painful as he'd remembered; by the end of the second count of ten, he felt as if each individual muscle fiber and tendon was on fire. Mortifyingly, his leg began to shiver with involuntary little contractions. There wasn't a woman alive who could admire a man who trembled like a baby fawn after twenty seconds of carefully bending his knee.

When they'd finished the fourth endless count of ten, Ilsa released her hold. She began to smooth both hands down his thigh and calf, over and over, as if she were gentling a nervous horse. "Take a moment to breathe. Then for this last count, let's try to go to twelve. Do you think we can do that?"

He only managed a disgusted groan in answer. "Wonderful," she replied, as if he'd given a far more enthusiastic affirmative. "We'll start on three. One. Two. Three. Breathe for me, Theo."

He was a sweaty, shaky mess by the end. And yet. As he sat up on the tabletop, there was definitely more range of motion in his left leg. Despite the burn of the stretching and a lingering deep ache, the leg felt less like dead weight. He swung it back and forth gingerly and then with more confidence.

Ilsa was grinning hugely at him. It was a lovely smile, warm and reassuring, but not the one he longed for. Instead of the carefree, flirtatious smile she'd given Nils Barson, her expression reminded him of the look you'd give a toddler taking his first steps.

"Thank you," he managed. "I almost hate to admit it, but this seems to be helping."

"High praise," she replied as she handed him his shirt. "I'll try not to let it go to my head."

"I mean it, though. Thank you. For … for everything. You didn't have to do any of this for me."

"I'm just happy I can help." God, the expression on her face was so very close to pity. It twisted in his gut, and he looked away to concentrate on buttoning back into his clothes.

He might as well make this easier on both of them and get everything out in the open. "Ilsa. I know we have … a past." He tested his weight carefully as his feet met the floor, putting the width of the treatment table between them. "But I'm glad you have a home here. I'm glad you've moved on, and I hope you know that I'll never stand in the way of that. And if Mr. Barson makes you happy, I'll be happy for you both."

For the first time in his memory, Ilsa did not have a ready response. He nodded respectfully as he let himself out of the little room and went down to the dressing room to make himself presentable again. His whole body pulsed with soreness, and every step he took jarred his muscles mercilessly. The pain throbbed in counterpoint to a growing headache, more than likely caused by his brain wrapping around itself in knots of jealousy and insecurity. Good thing he had already booked up to next month and didn't have to manage small talk to the woman at the front desk. He gathered his hat and cane and left Wilson's without another word to anyone.

As he made his way along the boardwalk, he began to walk faster. The chilly November air felt good. He put more weight on his bad leg, taking a savage pleasure in the stabs of discomfort he was inflicting on himself as he made his way back to his velvet-upholstered monk's cell in the St. Alice.

• • •

After her last appointment—thank God there was only one more after Theo—Ilsa flew through dinner and the end-of-day chores. She barely took time to nod at Jo and the girls as she crammed her little chip-straw hat on her hastily re-pinned hair, and she half ran past the buildings that stood between Wilson's and Doc Stryker's Saloon.

Once inside the tobacco-hazed bar, she found her quarry almost immediately. When he was in town, Nils was nothing if not predictable: same single tumbler of whiskey, same corner bar stool, every night for as long as she'd known him.

The big blond man jerked in surprise as she thumped him on the shoulder. "What did you say to him, you big oaf?"

"Ow! What did I say to who?"

"Don't play dumb with me. To Dr. Whitacre. He came in today and told me that he's glad I've 'moved on' and that he won't stand in the way of our love. What did you *say*, Nils?"

"I barely even talked to him. I walked with him on his way to his appointment. I told him that I saw you most days at Wilson's. Look, I told you I wasn't going to be any good at 'flirting.'" He rolled the word around awkwardly, as if it had filled his mouth with marbles. "You want to scheme, get Owen or Doc to help you."

"Owen is too married and Doc is too old. And it was just for that one night at the dance. I never told you to keep after him!"

"Aw, don't pout like that."

She pouted harder out of spite.

"Can I make a suggestion?"

"No. You already admitted you're terrible at this."

Nils raised his eyes to the ceiling, as if the stamped tin could grant him supernatural patience. "You could try talking to your doctor yourself."

"He's not 'my' doctor. And we did talk, that night. All he ever does is talk. Getting him to talk isn't the problem."

"Fair enough." He took a slow, considering swallow of his drink. "I could accidentally lock both of you in the pump house for a couple of hours."

Ilsa made a very unladylike scoffing noise in the back of her nose. "You men are all alike. If that's what I wanted, I could arrange it myself, and probably a lot better than you would."

"So you don't want to talk, and you don't want to, um—." One of Nils's more endearing traits was the ease with which he blushed. "You got his attention and made him apologize for acting like a *fjols*. What else do you need, exactly?"

It was an excellent question. She had been very successful at avoiding thinking about its answer for weeks, and she could probably manage another night or two. She shrugged.

"For starters? I want a drink."

Chapter 8

Harold Morse, the owner of the St. Alice, held court in the hotel's penthouse suite. Theo cursed him silently as he emerged onto the third floor landing of the main staircase. The climb had undone all of Ilsa's hard work from a few days earlier; his muscles and knees were seizing up in protest, and there was a sheen of sweat on his forehead: certainly not the way he'd hoped to meet his employer for the first time.

He mopped his face with his handkerchief and shook out his cramping right hand before knocking lightly at the polished oak door marked *Owner's Suite: Private.*

Morse opened the door himself. He was a surprisingly young man, perhaps in his very early forties, and rather undistinguished looking. Brown hair, brown eyes, medium height, wearing a brown suit of good cloth and only average tailoring. Theo had expected something a bit more dashing from the owner of a hotel as ostentatious as the St. Alice.

"It's a pleasure to meet you properly, Dr. Whitacre," Morse said as he shook Theo's hand. Oh good God, had they met before? Theo made an effort to keep his expression blandly pleasant as he raced through his recent memories. They had probably been introduced at that awful Welcome Doctor dance-that-wasn't.

And now he had waited too long to answer. Morse had released his hand and was looking at him expectantly.

"Oh," Theo blurted. "Yes, of course, a pleasure."

Morse let that pass without comment. "Step into my parlour, Doctor." Theo followed him into a room furnished as a combination of office and club lounge. A heavy desk and chairs sat directly in front of a large window with a stunning view of the lake and the mountains beyond it, framed on either side by tall bookshelves filled with large, leather-bound ledgers. Morse didn't head to his desk but veered left towards a pair of sueded leather chairs facing the room's large fireplace. Much like its owner, the room wasn't what Theo had expected. This inner sanctum was … cozy wasn't quite the right word. Comfortable, in a roughly masculine way.

"Drink?" Morse asked, pausing by a mahogany and brass sideboard.

"No, thank you," Theo replied. Morse nodded, poured himself a splash of something amber into a tumbler, and gestured for Theo to have a seat.

"So. How are you settling in?"

"Quite well, I think," Theo lied. "The facilities here are surprisingly modern. Um. Surprising for the region, I mean."

"You were expecting log cabins and whale oil lamps?" He couldn't tell if the question was a joke or a sign of Morse taking offense. Maybe he should have accepted Morse's offer of a drink—it was the middle of the day, but it would have given him something to do with his hands during these awkward pauses. "This may not be Manhattan or Paris, but that's the charm of the place," Morse said. "We're selling frontier vigour and clean mountain air, only with electric light and private bathrooms." Theo nodded. "That's part of why I brought you on. Along with Dr. Greyson, of course. The hot springs are well and good, but the St. Alice needs to attract patrons who are used to a certain level of polish, especially during the off-season."

He was window dressing, then, like the marble floors and the grand piano. An upper-class name for visiting Vancouverites to write home about: "You'll never guess who prescribed for my cough, dearest!" Theo smothered a sigh as Morse took a slow, deliberate swallow of his drink.

"At any rate. Glad you're enjoying the work and so on. Not really why I asked to see you, though. I'm afraid, Doctor, that we have to straighten out your habits outside of the office."

Theo stopped fidgeting with the handle of his cane and went quite still. "My habits?"

"Yes. This is a very small town, you know. You're the subject of quite a bit of speculation. And it's been brought to my attention that you've been patronizing Wilson's Bathhouse."

"Is that a problem? It seems to be a reputable establishment."

"Oh no, quite respectable. But it is a bathhouse."

"I'm afraid I still don't understand your objection."

Morse gave him the kind of condescendingly patient smile Theo had learned to detest over the years he'd spent as an invalid. "You are an employee of the St. Alice. And not just any employee, but the house doctor. It reflects poorly on all of us if you prefer to pay for services from Wilson's when you have access to those same services, free of charge, in-house. People will talk. They already are. The hotel and the town aren't the distinct worlds some people imagine them to be."

Theo felt like a first-year student again, being called out in front of the class for failing to do the reading. "I don't know that it's anyone's business where I go on my own time."

Morse's smile dropped away, revealing the shrewdness in his muddy brown eyes. "It's my business, Dr. Whitacre. And while you remain on my payroll, it stays my business."

Theo set his jaw. This was familiar territory. He'd had two decades of experience listening deferentially to variations on the tune of "as long as you're under my roof."

"I can't blame you for a misstep," Morse continued, lightening his tone again. "You're a medical man, not a businessman. And in a big town like Vancouver, nobody cares where you go or what you do. But as I said before, this is a small town, and people do care here."

"I see. I wasn't aware of the local politics."

Morse made a little grunt. "Politics. You're not wrong there, Whitacre. Don't take offense, but this isn't really about you. Our competition is the town's golden boy and mayor, and believe me when I tell you that's a tough needle to thread. Can't run the place out of business, but can't let it get too big either. And a little thing like where the hotel's doctor gets the knots worked out of his back can wreck that balance."

Theo grudgingly acknowledged the point. "If it's really that much of an issue, I'll cancel the appointments."

"Good." Morse drained the last of his tumbler and rose, their interview clearly at an end. "I should let you get back to your patients. And please, see about scheduling any work you need done with the concierge here. May I have your word on that?"

Theo levered himself up from the chair and shook the hand Morse proffered. "You have my word. Good afternoon, Mr. Morse."

Going down the stairs was almost as exhausting as climbing them, and by the time he'd made it back to his own room, he was sweating again. The physical discomfort paled in comparison to the larger irritation of Morse's condescension. He'd finally found something to enjoy in Fraser Springs, and he couldn't even have that without committing some kind of crime against capitalism and basic decency.

Still, Morse wasn't entirely wrong. People didn't come to Fraser Springs to rub elbows with miners and loggers. And reputation mattered, regardless of the town's size. Dr. Greyson had built a very lucrative career on the strength of social connections and was now enjoying an equally lucrative semi-retirement. His mother would never have allowed Greyson within an inch of her precious baby boy otherwise.

This kind of politicking was merely a fact of life, and one he needed to abide by. A few massages, no matter how effective, weren't reason enough to risk ending his career before it began. Ilsa would understand that.

He dashed off a quick note to Mrs. Sterling to cancel his remaining appointments, rang for the bellboy to run it down the boardwalk, and tramped back down to the office to see to another round of hypochondriacs and hangover victims.

Theo barely spoke to Dr. Greyson over dinner. Not that the good doctor noticed: their conversation was one-sided at the best of times, and the old man seemed tickled to have the floor entirely to himself. He was a sentence or two into yet another anecdote of medical disaster heroically averted when their waiter reappeared to clear their dessert plates. Theo stood abruptly, confessed to feeling unwell, and fled to his room. He kicked the door shut and hissed as pain shot up to his hip.

He was about to kick the door again—to teach it a lesson—when he was startled by a loud knock. He jerked the door open, ready to snap the head off of whichever unfortunate maid or bellboy he found on the threshold.

His terrible luck refused to take a break today: he was frozen in place, facing down five feet and four inches of Ilsa Pedersen. And she did not look pleased.

"You cancelled your appointments." It was a statement, not a question. That hadn't taken long. Morse was obviously correct about how quickly news traveled in this town.

"Good evening to you, too. Would you like to come in?" He wouldn't normally invite a woman into his room, but it seemed preferable to having whatever argument Ilsa was ready to have out in the hallway.

She swept past him and then spun on her heel to stare him down, skirts flaring around her ankles. "Those sessions were working."

"They were," he agreed, closing the door. "It's not …" He leaned against the doorjamb. "It's nothing personal."

"Then explain." She crossed her arms and shifted her weight onto one foot, jutting her hip out. If she weren't so clearly angry with him, she would be adorable.

"I had a talk with Harold Morse today." That surprised her—her mouth even dropped open a little.

"But he never talks to anyone."

"Well, he talked to me today. And he told me that it doesn't look good for the hotel if its house doctor is patronizing a competitor. Apparently, there's already been some talk."

"There's always some talk."

He shrugged.

"So what's the plan now? You're just going to hobble around in pain because it will make the St. Alice look bad if you don't?"

Put like that, it did sound foolish. "It's not up to me. I'm on the payroll here, so I do what the boss says."

She huffed an unamused little laugh. "As if you even need the money."

"It's not about the money," he shot back.

"Lucky you. You can tell Morse to mind his own business." Her anger intensified the faint Scandinavian accent of her childhood and gave her words an almost musical quality. Theo shook the observation away as unhelpful.

"That's not how it works. I gave him my word already. I cancelled everything at Wilson's. It's done."

She glared at him in silence for a long moment. "Nothing's changed with you, has it?"

She was baiting him, but he responded anyway. "What is that supposed to mean?"

"Someone gives you an order, and you roll over and show your belly right away. Who cares what you want, eh, as long as you don't get in trouble? Teddy's such a good boy."

His skin flared with an itchy tingle. "Don't call me that."

"What? Teddy? Teddy, Teddy, Teddy."

"Stop it. You're being childish."

"No. I'm all grown up. You're the one who's still trying to keep Mommy happy, no matter how much it hurts." And her voice wavered a little, right there at the end, and his chest suddenly felt hollow. A little of the fight seemed to go out of her, too. Her eyes were a little less narrowed, her voice a little less snappish, as she said, "So you're not coming back, then."

"I …" He hadn't thought about this part, in Morse's suite. Having to face Ilsa. Feeling like a coward.

Her chin lifted a fraction, and she uncrossed her arms and brushed her palms briskly down her faded blue skirt. "That's all I wanted to know. Have a nice evening, Dr. Whitacre." She turned for the door. His hand darted out to touch her elbow before he could stop to think better of it. She went very still.

"Ilsa, don't. I'm sorry." She breathed in, deeply, and turned to face him.

"You're sorry. For cancelling the appointments?"

"Yes. And for—for lots of things." She was so close, she had to tilt her head up to meet his eyes. Her eyes were so blue. Had they always been that blue? The last time they had been this close …

And then his lips were on hers. He wasn't sure which of them leaned first, closing those last four inches, and he didn't care. He remembered this. His body remembered this, how perfectly right they felt together. Her soft lips against his. The warmth of her breath. His hands skimmed her waist and that, too, felt right. He tasted her lips, and she made a soft sighing noise that sent pulses of warmth racing through him. It was as if an electric current made contact at every point where their skin touched, wherever her curves fit against the straight hard lines of his body. It had been so long, so goddamned long, since anyone had touched him like this. Held him. Wanted him. Not since he was sixteen, and Ilsa had—

He pulled away with a gasp.

"Christ. I shouldn't have done that." He jammed his hands into his pockets as he stepped back.

"Why not?"

"Why not?" he repeated. "Because ... because it's taking advantage."

She seemed sincerely surprised and still a little breathless. "It wasn't, though. At all."

"It feels that way. It's my fault you're even here. That you're ..." He had the good sense to not finish that sentence, at least. Even he knew enough not to tell a woman that she wasn't respectable. He shrugged, hoping she'd let it pass.

No such luck. "That I'm what? That I'm not working my fingers raw scrubbing muddy floors?" Damn. He'd angered her again, and they were right back where they'd been when she'd first barged in. Why couldn't he get this right? "You've seen my work. Up close, even. It's nothing to be ashamed of."

"No, of course not! I meant, you know, what you had to do in the past. Before you got this job." God, he hoped she wasn't going to make him say the actual, ugly word. Prostitute.

Her blue eyes suddenly went wide, and Theo braced himself for tears, for shouting, for a slap.

And then she laughed: a startled hiccupping sound at first that quickly swelled into a torrent of laughter she tried to hold in by covering her mouth with her hands.

"Your face!" she gasped. "Oh *Theo*, really?"

"What?" He was confused and a little offended. "What's so damn funny?"

"That's what you've been imagining all this time." She took a deep, shaky breath, steadying herself. "That I left your house under a dark cloud and became a tragic lady of the evening?"

"It's not funny."

"No, you're right." Her grin broke through again. "But you do realize there are stages between housemaid and whore, right?"

Of course he knew that. On an intellectual level.

"Then you never …?"

"No! Lord, no. I got a job the very next day. In a dance hall. Dancing." He must have still looked sceptical because she added, "With all my clothes on."

He had heard about dance halls, of course, although he'd never been inside of one. Workingmen spent their paychecks there on whiskey, music, and female companionship. But he had no idea how a woman could make an honest living as an employee in that kind of a place.

"Dancing with men?" he asked cautiously.

"It did tend to be men who wanted to dance with the ladies. And that's the only thing they paid for, besides drinks. Some of them offered, of course. Or brought little presents. But if anyone got grabby, he got thrown out on his ear." Ilsa smiled a little—apparently this was some kind of pleasant memory for her. Theo didn't like it, not at all.

"So you sold your time and your attention to any man who wanted to put his hands on you."

Her smile disappeared as if it had never existed.

"Don't. It wasn't perfect, but I wasn't ashamed of it then, and nobody's going to make me ashamed of it now. Especially you."

This time when she moved to leave, he simply got out of her way. In the space of ten minutes, he'd been called a coward, apologized for the worst mistake of his life, kissed Ilsa, and then effectively called her a whore. Twice.

The entire evening had been, without question, a disaster. He was losing everything good about his time in Fraser Springs. Not just the time spent with Ilsa; now that he wouldn't have it any longer, he realized that he was going to miss the camaraderie of the old-timers group. He'd finally found somewhere where nobody pitied him, where defects and pain and crookedness were old friends and not afflictions to be whispered about in hushed tones.

Worse, he'd insulted the last person on earth he ever wanted to hurt. Again. He just couldn't get out of the way of his own clumsiness and assumptions. He didn't know how he could make this up to her. He didn't even know if she'd let him try.

He lowered himself down on the bed and rubbed his temples. His back throbbed again, and the pulsing pain only reminded him that Wilson's and its treatments were off-limits to him now. The thought of anyone except Ilsa putting their hands on him like that made him flinch. So the knots would remain knotted. The tight muscles would still feel on the verge of snapping. And worst of all, without Ilsa, he was afraid that the hollow feeling in his stomach would stay that way.

• • •

Ilsa combed her fingers over her hair—everything still in place, still respectable. She couldn't look like a woman who'd just been pressed up against a hotel room door and kissed. She touched her lips, which still tingled. Even in the moment, she had known that she would regret kissing Theo. Stupid, stupid, stupid. She had been stupid for enjoying spending time with him, stupid for feeling safe with him, stupid for kissing him, for wanting to kiss him, for wanting to go right back into that room and kiss him again.

She had run out of second chances a long time ago. From her very first house when she was fourteen, where the master had had yellow teeth and would pinch her chest and always seemed to be waiting for her in darkened hallways. That man's wife had eventually hauled her back to the girls' home, claiming that Ilsa had displayed moral turpitude. She hadn't known what *turpitude* meant until she'd looked it up in a dictionary at the Whitacre's house, but she'd gotten the general idea right away. Four more employers with wandering hands, and four more wives who sent her packing with outraged silence or lectures about how Ilsa was leading their husbands into temptation. It was always her fault. Her body simply provoked men to lewdness, no matter what ugly uniform she dressed in. Some women just gave off an air of coarseness that couldn't be remedied.

And now, finally, she had landed in the perfect place. She had respectability. Protection. Dignity. Friendship. Enough pay to save for her future. So why did she seem determined to endanger that by marching up to a bachelor's rooms in a public hotel? And why had she wanted to kiss Theo so much? After years of attention from men who'd walk away from her the minute they got what they wanted, why did the one man she knew she should stay away from suddenly feel so irresistible? She didn't learn.

Theo was not the kind of person she could let down her guard for. Despite his bumbling and good intentions, he was dangerous. She knew exactly what rich people were like. They smiled and flashed those perfect manners at you, but they turned on you in an instant. And if you complained or fought back, you were only proving how inferior you were. Rich men especially seemed to be incapable of respecting any woman, especially one from a lower class.

Every time she had ignored this fact, she had paid for it. After her first kiss with Theo, she had resolved to end things before Theo's mother returned home. But what harm was there in enjoying their last few days together? And then his mother did come home, and of course, Ilsa had wanted to say goodbye. So she snuck into his bedroom and he wrapped her under his warm covers, and the bed was so much softer than her own little cot. Their whispered grand plans were punctuated with kisses.

"We'll be found out," she finally whispered. They lay facing each other, his strong leg over her thigh, his arms wrapped around her so her head was on his chest. Their bodies made sense pressed against one another. She was surprised to feel his erection pressing along her thigh, surprised that she wanted to feel it. "This is my last chance."

"What do you mean?"

"At the other places, the men were horrible. And their wives all thought it was my fault. That I liked it. But I didn't." Ilsa had to work hard to keep her voice to a whisper. "I didn't."

Theo tightened his hold on her.

"This is my last chance. The sisters sent me here because your father's so old and because …"

Theo snorted. "Because the poor crippled boy could never molest you?"

Ilsa laughed, despite herself. His erection pressed against her. His pajama bottoms hung low off his thin hips. It would take so little to tug them off. It would have been so easy: an inch or two here, a bit of fabric there, a man who was a little more insistent than Theo. Everyone from her parents to the sisters at the orphanage to countless employers had told her how dangerous this was, but here, with Theo, she could not summon any shame over it.

"We just have to keep it secret for two more years, until I can go to university." He paused. "We'll find some way. They can't get rid of you if I want you here."

But both of them knew that they could, and that they would, so he kissed her again.

"I won't let anything bad happen to you. Even if she fires you, I'll make sure you end up somewhere good. And then when I'm eighteen, I'll move away. And we can be together. I'm already learning how to walk with a cane. It will work out."

His voice was so earnest. Ilsa nodded. Things had never once worked out before. But it was hard not to trust Theo when his arms were around her. Not when everything had been so very difficult, and this did not seem difficult at all.

Except that it was. Ilsa shook the memory away. Nothing had changed. Nothing would ever change. He'd abandoned treatments that were helping him just because some rich so-and-so snapped his fingers. If he wouldn't stand up for himself, he certainly wouldn't stand up for her.

Luckily, no one was lurking in the kitchen when she slipped in through the back door. She did not have to explain herself or make excuses to anyone. She'd skipped out on dinner, so she slapped together a cheese sandwich and headed up to her room with it.

She was overworked, that was the problem. Her recklessness wasn't really about Theo; it was about her. She was on the edge of starting a new life, and that was scary. When you were scared, you retreated into old habits. Theo was simply one of those old comforts, like a forgotten favourite doll or blanket.

Still, every time she paused to look out the window, she found herself touching her lips, remembering how easily those inches of distance closed between them, how little their bodies had forgotten about each other. Kissing Theo was the first time she'd felt thrillingly alive in months. Perhaps in years. She deserved to feel that way more often. She would simply have to find a thrill that wasn't attached to a man from the richest, most awful family in Vancouver.

Her heart pounding, she retrieved the hatbox from under the bed. She took out her pencil and paper and began to write before she lost the nerve.

Dear Mr. Hayley:

I read your advertisement for brokerage services in *The Vancouver World* with great interest.

No. She should get right to the point. She took out a fresh sheet of paper.

As per your advertisement in the Sept. 1912 edition of *The Vancouver World,* I am writing to request more information about your brokerage services.

That sounded awkward. Another sheet.

I am writing in response to your advertisement for brokerage services, as advertised in the September 1912 edition of *The Vancouver World.* I plan to relocate to Vancouver to open a small sundries business. After much research, I believe that your prices are the most competitive, and I would like to meet with you to discuss this opportunity further.
Would you be available to meet

She paused. Jo's baby was due in late November, just two weeks away. Should she try for early December or around Christmas? Maybe January. No, if she didn't do it now, she would never do it.

Would you be available to meet in early December?
Yours most sincerely,

I. Pedersen

She wasn't sure what Mr. Hayley thought about women opening businesses, so she decided to remain on the safe side by using her initial. There. Done. She tucked the letter into the hatbox and shoved everything under the bed.

The triumphant rush of stuffing the letter into an envelope and addressing it had gone a long way to overpowering the thought of kissing Theo, and it was much more productive in the long run. Once she moved back to Vancouver and answered only to herself, she could daydream about kisses any time she liked.

Chapter 9

Theo spent a night of broken sleep and nightmares. In one, he was sixteen again, in a carriage with his father, traveling through the snowy Vancouver streets. They pulled up to the brothel. He cried out, tried to leap from the carriage, but it was no use. And then he was in the hotel room, kissing Ilsa, only this time he lowered her down onto the ridiculous velvet bedspread. Their bodies fit so well together, the knots and hooks of her dress seemed to fall away, and the rising sun cast shades of red and gold over her pale skin. She was so beautiful. But just as he reached out to touch her, she was yanked out of his bed by Dr. Greyson. Theo tried to pull her back, but he was frozen in place, paralyzed as if he were trapped in amber.

He woke up thrashing in the tangled sheets. The dream had seemed so real that he was surprised to realize he was, in fact, alone in the room. He took a few deep breaths. No Dr. Greyson. No Father. And most of all, no Ilsa.

That last one was his fault. He had chased her away. Every time things seemed to be growing easier between them, he found a way to make them difficult. He sat up in bed and fumbled for his spectacles. The blur of shadows and dim, early dawn light crystallized into the shapes of his wardrobe and dressing table. He took another breath.

The dreams tugged at the edge of his vision. He could almost see her by the door as she had been last night, closing the few inches between them, raising her chin up to meet his lips.

If he stayed in this room, he would never have to stop imagining how her lips felt, how they tasted, the little sigh she'd make when his hand brushed her waist—

No. Enough. He lurched out of bed and stumbled across the room to the sink. He splashed cold water on his face and dressed as quickly as he could.

As he descended the stairs for breakfast, the porter met him.

"You're up bright and early, Dr. Whitacre." The porter lowered his voice. "Mr. Enderby took ill yesterday evening. Dr. Greyson says it's the flu but," he hesitated, and then hurried on, "that recipe you gave me before, with the salt and the sugar—can you write that down for me? It worked such wonders on Mrs. Deighton. Mr. Enderby seems to be getting worse and worse, you see, and he's such a frail old man to begin with."

Well, then. Dr. Greyson had been seeing patients without him, sending him to tend to the rashes and headaches and taking the most serious cases for himself. He knew he should defer to the senior physician, but Theo's first oath was to his patients: to do no harm. If Mr. Enderby had the same illness Mrs. Deighton had, the dehydration could be fatal.

"Do you have a pencil?" The man fished a yellow stub and a scrap of paper from his pants pocket. Theo spoke as he wrote: "One quart of water to a boil for several minutes, add six tablespoons of sugar and half a tablespoon of salt, then let it cool. Get him to drink as much of it as he can. Have there been any other cases?"

The man looked nervously down the empty hallway. "You didn't hear this from me, right?"

At that moment a stout, balding man wrenched open the door that led out to the stairwell. "You there! Call the doctor." The man's thin white moustache quivered, and he was sweating profusely.

Theo raised his hand in greeting. "I am the doctor. What seems to be the trouble, sir?"

"My wife is ill. Very ill." The man grabbed Theo by the arm so roughly that it almost knocked him over.

He shook himself free, stepped back, and straightened his coat. "Calm yourself, please. What room is she in?"

"Room 315. She was perfectly well last night, and now she can't even keep a sip of water down."

"I'll get my bag and meet you there in five minutes." The man opened his mouth to object. "Five minutes," Theo repeated firmly. The man nodded curtly and headed back to the stairwell.

"You'd better double that recipe," he told the porter quietly. "Mr. Enderby first, then meet me in 315. We can talk after."

When Theo entered Room 315, the woman in the bed seemed to be a carbon copy of Mrs. Deighton: same ashen skin and cracked lips. Same unresponsiveness. Theo put the back of his hand to her forehead. No fever. He pinched the skin on the back of her wrist. She, too, had terrible dehydration.

"When did this start?" Theo asked her husband.

"A few hours ago. We came here to treat her rheumatism, not kill her!"

Theo put a hand on the man's shoulder. "She won't die, sir. She needs rest and fluids, but she's not feverish. That's a very good sign. I'll have the staff bring up a restorative, and your wife must drink as much of it as possible."

The man nodded. "Is it food poisoning, do you think?"

"I don't believe so," Theo said. "Travel can weaken the body's defenses, so it's possible she picked up something along the way. I'll come back in an hour or two to check on her and do some tests. But as long as she stays hydrated, I believe we can have your wife back on her feet in a day or two."

This seemed to defuse some of the anxiety in the little room. Perhaps he had learned a thing or two about bedside manner after all.

He found his porter waiting for him in the hallway with a large, covered pitcher.

"Thank you. Make sure that stays full, will you?" The porter nodded gravely. "Oh, and I don't think I ever caught your name."

"Porter." Theo must have looked confused, because the man smiled at him reassuringly. "My name's James Porter. It's easy enough to remember. Or you can call me Jim. And I'll take care of things here, Doctor."

Three cases so far, all with the same startling symptoms. Theo needed to get samples from the hotel's water supply. If Dr. Greyson thought that the St. Alice's reputation would suffer because someone dared to utter the word *cholera*, he was in for a real shock if patients began dying from it.

Theo ordered tea with breakfast to ensure that the water had been boiled. As he ate his porridge, he jotted a list: cisterns, pumps, water pipes, springs, drains, streams, latrines. He racked his brain for more, but damn it, he was a doctor, not a plumber. With proper discretion, he could get samples from within the hotel easily enough. But what if the source of the problem lay somewhere outside in the town? He couldn't exactly walk up to everyone he met and say, "Good morning! Have you or any of your loved ones experienced any sudden vomiting and diarrhea? No cause for alarm. Lovely weather we're having."

He needed someone who could talk to people without raising suspicion. Someone who knew the layout of the town in great detail. He needed someone he could trust and who would be trusted by others. His list of candidates was very short. There was, in fact, only a single name. Theo took another sip of his tea.

Blast. It looked like there was going to be grovelling in his immediate future.

• • •

Haggling for provisions this morning had provided the perfect outlet for Ilsa's pent-up disappointments. She'd negotiated a penny a pound off the bulk price of onions and even gotten the butcher to throw in some eggs for free along with the roasting chickens.

Laden with the spoils of her victory, she made her way down the boardwalk. As Jo's confinement drew nearer, more and more tasks had fallen to Ilsa, and it was all beginning to feel like too much to handle. But the shopping was one chore she didn't mind doing. Jo, as the mayor's wife, had to play nice and leave generous tips, but Ilsa wasn't bound by such rules. The general store's clerk in particular was a pompous windbag who loved to deliver monologues on the proper way to do anything and everything. A sweet smile and a few well-placed compliments, and Ilsa could name her price. Her dance hall training came in handy sometimes. And besides, sharpening her haggling skills was good practice for when she had suppliers of her own. Every chore she took over from Jo was both a distraction from her plans and a small lesson that would help her own enterprise thrive.

"May I speak with you?"

Ilsa's daydreams of haggling ruthlessly with Vancouver merchants were interrupted by someone touching her shoulder. Theo. So the universe couldn't grant her this one moment of victory. "You may not."

"May I walk with you, then?"

"You may walk wherever you like."

Theo haltingly fell into step beside her, his cane clacking on the planks. "I'm sorry," he blurted out. "I know I'm always apologizing to you, but I behaved badly."

"Again," she said. "You behaved badly *again.*" She stole a glance at him out of the corner of her eye. His cheeks were pinked from the effort of keeping up with her, highlighting the dusting of freckles across his nose and cheeks. Not that she cared. She was annoyed. And annoyed people did not notice the boyish freckles on their annoyer's cheeks. Still, she slowed her pace.

"Yes, again," he agreed. "I can't seem to help but foul things up."

She sighed. He was maddeningly sincere. Like a puppy dog that didn't mean to destroy your favourite shoes and wants so badly to do better, but for which shoe chewing was simply an uncontrollable instinct.

"I never intended to insult you. I spent so many years imagining all the terrible things that could have happened to you, I guess I couldn't wrap my head around the fact that you'd been fine all along. Better than fine. And then I assumed you were spoken for. So I was surprised when ..." he trailed off. "None of that is an excuse for losing my temper. I'm sorry."

And now she felt guilty, too. He might be at fault for most of last night's debacle, but she should at least own up to her own part in it. "By spoken for, you mean Nils Barson?" He nodded, looking miserable. "Nils and I are good friends, but we are only friends. He's never been interested in anyone for as long as I've known him. And he's off trapping fur all winter, so he smells like a muskrat half the time."

"But you spent all night dancing with him. You were flirting."

Ilsa shrugged. "He's a good dancer. I'm a good flirter. And"—she gathered her courage—"and I may have wanted to make you a little jealous." Theo brightened immediately, whether from the news that she was not madly in love with Nils or that she'd cared enough to want to make him jealous, she wasn't sure. Perhaps both.

She couldn't suppress a smile. "I suppose it worked a little too well. I just wanted to show you that I was happy here. And successful, I suppose."

"That's all I ever wanted for you." They walked a few more steps in silence, and he added, "I'd like us to be friends again, Ilsa. I'd like that very much."

Maybe she was weak. Maybe she was an idiot. "As long as you're in town, we may as well be civil. But you can't keep sulking and snapping at me. I'm not your servant, and you can't treat me like one. Agreed?"

"Agreed. I promise, this will be the last time I have to beg your forgiveness."

She laughed. "I doubt it."

He smiled back. "You're probably right. But I'll try." His expression became serious. He lowered his voice and leaned in a little closer to her. "Now, if I'm out of the doghouse, I wondered if you might help me with a sensitive matter."

She hesitated a moment, then nodded. He'd just finished assuring her that he never meant to insult her, but there were a limited number of topics a grown man would consider "a sensitive matter." Theo took her arm lightly and steered her off the boardwalk and into a narrow little alleyway between two buildings. She braced herself for something awful, or awfully awkward.

"You really can't tell anyone."

"I won't," she said.

"I need to find out if anyone in Fraser Springs has suddenly taken ill," Theo said quietly. "And I need your help getting samples from all the water sources in town."

Well, this was definitely more intriguing than the price of onions. Not as intriguing as if he tried to kiss her again, but interesting nevertheless. "Why?"

"Because …" She had to lean in to hear his whisper, and the sensation of his breath on the tiny hairs of her ear sent a shiver through her. She ruthlessly suppressed the feeling. Theo was her friend now. Just an ordinary friend, like Owen or Nils. "Some people at the St. Alice are sick. Very sick. I think it's a waterborne illness, but Dr. Greyson won't even let me take samples from the patients. So I need to be very discreet. If this gets out, it could cause a panic. But if there's something in the water supply, I need to find it sooner rather than later."

"What kind of sickness?"

"Vomiting and severe diarrhea."

She wrinkled her nose. "I haven't heard of anything like that going on, but I'll ask around. Is there anything we should do at Wilson's? Jo can't afford to get sick, not this far along with the baby."

"Boil your drinking water. But you can't tell anyone why until I know if there's a real threat. Maybe you could just say that you saw the water was a bit cloudy?"

"I can do that. If Jo—if anyone is at risk, I'll do everything I can to help."

"If you could get me a few samples from some water sources, I would be eternally grateful."

"And you need to know if anyone outside of the St. Alice is sick in the same way?" He nodded. "Okay. How should I reach you?"

"You can send a note to me at the hotel," he suggested. "Anonymously."

She shook her head. "Not a chance. If you start getting messages from secret admirers, somebody will stick their nose into that before you can blink."

He thought for a moment. "Could we meet in person? The spa in the hotel basement is empty after hours."

So they were back to sneaking around. Just like old times. But she had already pushed her luck by going to his room alone. If anyone had seen her, her name would be volleyed along the town gossip lines for months. "Did you hear that Ilsa Pedersen was seen entering Dr. Whitacre's hotel room?" would become "Did you hear Ilsa Pedersen was caught stark naked in Dr. Whitacre's bed? She's an infamous hussy, you know." Which would somehow become "Ilsa Pedersen has been boldly seducing men all over town, never taking no for an answer."

It was probably proof that she should avoid Theo altogether. Plenty of men would be happy to be seen in public with her. All the same, she couldn't afford to sit by and watch her friends and neighbours become sick.

"I can slip out after supper. And there won't be as many people out and about after dark." Fraser Springs was usually quiet after eight, but not so closed down that her presence in the street would be remarkable. "Prop open the boiler room door, where they make the coal delivery, and I could meet you there." He nodded, his green eyes intense behind his spectacles. "I might need a few days to ask around. Would Sunday be too late?"

"I don't think so, no. So Sunday night, eight thirty?"

"Sunday night," she agreed.

"Thank you," he said, touching her shoulder. "I owe you. Truly."

She never learned. Not thirty minutes ago, she had never wanted to see his face again, and now she'd agreed to do favours for him and sneak around with him after dark.

This was what she got for wishing for more excitement in her life.

• • •

Buoyed by Ilsa's cooperation, Theo returned to the hotel and managed to stealthily retrieve water from three different sources. Dr. Greyson would be having his nap—the old man referred to it as his afternoon recess—by now, giving Theo plenty of time to put the samples under the microscope.

When he opened the office door, however, two faces stared back at him in surprise: Dr. Greyson and Mr. Morse sat on either side of the wide desk that took up the majority of the room's space. Dr. Greyson's hands were curled white-knuckled around his cane, and he was red in the face. Morse's whole body seemed coiled tight, like a spring.

"Teddy!" Dr. Greyson barked. "Where the devil have you been?"

"Good afternoon," Theo said, trying to recover from his surprise. "My apologies. I didn't realize you were in conversation." He took a step backwards.

Morse noticed the test tubes in Theo's hand. "Wait a moment. What are those?"

"Uh …" Theo looked down. "Water samples, sir."

"They're nothing," Greyson blustered. "Since I have expressly forbidden wasting time on science experiments."

Morse took one of the glass vials out of Theo's hands and held it to the light. "What, precisely, are you testing for, Dr. Whitacre?" The calm in his voice was edged with warning.

"Contaminants," he replied carefully.

"Contaminants. I see. So you disagree with Dr. Greyson that my guests are experiencing a bout of stomach flu?"

There was no good answer. "I think that, in cases of sudden illness, one can never be too careful. I am merely trying to eliminate the possibility of other causes."

Morse's voice remained even, but Theo could see the muscles of his jaw tensing. "Causes such as?"

Theo sighed. He could feel Dr. Greyson's anger radiating at him. "I believe it might be cholera, sir."

"Nonsense!" Greyson exclaimed. "Young doctors see every horse as a zebra, always looking for the most exotic option."

"Given that the patients do not present with fever or muscle aches, I cannot in good conscience accept that this is merely a case of influenza. It's irresponsible to ignore the possibility of an outbreak of something worse."

Morse had begun to pace while the two doctors bickered. "An outbreak. So one of my overpaid doctors thinks the fact that six paying guests are puking their guts out is no cause for concern, and the other is ready to declare my hotel a festering cesspool. Wonderful. You're both lucky it's not peak season."

"If I may … " Theo began.

"You may not!" Greyson said.

"If you're about to tell me I'm the captain of a plague ship, I don't want to hear it." Morse snatched the rest of the samples from Theo's hands. "You need to spend more time with your patients and less time with test tubes. And you," he glared at Greyson, "are lucky that whatever sugar water he's prescribing seems to be working a damn sight better than your bloodletting, because ..." He bit back the remainder of his sentence. "The two of you had better get this under control. Quickly, or you'll both be on the first boat back to Vancouver."

With that, he strode out of the room, the test tubes still clenched in one fist. Greyson held on to the back of his chair, staring at his hands. Theo steeled himself for the dressing down.

But the old man just sighed and waved him towards the door. "Get out. You've done enough."

Theo could deal with accusations and lectures. Shouting no longer bothered him. But this casual disregard was something he'd never encountered before. It should have been a relief, but somehow it felt worse.

"Yes, sir," he said softly and left the room. Maybe Greyson was right, and that he was wrong about the possibility of cholera. The older doctor had decades of experience. He had seen epidemics before. But if he was so confident it wasn't cholera, why did he care if Theo wasted a few hours of time staring down a microscope? Was he worried that something else might be discovered? Or did he just dislike modern methods—or Theo—in general?

The doubt only added to the frustration of his thwarted testing. He would have to replace the water samples Morse had confiscated. Perhaps Ilsa would find something of value, and he wouldn't need the lab tests at all. If nothing else, at least he seemed to be back in Ilsa's good graces. That alone kept the day from being a total loss.

• • •

Ilsa's purchases weighed her down with each step as she continued her errands. She should have told Theo to go to hell. She shouldn't have talked to him in the first place. Even their brief conversation had drawn stares and little whispers from people on the boardwalk. Theo seemed oblivious, but she knew that look so well. Even here, away from Vancouver's elaborate social stratification, no one could look at them together without getting a gossipy glitter in their eyes. Even though she was no longer wearing an itchy wool costume or a frilly hat, Theo probably still saw her more like a maid than a friend: running errands for him, doing the difficult work he couldn't do himself, up for the occasional quick kiss in an empty room.

But she'd agreed to help, and now she had a potential epidemic on her hands. How on earth would she get the answers to Theo's questions? It simply wasn't a natural topic to bring up with the baker, or the cobbler, or the boy at the counter of the dry goods store. Happily, it didn't take long for the answer to appear. Mrs. McSheen stood at the entrance to Wilson's Bathhouse, adjusting her hat. This one was made of crushed velvet and covered with silk vines and floppy artificial leaves. A bunch of purple glass grapes on the brim shivered with each step.

Ilsa squared her shoulders. Theo had no idea how much he was going to owe her for this. "Mrs. McSheen!" she called out cheerfully. "How are you today?"

Mrs. McSheen stopped and the little glass grapes tinkled. She gave Ilsa a look that could only signal Deep Moral Outrage, which happened to be Mrs. McSheen's default mood. "I would be a far sight better if that employer"—she emphasized the word as if it were foreign to her—"of yours weren't so stubborn! A baby due at any moment, and where do you think I saw her just yesterday?" She paused long enough for dramatic effect but not long enough for Ilsa to attempt an answer. "Walking. Walking along the street, publicly, where anyone could see her."

Ilsa gave her a sympathetic grimace. "That's why I've taken over most of the shopping," she said, nodding down at the heavy packages in her arms. "Mrs. Sterling really should be in bed."

"It's obscene, is what it is." Mrs. McSheen gave no indication that she had heard Ilsa. "Why, when I was expecting, I did the correct, Christian thing and stayed indoors the minute I started to show, and saw visitors at proper calling hours. All my female friends and relatives have had proper confinements. Everyone knows it's not healthy for a woman to exert herself when she's in the family way."

Where Ilsa had grown up, women had cleaned fish and hauled nets right up until they gave birth, then returned the next day with their newborns swaddled to their chests. Apparently, some of the things "everyone knows" only applied to the wealthy.

She nodded sympathetically anyway. "Actually, Mrs. McSheen, I'm glad I've run into you. And just in time, too!"

Mrs. McSheen pivoted from her tirade against walking and onto this new topic with a dexterity of a falcon. "Why do you say that?"

"I heard that someone fell seriously ill last night. As the head of the Convalescence and Spiritual Uplift Brigade, I assumed you'd already be at the poor soul's bedside," Ilsa said. "But since you're on your way there, is there anything I can do to help?"

Mrs. McSheen's cheeks darkened from Deep Moral Outrage pink to Poorly Concealed Embarrassment red. "Oh! Yes! Well! I was just on my way! You don't know how tiring it is to be on so many committees. I would love to stay and chat, Ilsa dear, but duty calls." As Mrs. McSheen bustled off, Ilsa smiled and let herself in through the front door rather than hauling her load around to the back porch.

Inside, Jo was dusting the sill of the big plate glass window. "You look like the cat that ate the canary. Successful trip?" she said.

"Maybe too successful," Ilsa said. She dumped the parcels on the front counter, then shook out her arms to restore the circulation to them. "I saved us twenty-five cents this week, thank you very kindly. And I got us free eggs. I can make a pound cake for Sunday supper."

Jo grinned. "An excellent idea. Did Mrs. McSheen catch you on her way out?"

Ilsa rolled her eyes. "Yes, and I heard all about your indecent walking habit. She's not entirely wrong, though. You should be sitting down. Or in bed."

Jo made a face. "I'm fine. It's just dusting. I was going out to get the kindling, and the window was a disgrace." Ilsa guided her by the shoulders and turned her around to face one of the two armchairs that constituted their reception area. Jo hesitated, so Ilsa gave her a little nudge in the small of the back. "All right! Fine." Jo levered herself into the cushioned chair. "But just for a minute, because we really do need to fetch in more kindling. Nils seems to have gone off on a wander."

Nils had a habit of disappearing for weeks or months at a time without notice, usually picking the exact worst time to do so. "I don't care if Nils is on the moon. You're nearly nine months pregnant. I'll take care of the heavy lifting." She patted Jo on the arm. "I hate to admit it, but Mrs. McSheen was right. You're stubborn as a mule."

Jo pretended to sulk, even as she sank back into the chair and allowed Ilsa to prop her feet up. "Never thought I'd see the day you'd take Mrs. McSheen's side over mine."

Ilsa began to knead Jo's shoulders by way of apology for her disloyalty. Jo grunted in appreciation. "You are going to take the afternoon off and … knit little hats," Ilsa said. "Or whatever big fat pregnant ladies do. And I'm going to take over dinner, too. No arguing."

Jo sighed. "Yes, master. When did you become so extremely annoying?"

"I learned from the best. Now, off with you!"

With Jo begrudgingly resting upstairs, Ilsa set out to tackle the woodpile. She rolled up her sleeves and tied on a heavy canvas apron from the toolshed. It had been months since she'd split kindling, but the combination of the crisp late-autumn air and the heavy labour felt glorious.

She was halfway through her chores when Mrs. McSheen returned, ducking her head to fit her hat through the kitchen porch doorway. She launched directly into a monologue without so much as a how-do-you-do.

"The Johnson baby has the croup, Mr. Peterson sprained his wrist doing some fool thing with an accordion, and Mrs. Martin has a touch of dropsy, which I personally believe is caused by eating entirely too many sweets. Why, I saw her buying both a bag of toffees and a brick of chocolate, and you know that her husband doesn't touch the stuff on account of his sugar diabetes," she reported. "Certainly no deathbed vigils worth rushing around town for." Ilsa had never understood why Jo seemed to have so much trouble managing Mrs. McSheen. You simply had to wind her up like a tin toy and set her loose in the direction you wanted her to go.

"That's so strange. Perhaps it was one of the poorer families who live out past town."

"That lot. You'd know more about them than I would. Although I will say that they all come scrounging for handouts whenever one of their tots gets so much as a runny nose."

The sweet smile that had helped her to secure discounts was now deployed to pacify Mrs. McSheen. "I'm so sorry. I must have misunderstood. Or maybe one of the hotel guests fell ill?" she suggested.

Mrs. McSheen gave a dismissive huff. "I don't lose sleep over hotel guests. Not when they have not one but two doctors to tend to them."

She spent the next thirty minutes listening to Mrs. McSheen's complaints about how certain hotel guests who should remain nameless—she, of course, went on to name names with great specificity— thought they were superior to the people of Fraser Springs, and how her niece was acting like a wild hoyden now that she was feeling better, and if she kept it up, she wouldn't be fit for marriage to even the lowliest rag-and-bone man, and how with winter coming, her joints were aching more than ever. Ilsa nodded along until she thought her head might roll off her neck. Finally, Mrs. McSheen swept out as abruptly as she'd arrived, leaving Ilsa alone with the answers Theo needed.

She pushed them to the back of her mind. From what Theo had told her, this lack of news was actually the best-case scenario. It seemed that the illness was restricted to the hotel and— annoyingly—Mrs. McSheen had made a good point. The guests already had access to the best medical care the town could offer. She would see Theo soon enough. But for now, she had water to boil, a dinner to prepare, a wandering handyman to track down, a new business to plan for and, if she were lucky, a few hours of sleep to sneak in. Secret missions would have to wait.

Chapter 10

The days seemed to drag until Sunday night finally arrived. There had been no new illness in the hotel since Wednesday, and the stricken guests had all recovered. From what Theo could tell, Morse seemed to have kept the entire business remarkably hushed up.

In the daytime, the basement-level spa of the St. Alice Hotel was a bustle of patients and white-smocked attendants. Unlike Wilson's, where patients bathed communally, hot springs water was piped into partitioned rows of large tubs so that patients could soak in privacy. The tubs were decorated with elaborate tile mosaics and spouts shaped like little cherubs, making it look as if the tubs being filled with the spit of chubby winged babies: not the most relaxing notion, but Theo supposed the spa guests found it a classy touch. Nothing was purely utilitarian here. Even the lowliest supply closet was flanked by white plaster columns.

In the half dark, however, the basement looked abandoned. The only noise came from the fountain in the centre of the room. Spring water burbled out of a jug held aloft by a bronze woman dressed in Grecian robes. Below her, four bronze fish squirted water out of their mouths and down into the marble basin. In the light from the stairwell that led up to the hotel lobby, the fountain cast a feminine shadow along the tiled floor. Theo kept turning, expecting to see Ilsa. He'd propped open the back door with a rock. The St. Alice didn't have a night watchman, so he didn't anticipate any trouble.

To distract himself, he flicked on the lamp behind the marble attendants' station and laid his equipment out on the long counter: pipettes, slides, mounting supplies, a Bausch & Lomb microscope that he cosseted like a beloved child. He picked up a glass slide mounted with a slice of leaf and clipped it onto the stage. Viewed through the eyepiece, the ordinary leaf transformed into an elaborate latticework of cell walls. Theo twiddled the knobs, calibrating the lenses' delicate focus. He loved this process. It was like getting a private look into a world that only God had been able to know.

Theo looked away and rubbed his eyes under his spectacles. He'd lit only one lamp, which wasn't an ideal light source, but it would have to do. He couldn't trust that Dr. Greyson wouldn't go snooping in his study, and it wouldn't do to bring Ilsa back to his rooms. No, this would have to suffice.

"What are you looking at?" came a quiet feminine voice, startling him out of his reverie.

He spun around. Ilsa stood just inside the propped door, carrying a cloth satchel bulging with something he suspected was glass, since it clinked softly as she walked towards him.

"A leaf. Just killing time until you got here."

Ilsa walked slowly around the room, sizing up the competition. She ran her hands over two wooden cherubs that stood guard over a chromed towel rack. "I'll give them one thing, they certainly have us beat when it comes to baby angels." She kept her voice to a whisper, which somehow made the faint lilt of her accent more pronounced.

Theo grinned. "But I hear the staff at Wilson's are far superior."

She smiled back at him. He did love to see her smile. "Speaking of which. Since you're not allowed to come to Wilson's, I brought massage oil in case we have time to work on your legs." Before he had time to respond, Ilsa rustled through her purse. "But first:

samples of the water from the pump at Wilson's, the soaking tub, and the lake."

She handed Theo three little jam jars filled with water. Attached to a string tied around each bottle was a little paper tag that explained the water's origin.

"Thank you," he said. "These are perfect."

"And I asked around. Nobody's sick outside of the hotel. The Johnson baby has the croup, but otherwise we commoners are a healthy lot."

"That's disappointing." Ilsa tilted her head and gave him a look. Oh. "I mean, not disappointing that you're healthy. That's wonderful. Of course." He set the little jam jars down on the marble countertop with a clink. "Anyway, I should take a look at these." He selected a slide and cover slip, then picked up the pipette, calming himself with the familiar routine.

"Is that a microscope?" Ilsa asked. He startled a bit—she was closer to his shoulder than he'd expected.

"Yes. Do you want to see?"

She nodded and sat down at the bench. "What do I do?"

"Look into the eyepiece."

She leaned in close, and then frowned. "I can't see anything."

"Close one eye, then look into the eyepiece with the open one." She squinted into it as if she were sighting down a gun barrel.

"I still don't see anything."

"Here, let me help." He stood behind her and covered one of her eyes with his hand. Her eyelashes brushed against his palm.

"Look now," he said softly. "It should be in focus."

After a moment of silence, Ilsa gave a little gasp. "What is that?"

"A fern."

"Look at the patterns!"

He had to remember to keep his voice down. It didn't take much to set him rambling about microscope slides, especially if he had a willing audience. "I know. It always reminds me of stained glass."

She looked up, and he removed his hand from her face. He hadn't meant to let the edge of his thumb linger along her cheek, but it was so soft …. He jammed his hands into his pockets.

"What are you looking for in the water?" she asked.

"I'll show you." He opened the jar marked "Lake" and used a pipette to siphon up some of the water. He placed a drop carefully on the glass side, then slid a round cover slip over the top.

Ilsa stood to allow him to sit down at the microscope. He peered into the eyepiece and adjusted the viewer. A teeming world came to life before his eyes: jagged salt and iron crystals, some bits of plants and algae, a few tiny cyanobacteria and miniscule insects, but not one single cholera bacterium. They were distinctive enough that he wouldn't have missed them. "This one's clean," he said. "You can take a look." He got up and offered her the seat.

Ilsa looked into the microscope again. "All that's in our water?"

Theo nodded. "It's all totally safe. If there were cholera here, you'd see something that looks like tiny sausages with long, skinny tails."

That drew her attention. "You're looking for cholera?" she hissed, her eyes wide with alarm.

"Just an example," he hastily explained. "I can't be sure exactly what I'm looking for at this point. But your water is definitely safe."

"Did you see much cholera when you were doing your training?"

"No, not really. I have a special interest." He had to fight to keep the enthusiasm out of his voice. The field was esoteric even by the standards of his medical school, and he hadn't had anyone to talk to about it for months. "Epidemiology is a new field, but very promising. In less than a decade, some doctors think that we'll have stopped these outbreaks entirely. And these little creatures hold the key to it all."

To his surprise, Ilsa was looking attentively at him. "Is that more interesting than doctoring?"

"Let's just say that a Cryptosporidium has never asked for my calling card, and a Giardia lamblia has never tried to introduce me to its daughter."

She smiled again: even in the dark, he could see the colour in her cheeks. He longed to touch them again. "Fair enough. So do you want to be an epidemiologer?"

"—ologist," he corrected. She'd even attempted the proper term. His mother dismissively referred to it as "that germ nonsense." "I do. But I need to go to Europe for more training. Dr. DuBois in Paris has already agreed to take me on."

"So you're going to Paris?"

"It's not that simple."

"I would imagine it's simpler for you than it is for most anyone else." She gave him a reassuring smile. "You're already a doctor and you can afford the ticket."

He shrugged. She was right: he had advantages that the average medical student could only dream of. But it wasn't a simple matter of booking a steamer and brushing up on his French. Not with the parents he had. He changed the subject. "Shall we start on the rest of your samples?"

Over the course of an hour, they studied the contents of Ilsa's jars as well as the samples he'd taken from around the St Alice. He saw spores and minerals and bacteria, but no cholera. And no Giardia lamblia, or Cryptosporidium, or any other microbe he knew that might cause illness in humans. For days, he'd nursed visions of bursting through Greyson's office door, brandishing the slide with proof of his theory. The old man would be forced to admit that Theo had been right, that Dr. Whitacre had saved the day, thank you very much, and maybe modern science wasn't so bad after all. But here he was, in the odd position of being unhappy that a town had clean water.

If it wasn't cholera, then what was wrong with the hotel's guests? Maybe he simply hadn't located the correct source yet. "Is there anywhere else the town gets its water? A well, or another spring somewhere?"

Ilsa nodded. "There are two streams farther up the mountain. They're out of the way, though."

"I'd like to check them."

"I could show you next week. I get almost all Sunday off."

He paused. "I don't want you to waste your day off on what might be a fool's errand."

"It's no trouble. It'll be good to get away for a little bit. It's a nice walk—there are some beautiful views."

"Then, yes. Thank you. You've already helped so much."

Ilsa smiled. "It's been interesting. And I've never seen anything through a microscope." She looked around the darkened basement. "I don't have to be back for another half an hour. Can I look at something else, besides the water?"

"Of course." He had a small box of calibration slides packed away neatly in the microscope case, although he hadn't used any except the fern in years. He slid the little wooden box open and pulled out a slide at random: "Silk: Cocoon of *B. mori.*" He began to place it into the clips, and paused. "Would you like to learn how to set this up yourself?"

"What if I break it?"

"You won't break it. You have a very light touch." And even if she broke every last slide he owned, it would be worth it to make her happy.

• • •

On her last visit to Vancouver, Ilsa had paid a penny to look through a kaleidoscope at a fair. She'd been stunned by the swirling colours and patterns. But this was so much better. One slide led to another, then another: a feather, a thin section of bone, a fly's wing, a piece of purple onionskin.

How lovely to sit beside Theo and talk about this magic lantern show created by such everyday things. Everyone she knew in Fraser Springs listened out of the corner of their ear, especially the men. How many times had she tried to tell a potential suitor something about her day or her own interests, only to find that he was staring at her chest, or looking out the window, or counting the seconds until it was his turn to speak again. Tonight felt different. Whenever she asked a question or tried to describe what she saw, Theo responded quickly, alert to her every word, trying as hard to listen as to explain. She was used to male attention, good and bad. But being taken seriously, as if her thoughts and opinions mattered? That felt like a gift.

When the slides ran out at last, they lapsed into silence. She wasn't sure exactly when it had happened, but Theo's arm was nestled around her waist. She stretched out her neck and rolled her shoulders, which were stiff from stooping over the eyepiece for so long. He snuggled her closer, and she leaned into the comfort of the connection, resting her head against his shoulder. He smelled … expensive, like milled soap and heavy cloth and tasteful cologne.

Neither of them said a word. She listened to the water in the fountain, the hum of the pumps and generators somewhere farther off in the basement's depths, to the gentle rush of Theo's breathing, and the steady thump of his heartbeat.

Sharing secrets in whispers under the cover of darkness with Theo was so easy and familiar. And yet unfamiliar: he simply wasn't the same person as the frail young man she'd loved in Vancouver. He was stronger now, broad and tanned, and he carried himself with the confidence that came with education and skill and fashionable clothes. She indulged herself, letting her fingers stroke the impossibly soft wool of his lapel, and he shifted on the bench so that she was practically sitting on his lap.

She knew that if she looked up, she would want to kiss him. *Do not kiss him*, she lectured herself. *Don't you dare kiss him.*

He took one of her hands in his, very lightly. A chorus of voices in the back of her head—her parents, the sisters at the orphanage, the town gossips—all chanted "pull away, pull away." He stroked her palm with the pad of his thumb once, and then again.

What the hell. Life was short.

She grazed her lips across his, like the brush of fingertips across silk. He inhaled sharply, holding himself perfectly still against the gentle friction of her kiss. She tasted the corner of his lips, just a quick little flick with the tip of her tongue, and he let out his breath in a low groan. His arms tightened around her.

When they'd kissed last week, their tempers had both been flaring. They'd embraced with a passion, an intensity, that she would never have predicted from the sweet, sensitive boy of her memories. His touch now was different, too. Not a racing fire, but a soft, inescapable warmth—like sliding into the hot springs themselves.

She settled herself more confidently into his lap and felt his hard length pressing against her thighs. He wanted this. Wanted her. The knowledge was almost as intoxicating as the slide of his lips on hers, the taste of his skin under her tongue.

He angled his head to deepen the kiss, and she followed his lead eagerly. Then his spectacles banged against her nose, and they pulled apart, grinning.

"I should go." She sighed.

"Don't." He raised her hand to his lips. The old-fashioned gesture melted what little was left of her common sense and left her strangely embarrassed in a way that their kissing hadn't.

"When did you become so charming?" Flustered, she hid her face into the crook of his neck.

"Medical school," he replied, smiling. "They offered a class on seducing beautiful women, right before pharmacology." She giggled at the terrible joke. His skin between the edge of his starched collar and the stubble of his chin was so soft. She pressed a kiss just there, and then another, along his jawline and up to the shell of his ear.

He made a low, throaty noise and shifted uncomfortably beneath her. She pulled back. "Am I too heavy? Your leg—"

"My damned leg isn't the problem. If you keep teasing like that, we're going to need to change positions. Dramatically."

She gave a provoking little wriggle. "So Dr. Whitacre isn't made of stone after all."

"Debatable." He unhooked his spectacles from around his ears and set them down carefully next to the microscope. "If you're going to kiss me, do it properly."

He didn't even realize how much fire he was playing with. She bit her bottom lip to suppress her grin, and slid off his lap and the bench.

"Wait! I didn't mean to—" His apology was cut short when she hiked her skirts and petticoat up to her mid-thigh and straddled him, face to face, with her knees on either side of his hips. He gaped at her like a hooked fish.

"You did say 'dramatically.'" And she took his face between her hands and kissed him with all the hunger and frustration of weeks—years—of false starts and disappointments. Tongues tangled, hands grasped and clutched and pulled. He tugged her hair loose from its pins, and it tumbled down around both their shoulders. He rocked his hips beneath her, helplessly trying to increase the pressure, the friction. She rolled with him, urging him on with gasps and murmurs of pleasure.

He took one of her earlobes between his teeth, nipping hard enough to make her gasp. "God. Ilsa," he ground out, his whispered words caressing her ear. "You feel so good. I—"

A loud metallic clanging startled them apart like rabbits. Ilsa thought her heart would explode. "Jesus!"

"It's just the boilers. Or a pump. Something." Theo sounded as startled and breathless as she felt. He moved to pull her back onto his lap, but she held his hands at arm's length.

"It's like the clock at Cinderella's ball. I really have to get home now, or I'll turn back into a pumpkin."

"I don't think that's what happens in that story," he objected. But he smiled back at her and released his hold. "Would you like me to walk back with you?"

She shook her head, tucking her hair haphazardly back into its pins. "It's fine. There's nobody out at this hour."

He gave her a concerned look but nodded. "I'll just see you off, then." When he put his spectacles back on, the mischievous glint in his green eyes magnified. "If nothing else, the cold air should help me compose myself before I have to take a stroll across the lobby."

The late autumn wind whipped down from the mountain, creating little eddies of mist around her feet as she hurried down the boardwalk. Every time she turned around, she saw Theo watching her loyally from his place by one of the columns of the St. Alice. She wanted to wave but didn't, in case anyone was watching from a window.

Wilson's Bathhouse was quiet as she snuck inside. She made it to her bedroom without encountering Jo or any of the other girls in the hallway. Things really had changed. Normally, Jo had the hearing of an owl and would have been waiting on the landing as soon as she heard the door creak open. But Jo was tired and distracted these days, and Ilsa knew she should be glad for the privacy.

She changed into her nightgown, gave her hair a quick comb, and braided it in a single plait over her shoulder. Better to keep this to herself. Her recklessness would only worry Jo. Entering

Theo's room in broad daylight was one thing, but jumping on top of him in a public place was entirely another.

What was it about Theo that made her stick her neck out? Was it simply the thrill of reclaiming something she'd lost years ago? Or maybe this wasn't about Theo at all. She was planning to leave Fraser Springs and start a life of her own. Maybe she was drawn to him because he wasn't planning to stay here, either. Even if he never went to Paris, Theo wouldn't tie her down here. She couldn't afford to fall in love and get married, not for a long time yet. It would throw the brakes on years of planning; her savings would become her husband's savings, and that was unacceptable.

Theo's family would never allow him to marry someone like her, and she had no illusions about his willingness to choose her over them. Look how long their childish pledges to be together forever had lasted: a few months. He'd changed, she reflected as she slipped under her covers, but people didn't change that much. He might claim to not want a high-brow wife now, but he'd feel differently when he needed a well-bred hostess to help advance his career. Or maybe he'd want a wife with a college education of her own, someone he could really talk to about his interests.

No, they were both bored and a little lonely, just as they had been the last time. Theo was the perfect man for her life at the moment, really. Handsome, attentive, and temporary.

Chapter 11

As usual, five in the morning arrived entirely too early. Her first impulse was to turn over and go back to sleep. It was still dark. The faintest trace of frost hazed over her window, and even though she doubted it had snowed overnight, the air smelled like it was going to. It took all her willpower to slide her legs from beneath the down comforter's warmth. She dressed, scrubbed her face in the cold water at the washstand, and quickly twisted her hair up in a simple knot.

She opened her door to find Owen standing there: half-dressed, with his shirt untucked and his whiskers unshaved. That wasn't all that unusual for him, really, especially when he had a writing deadline. What froze Ilsa in her tracks was the half-wild expression on his face.

"The baby's coming," he blurted out.

That brought her fully awake. "It can't. It's too early." That just made Owen look like he was trying to swallow a caterpillar, so she took a deep breath. She was clearly going to have to be the calm one today. "Okay. If it's time, it's time, and that's all there is to it. When did the pains start?"

"On and off all yesterday, but she just woke me up and told me about it now."

Ilsa suppressed the urge to go and shake her best friend until her teeth rattled. How very like Jo to suffer in silence. "Go tell Annie she's in charge of breakfast, and then light a fire in the stove.

I'll sit with Jo." Owen looked relieved at her bossiness and hurried down the stairs.

She found Jo in her bedroom, curled up on her side on top of the covers.

"Owen told me it's time," Ilsa said.

"I don't know if I can do this," Jo whispered.

Ilsa sat down at the foot of the bed and squeezed Jo's ankle reassuringly. "Of course you can. You're Josephine Sterling. Didn't you run your own business after your husband passed away and the entire staff deserted you?" Jo nodded. "And didn't you make a success of that business while seducing Vancouver's most eligible bachelor?" Jo managed a weak smile at that one. "Then you can do this. Besides, if Mrs. McSheen can do it three times, you can do it once."

Jo grimaced. "If you make me start admiring Mrs. McSheen, I will never forgive you."

"I'm just telling you the truth. Women do this every day, and you are an extraordinary woman. I'm not worried a bit."

Jo stifled a moan as a fresh wave of pain rolled over her. Ilsa held her friend's hand, and Jo gripped it hard enough to whiten both their knuckles. "It's okay to make some noise. You won't shock anyone in this henhouse. Breathe through it."

When the contraction passed, Ilsa went downstairs to get water for Jo, spent fifteen minutes doing the scolding that Owen seemed unable to do, and returned upstairs. Then it was back down again for towels, hot water, a check with Annie to make sure her clients had been taken over by other masseuses, finding busy work that would get Owen out from under everybody's feet (Go find the midwife! Go look for Nils!), then back upstairs to check on her friend. When Owen returned, he had no good news to report. Nils had definitely packed his gear and left town for the season, and the midwife was up the mountain attending another birth.

By evening, the whole of Wilson's Bathhouse practically vibrated with nervous energy. Jo's pains came regularly, but they'd been stuck at three-minute intervals since noon. Jo's labour seemed to have stalled, leaving her weeping and exhausted after a day and a half of pain. Ilsa had helped her walk circuits around the room, had sung silly songs with her, stroked her hair, rubbed her back through the contractions. She had seen her fair share of births, and the ugly fact was that this one was going badly.

"Where are you going?" Jo asked weakly when Ilsa entered the bedroom with her coat on. Jo was usually so calm and self-controlled, but now her voice wavered and cracked.

"Annie is coming up to sit with you. I'm going to get the doctor."

Jo nodded. Her face was sweaty and haggard with fatigue. Ilsa hustled back down the stairs, dragged Annie out of the kitchen, and then broke into a run down the boardwalk. The temperature had dropped and ice slicked the planks, but she moved as quickly as she could. The hotel doctors didn't prioritize outside patients, but if Dr. Greyson wouldn't come, she knew another doctor who owed her a massive favour.

• • •

Even the routine practice of writing patient notes was hell with Dr. Greyson looking over his shoulder. He insisted that Theo write them in his presence so that he could provide his usual "guidance." It was past dinnertime. If only the water samples had turned up something important. Then he'd be the one doing the lecturing.

Still, it was hard to be in a bad mood when events had taken such a positive turn with Ilsa. He kept thinking about the little grin on her face as she wiggled against him, teasing him—

"What have you written up for Mrs. DeMonte?" Dr. Greyson delivered the question with his feet up on a settee and one of his cigars just inches from his lips. A haze of smoke filled the room.

"Patient presented with red, fluid-filled pustules located on the upper chest."

Dr. Greyson waved the cigar. "Now 'pustules' is an ugly word, don't you think? I associate it with adolescent spots. Mrs. DeMonte is one of the New York DeMontes, so surely there's a better term."

Theo suppressed a sigh. Someone should have told him earlier that the wealthy were not afflicted by acne; it would have made his adolescent years much more pleasant. "Pustule is an accurate description, is it not?"

"I find that 'blain' is a much better word. A softer word."

"Does blain not imply that the lesion was a blister? When really, what we're looking at is common acne."

Dr. Greyson's expression soured. He puffed away in punitive silence, looking out the window.

"Would you like me to change it to blain?" Theo asked after many long minutes.

Dr. Greyson let the smoke exhale slowly and deliberately. "The last time I checked, I was the senior physician, and this was not a debate club."

"Understood," he said, crossing out "pustule" and replacing it with "blain."

"No one likes sloppy notes, Teddy. Sloppy notes are a sign of a sloppy practitioner. You'll have to rewrite the entire page."

Mercifully, a knock on the door prevented Theo from responding.

"Come in," he called.

Even more mercifully, the door opened to reveal Ilsa Pedersen. With her pink cheeks and blond hair askew, she looked like an angel.

"Good evening, Miss Pedersen," he said. He took his time setting his pen back into its well so that Dr. Greyson couldn't see the heat he suspected had risen in his cheeks. "What can I do for you?"

"It's Jo. The baby is coming, and the midwife is nowhere to be found and it's ... it's not going well."

Dr. Greyson looked sceptical. "When did her labour pains start?"

"Yesterday. But now she's ... she's stuck."

"Ah. Well, it's a first baby, isn't it?" Ilsa nodded. "They do take time. When Mrs. Sterling is ready, I'm sure Mrs. Parsons will have turned up." With that pronouncement, he settled contentedly back into his chair and set his hands on his belly. There was no happiness to compare to a doctor learning that he didn't have to go on a house call in cold weather.

Ilsa took another step into the room. "I've seen births before, and this one is taking too long. And the midwife has taken off to Lord knows where, and we have no one to help." She looked towards Theo.

He tried to sound casual. "I don't mind taking a glance. We were just finishing up here anyway." In truth, his limbs were buzzing. He had never delivered a baby by himself before.

Dr. Greyson snorted. "Waste of time, but it's your time to waste. Have you checked over at Doc Stryker's for your missing midwife? Seems a likely place to find a tradeswoman."

Theo ignored him, grabbing his doctor's kit in one hand and his cane in the other. If only he could take a moment to review the obstetrical chapter in his reference book. Then again, it certainly wouldn't soothe Ilsa's nerves to see him frantically flipping through pages. No, at this point, he either knew it or he didn't.

As they made their way down the boardwalk, Theo tried to keep pace with her. She kept striding ahead, then stopping and waiting for him to catch up. She didn't say anything, but her whole body radiated impatience. He went as fast as he could, the doctor's kit banging against his leg.

Finally, they reached the bathhouse. When he'd walked into Wilson's before, he'd been greeted by the busy sounds of staff and clients bantering or enjoying a meal. But today, it was silent except for a low keening that came from upstairs. He didn't see Mr. Sterling, which was too bad because he doubted that he and Ilsa alone could move Mrs. Sterling, if that became necessary. But a husband attending his wife's birth would be very strange indeed.

"She's upstairs."

"I'll need to wash up: hot water, carbolic soap, and clean towels." It felt strange to boss Ilsa around, but someone would have to be his nurse.

Ilsa nodded and he followed her into the kitchen, where two huge pots of water were boiling on the stove. She poured some into an enamel basin and set the soap beside it. Theo shed his jacket and rolled up his sleeves, carefully scrubbing his hands with the soap, plunging them in and out of the scalding water. This part of the ritual soothed him: forearms, hands, fingers, then fingernails, counting to twenty for each. He had practiced it hundreds of times during his training. As he scrubbed, Mrs. Sterling's moans drifted down the stairs.

"Do you have to scour your skin clean off?" Ilsa asked. A stray curl hung by her eyes, and she blew it away with an impatient huff.

"This is the most important step. Even one germ could cause a fatal infection. We'll need more hot water and clean towels upstairs. Your turn. Everyone assisting has to wash up."

Ilsa sighed and plunged her hands into the basin. "Ow! It's *hot*."

"Don't be a baby." Her only response was a narrow glare, and she began wringing the bar of soap in her hands with an exaggerated motion. After a few seconds, her shoulders dropped and she looked back at Theo. "I'm sorry. I'm just worried. Thank you for being here."

"I'm happy to help." He did not mention that he was also happy for the opportunity to attend a potentially complicated birth. "Now, make sure to dry thoroughly, even under your fingernails."

Ilsa sighed but obeyed. "Yes, doctor."

"And I'll have none of your sass, Nurse." That won him a wan smile and a smack across the arm with her towel.

That done, they headed upstairs. The moaning grew louder. As he walked through the bedroom door, he squared his shoulders. Whenever he entered an operating theatre, he pretended that he was walking onto a stage. He transformed into someone entirely different: Dr. Whitacre, a man who stood a little straighter, who always knew what to do, who projected calm competence at every turn.

"How are you doing, Jo?" Ilsa asked. Jo Sterling was propped in bed with her knees up. Her face was red and sweaty, and she was breathing heavily.

Mrs. Sterling turned to Ilsa. "I thought you were getting Dr. Greyson. Has this one even done this before?"

Theo smiled in what he hoped was a reassuring manner. "Of course." He approached her bedside. "And the births I've attended have all ended well for mother and baby." That part wasn't technically a lie, since the only delivery he'd participated in was his own, and he'd lived to tell the tale. "Now, may I examine you?"

She looked at Ilsa, who was standing beside the bed. Ilsa nodded. "Yes," Mrs. Sterling said finally.

"Excellent. I'm going to tell you exactly what I'm doing, and if at any time you need me to stop, you just say so. Ilsa will hold your hand in case you need something to squeeze."

Mrs. Sterling nodded.

Theo pulled a chair up to the bed. After a few minutes of careful probing and palpating, the problem seemed clear. The baby was very close to being born, but the head was face up: not an ideal position. Worse, the placenta might have grown partially across its way as well. No wonder the poor thing was stuck.

Though he tried to recall his textbooks, his brain instead reached for the voices of the women who had been employed as nurses throughout his childhood. They'd all been stout Irish or Scottish women with open, friendly faces, and they'd talked candidly to each other about births they'd just attended. Theo had drifted in and out of sleep to stories about who had bellowed like a heifer, who had wailed like a banshee, who had pulled through unexpectedly, who had called out for a former beau instead of the baby's father, who had been beyond help. One phrase stood out to him now: *Give me a sturdy stool and a good push, and I'll give you a baby in two shakes of a lamb's tail.*

"Very good. Mrs. Sterling, I know you're tired. I believe you simply need a little help from gravity. Ilsa, can you fetch me a stool?" Ilsa nodded and hurried out of the room.

"Have you experienced any bleeding at all in the past month or two?" he asked.

"A little. Not enough to fuss about."

That could confirm the possibility of placental previa. He could only pray it was minor and that she wouldn't haemorrhage. "You're doing wonderfully," Theo said.

Another pain rolled over her, and she cried out.

"It's okay. Just take deep breaths. Every pain is another step closer to having this all done with." She breathed. "There you go. Just think of all the many, many women who successfully gave birth for you to get here. Your mother, your grandmother, your great-great grandmother."

"My mother—died—in—childbirth," Mrs. Sterling gasped between breaths.

He winced. "And modern medicine has come so far since then."

Ilsa's entrance offered him an easy out. She was quick, he would give her that. Mrs. Sterling's pain passed, and she collapsed back against the pillows, panting.

"Before your next pain comes, I'm going to move a few things around, and then Ilsa and I are going to help you lower down onto this stool. And Ilsa is going to sit on the bed behind you, and you just lean into her."

"I can't," protested Mrs. Sterling. He motioned to Ilsa, who began helping her swing her legs to the side of the bed.

He stood over her and gave her what he hoped was his most doctoral look. "You very much can and you will. With a sturdy stool and a determined mother, I can get this baby out in the next few minutes."

That seemed to work. Together, Theo and Ilsa lowered Mrs. Sterling to the stool. Nothing seemed to faze Ilsa, not the vice grip Mrs. Sterling had on her hand, not the sight of blood, not the difficulty of moving a pregnant woman in labour.

Soon, Ilsa was seated on the bed, steadying her friend between her knees. "That's it," she murmured. "You're doing so well. Everything's okay."

He knelt between his patient's legs and adjusted her nightgown to provide at least the illusion of modesty. "When your next pain comes, you need to focus all your energy on pushing this baby out. Slow and steady, and don't let up." He stealthily reached down into his bag and removed the scalpel in case it was needed. No need to stress Mrs. Sterling's frayed nerves by brandishing a knife around.

As the next pain came, Mrs. Sterling arched her back into Ilsa.

"Push," he and Ilsa said in unison.

The baby's head crowned onto his waiting palm. "One more push," he urged.

Theo's hands seemed to know what to do without his brain's help. As the next contraction came, he gently twisted the baby's tiny shoulders until it was delivered right side up. He wrapped it in a towel and began wiping gunk from its nose and mouth, then gave it a few taps on the back with the heel of his hand. It opened its eyes and gave a long, wavering cry. Mrs. Sterling and Ilsa both laughed with slightly manic relief. The baby was scrawny, but otherwise he seemed to be holding a completely healthy baby girl.

Theo looked up. Ilsa was staring at him with wide eyes, waiting for him to say something. For a moment, the room hung in stillness: Ilsa's blue eyes, her pink cheeks, the baby wailing and squirming in his arms. He had done it. He had known what to do. He had done it exactly right.

"Is he okay?" Mrs. Sterling asked.

Theo retrieved two clamps from his bag, then cut the cord with the scalpel. "She's perfect."

"It's a girl!" Ilsa exclaimed.

"Oh, my God. A girl." Mrs. Sterling breathed. "A girl."

"We're not out of the woods yet. Ilsa, will you keep our new arrival company?"

She took the baby over to the gently steaming washbasin on the other side of the room and began wrapping her in a towel. Theo devoted his entire attention to delivering the afterbirth, which arrived broken. While he made sure that all the pieces were there, Ilsa came over to reunite mother and baby. After a few tense moments, he let out a relieved breath. There was, thank God, nothing left behind and no indications of hemorrhaging. "Congratulations, Mrs. Sterling," he announced with a wide smile. "My work here is done."

The newest mother in Fraser Springs gave a hoarse little chuckle. "Please, call me Jo. I think we know each other well enough by now."

As he washed his hands, he looked over to see Ilsa kneeling next to the bed, cooing to the swaddled baby girl cradled in her friend's arms. Ilsa's hair glowed like a halo in the lamplight. He felt a rush of pride: she had proven herself more capable and empathetic than many of the nurses he'd worked with. Perhaps being a practicing physician wouldn't be so bad if he had someone like Ilsa at his side. No, not *like* Ilsa. He could do anything, as long as he had Ilsa with him.

She raised her head and smiled at him.

"Good work, Dr. Whitacre," she said quietly. From her, the words meant more than any diploma he could ever earn.

* * *

Ilsa got Jo cleaned up and back into bed. She took care of the bedding and towels, and sent Annie to retrieve Owen from Doc Stryker's. Soon, Jo's bedroom was filled with the proud father and most of the girls, all of them babbling over the new arrival. Little Sarah was a beautiful baby, with alert eyes and a miniature tuft of dark hair.

None of them had a clue that the room had been nightmarish just an hour ago. The entire time, she'd wanted to run away screaming. The blood, the crying, even the horrible handwashing routine. Thank God she wasn't a nurse. She'd barely managed to keep from vomiting when she'd seen Theo piecing together the afterbirth like a jigsaw puzzle. She would take bunions and achy backs any day.

Theo knocked politely against the frame of the wide-open door— he'd gone downstairs to finish cleaning his knives and whatnots in the kitchen—and was greeted with a chorus of thanks and hand-shaking. "I'm just here to say good night. If it's all right, I'll drop by in the morning to check on you, Jo."

"Of course. Thank you again, Doctor."

A grin broke through Theo's professionalism. "It was my pleasure. You did all the hard work. I just managed to avoid dropping her."

Owen and Jo both chuckled feebly at the joke; Jo could barely keep her eyes open, and Owen wobbled with relief and Doc's best whiskey.

"I'll show you out," Ilsa said.

They walked down the stairs in silence. She was suddenly aware of how heavily he was leaning on the bannister—he must have left his cane downstairs. He had handled everything so assertively that she had totally forgotten about his limitations. Well, it had been a stressful time. Emotions were running high, and tonight hadn't been about Theo or her. Thank God he had been there and had known what to do. She didn't want to think of what might have happened if she'd listened to Dr. Greyson.

The baby was here. Jo was okay. It was all okay.

"Do you mind if I wash up a little better before I leave?" Theo asked. "It might start a bit of a panic if I wander back into the lobby in this state."

"Absolutely." Ilsa freshened the hot water in the basin and found him a comb and more clean towels. One of the benefits of living in a bathhouse: an endless supply of towels.

"Thank you again," she said. "I'm glad you were here."

Theo looked up at her: that studious glance, that slight smile. "I'm glad I was here too," he said. "And thank you. You were an outstanding assistant."

Ilsa smiled. "We were a good team."

"We were," he said, beaming. "If I didn't think half of Fraser Springs would question my motivations, I'd try to poach you to come work for me."

"You couldn't afford me." Because I wouldn't do that again for a million dollars, she added silently.

"Probably not. Well. I'd better go. Paperwork awaits." He picked up his cane from where it had been leaning, forgotten, against the doorway. "Until tomorrow. In the meantime, see if you can get Jo some iron-fortified biscuits and some mutton tea. And if you can find a dark beer, so much the better. It helps with milk production. Only dark beer, though. Not ale." He was babbling now. It was adorable.

"I will," she said.

"If she develops a fever or starts bleeding heavily, come and get me right away. Doesn't matter the time. If you have any questions, any at all, it's better to ask. Just come and get me."

"I will."

On his way out the door, he leaned in and brushed his lips against her ear. "And I hope very much to see you again on Sunday," he whispered.

She flushed. "I wouldn't miss it," she whispered back. Part of her wanted to tug him into the pantry, but she could hear Annie and Jean chattering right outside the kitchen. There was risk, and then there was foolish risk. She would see him soon enough.

After he left, Ilsa busied herself by preparing the tea for Jo. She arranged iron biscuits on a tray, strained the tea, and put it in their prettiest teacup. The towels and bedding would have to be boiled and bleached. The dough for tomorrow's bread hadn't even been started; they were behind on that, not that anyone would blame them. Did they have enough towels left for tomorrow's clients? She would check. With Nils gone earlier than she'd expected, their woodpile was low. Perhaps they could borrow some from Doc Stryker to tide them over until morning. She would have to be up at dawn to get it all ready.

When she carried the tray up to Jo, Owen was standing over Jo with his hand on her shoulder, staring reverently at her and their child. Jo, pale and half asleep, smiled up at him. Ilsa's heart clenched in her chest at the perfect scene of domestic bliss. She felt like she was stepping into one of the maudlin paintings that Mrs. McSheen insisted on hanging in the Anglican fellowship hall.

"Doctor's orders," Ilsa said. "Mutton tea and biscuits."

Jo wrinkled her nose at the brew, but carefully passed Sarah to Owen and took the cup anyway. "Your doctor seems nice."

"He's not my doctor."

Jo smiled. "You seem quite fond of one another, though." Still meddling, even when she'd just given birth an hour ago.

Ilsa breezed past the topic with a smile. "I'm glad it all worked out. He said some dark beer would help you get your strength, so I'm going to pop over to Doc's. I'll be back soon. I'll get Annie to start the bread and Jean to make us some more salve for the morning."

"You're working too hard," Owen said,

"Bah. I'd make you do all of it if you weren't foxed. Jo, when I come back I'll braid your hair. You look a mess."

Midnight came before Ilsa had a chance to pause for a breath of fresh air. She lingered by the kitchen garden, inhaling the spice of fallen leaves, woodsmoke, and the ever-present mineral tang of the hot springs. The wind was sharp this time of year, but she barely felt the cold. She kept thinking about Theo's hands around hers, his whisper against her ear. It was like being sixteen again: wonderful, and annoying.

She had been so afraid for Jo, and then Theo had stepped in and taken care of everything. He would likely make some asinine comment the very next time she saw him, and she knew that he would be out of her life again sooner rather than later, but for now? All she could think about was his broad shoulders, the gentle, reassuring confidence with which he'd delivered Jo's baby, and the way his lips felt against hers. And for now, that was all lovely. The disappointments of real life would be here soon enough—she would enjoy a little fantasy while she could.

Chapter 12

The satchel had been a mistake. Theo knew it the moment he set out along the boardwalk. He'd begged it off the porter; apparently the St. Alice Hotel provided guided nature picnics in the summer. But the two enamel cups tied on the side of the canvas bag clanged like a tinker's pack, drawing stares from the townspeople as he walked. So much for keeping a low profile; he might as well have worn a sandwich board advertising his intention to go looking for those water samples he'd been forbidden from collecting.

He met Ilsa on the outskirts of town, where even the gravelled path that led back to the boardwalk disappeared. "Setting off for the territories?" she asked, grinning at him.

He grimaced. "I may have overprepared. In case we end up lost." In truth, his experience with hiking was limited to being pushed in a wheelchair through Stanley Park while a nurse prattled on about how the fresh air would do him good in all sorts of ways. He wasn't going to turn down a chance for an excursion in the real outdoors, even if his leg made him pay for every step. Plus, how often did he get to enjoy a picnic lunch with a beautiful lady? He'd had to use all his limited charm to secure said picnic lunch from the cook.

Ilsa laughed. "If we get lost going up the side of a hill and back, we deserve to have bears eat us."

After weeks of frosty weather the sun had reappeared, coaxing the pine scent out of the trees. Even in his coat felt too warm. Ilsa was right: the path was only gently inclined and clearly marked by little stone cairns. The hike was more like a leisurely stroll.

"Well, thank you for taking time to be my courageous mountain guide. I imagine the Sterlings' new arrival has you very busy."

Ilsa sighed. "I forgot how much babies cry and how much laundry they make. Poor Jo. It's been a bother."

"I'm sure she's grateful for your help."

Ilsa kicked at a large pebble on the path. "She is. With her out of commission, I'm the only one who can whip those girls into action. They have the attention span of squirrels." He smiled at the adorable way she pronounced "squirrel." Her cheeks were pink from the walk, and her bright blue scarf set off her eyes.

They heard the stream before they saw it. "Is this the place?" he asked.

She nodded. "We should be close. Anywhere around here."

"People walk this far every day to get water?"

"Not many people draw from this stream that I know of. And those that do usually pump from farther down than this."

"Why not just use the water from the hot springs?"

"Because nobody drinks the hot springs water."

Theo knelt down, using his cane for stability. He dipped the test tube into the water. "Why not?"

Ilsa shrugged. "No one ever has. Why bother with something that tastes like vinegar when there are so many streams around?"

Perhaps the so-called "vitality water" the hotel was bottling for its guests was making people sick. That would explain why only people at the St. Alice fell ill. He tucked the sample into his satchel, and they continued trudging uphill to the next stream. Theo wasn't sure whether it was Ilsa's long-ago treatments or the pleasure of her company, but his leg barely bothered him at all.

"So what's your plan, once you have this water business sorted out?" she asked.

She asked the question lightly, but there was a note of real curiosity. His first instinct was to laugh the question off. "If I get caught with these samples, I won't be staying a week." He glanced away, up into the trees. Two little grey birds were squabbling over a pinecone, and the canopy echoed with their dispute. If he couldn't even tell Ilsa, how would ever be able to talk to anyone else about his ambitions? "There's a university in Paris that's developed a model to track measles outbreaks before they become deadly, and another in Göttingen doing some groundbreaking work with milk-borne scarlet fever. I had interviews arranged, even a fellowship offer from Dr. DuBois in Paris."

"So what happened?"

"It depended on … a lot of factors."

"Factors like your parents?"

Of course. Ilsa knew what he was up against better than perhaps anyone else in the world. "Yes. Exactly. It's maddening. If I wanted to sail across the Atlantic and spend a year sitting in cafes all day and getting drunk all night, Father would pay my way in a heartbeat. But if I want to go to continue my education?" The words poured out of him; he probably sounded like a whiny child, but he couldn't stop himself. "The chances of my going to Europe are more or less nil. Apparently, a man of my standing exists to sit on advisory boards and host charity balls, not muck around with sick people and diseases."

"That's ridiculous," she agreed.

"I worked so hard to get out of that bed and then to make it through my degree. I assumed that they'd be pleased to have a son who's something besides an invalid. But I honestly think they preferred me when I was helpless."

He'd never said that out loud, even to himself. It was an ugly thing to admit.

Ilsa touched his arm and they stopped again. "Well, if it's any consolation, I prefer this version of you."

The thumping in his chest suddenly didn't seem related to the exertion of the hike. "You do?"

"Of course. You've been out in the world, and you're a doctor now. A good one. And you finally grew into your gigantic ears."

He blinked, hard, as if she'd slapped him instead of paying him the nicest compliments he'd ever received. Ilsa just smiled and then pointed up and to her left.

"That's the last one, I think. Crow's Nest Creek." He could see the sunlight glinting off another stream; in that direction, the trees gave way to scree and boulders and then a meadow that sloped downwards towards the town. He could see the bright, green-tinged waters of the hot springs, and the next range of mountains in the distance, gray and purple against the blue sky. The view really was breathtaking up here. This time, Ilsa took the test tube from his satchel before he could object, and darted off to gather the sample herself; she was halfway to the stream before he even realized what was happening.

He certainly wasn't going to chase after her. He propped himself in the shade of a large limestone rock, roughly the size and shape of a bear, and settled in to wait for her. He took a long pull from one of the two canteens of boiled drinking water Ilsa'd had the forethought to bring along. He nearly choked when Ilsa popped out from the other side of the boulder, shouting "Ha!" like a child playing hide-and-seek.

"Brat!" he yelped, wiping his chin with the back of his free hand.

"Stick-in-the-mud," she replied. "*That* hasn't changed. I'll trade you this lovely little tube for that canteen."

He handed it over and tucked away the last of the day's samples while Ilsa drank. She drained the canteen and then hopped up nimbly to sit on the bear-shaped boulder. "Break time. I'm not much for these long hikes."

"So a career as a mountain guide is out. What's your backup plan?" It wasn't his cleverest conversational gambit, but he'd been dying to ask her more about her past and her hopes for the future.

"Pirate," she said without hesitation.

"No, be serious. I told you mine. What's your big, complicated dream?"

"Pirate," she insisted. "What could be more complicated than the life of a lady pirate in this day and age?" He glared at her, and she laughed and gave in. "Promise you won't tell Jo?"

"Cross my heart."

"I haven't told anyone about this." She picked at an imaginary thread on her skirt. "I make a bit of money on the side by updating people's old dresses. Add some lace, drop a hem, cut away a flounce: presto! Brand-new dress. But it's hard to find the right materials. I want to open a little sundries store for that."

"Don't women just buy new dresses every year?"

Clearly, he'd said something wrong, because Ilsa looked at him as if he'd grown an extra nose. "A brand-new dress, a nice one? That's forty dollars at least. Your mother's evening gowns probably cost upwards of a thousand dollars each. And then capes and gloves and hats to match."

Was forty dollars a lot of money? Theo had never really handled the financial side of anything. Even in Fraser Springs, his bills were forwarded to his father's bank in Vancouver. He didn't dare ask, nor did he dare to volunteer his mother's opinions of women who wore "last year's dress." "It sounds like you've thought a lot about this," he said.

"You don't think it's a good idea?" She looked disappointed.

"No! I mean, no, I didn't mean that. I don't know much about women's fashion. But it sounds like you do."

Again, that didn't seem to be the answer that Ilsa was looking for, because she fell silent.

"So you would move to Vancouver and start a business," Theo tried. "You don't want to settle down instead, start a family of your own?"

"I've haven't had a family for a long time, and it hasn't killed me yet." Ilsa closed her eyes and tipped her face up to the sun.

"You're not exactly an advertisement for happy families yourself." Wasn't that the Lord's honest truth? She looked back over at him suddenly, like a cat startled awake from its sunbathing. "You're not married, are you? Or engaged or whatever?"

He laughed at her sudden, very belated concern. "No. Although not for my mother's lack of trying. She still keeps inviting debutantes to extremely formal family dinners. With any luck, they're starting to give up on me. And at least Father's too decrepit to try dragging me off to a whorehouse again."

Damn it. He had not meant to say that. He'd never mentioned that humiliating incident to anyone.

"That sounds like a story I haven't heard." And Ilsa wasn't going to let it pass, either.

Theo sighed. In for a penny, in for a pound. "After we got caught," he said carefully, "my father decided to make 'a real Whitacre' out of me."

He could still recall the decade-old memory in crystalline detail. He'd known at once that something was wrong when his father had come down to his room. The old man rarely left his study, preferring the company of his cigars and his brandy.

"I told him I was going to go find you. And he just laughed and told me to get my coat. He loaded me up in that ghastly old carriage—they still have it, by the way. The same horses and everything. They must have one hoof each in the glue factory by now, and it's not as if we can't afford a motorcar."

"Theo," Ilsa prompted. No, she absolutely wasn't going to let him back out of this, it seemed. He leaned back against the warm boulder to take some weight off his leg and to avoid looking at her for the rest of his ugly little tale. "He kept slapping me on the back and giving me his flask to drink from. I think it was the proudest he's ever been of me. He told me I'd just gotten a little confused, that 'having urges' was natural, but you've got to take care of it in the proper time and place. And that he was going to show me around one of the proper places."

"Oh."

"Exactly. It was an absolute nightmare. The place reeked, and the women all looked miserable, and Father was half drunk and kept telling everyone not to worry about my leg, because my pecker still worked." He'd also insisted that the madam rustle up "a blond one with big titties" to suit his son's newly discovered tastes. "He got me hustled into a bedroom with some poor girl, and almost as soon as the door was closed …" God, it really had been the worst night of his life. "I was a mess. I started bawling, and then I vomited. Everywhere. The girl started crying, too, and the madam dragged my father upstairs to take me home."

Even telling the bare outline of that night made his stomach churn. He wasn't sure he wanted to admit this next part; wasn't sure he even needed to. He took a deep breath and spoke quickly, before he lost his nerve. "I've avoided it ever since. All of it."

A moment of gut-wrenching quiet passed before Ilsa spoke. "Wait. You're … all of it? Not with anyone?"

"Well," he began, but he didn't have any plan for completing the sentence. He attempted a reassuring smile and then looked away, over the lake.

"Hey!" She kicked his arm with her booted foot. "Look at me."

When he turned back, she wasn't laughing at him or giving him the look that always meant "poor Little Teddy." She looked, actually, quite serious. As if he'd told her a riddle that she couldn't quite puzzle out. She slipped down from her perch and touched his cheek, as if to smooth away his embarrassment.

"Oh, Theo. You've been carrying that around for all these years?"

Her blue eyes were bright with an emotion he couldn't quite place, something more like affection than revulsion. Relief coursed through his body like adrenaline. He'd told her his most shameful secret, and not only was she still here, but she was also still touching him. From the moment she had walked into the room in Wilson's Bathhouse, he'd acted clumsily, hurt her feelings more than once. And yet, here she was.

Her hair had loosened from its pins during her scramble to and from the stream, and when she sat with her back to the sun, it formed an aura of light around her face. Her lips were parted, just slightly, and her cheeks and the tip of her nose were flushed pink from the crisp air. He reached out and tucked a stray curl behind her ear. Touching her before, in the darkness of the St. Alice's fountain room, seemed completely natural. But here, in broad daylight and in the open air?

He felt like taking a risk. His limbs buzzed with six years' worth of wanting to take a risk, to try again. He erased the last inches between them, and he kissed her. Not tentatively this time, but with the hunger and confidence of that glorious night in the basement. Ilsa melted into him immediately, weaving her fingers into his hair to pull him closer.

After an intoxicating minute, she pulled back. "You can't be a virgin," she said breathlessly. "You're too good a kisser."

"First off, men aren't virgins." She looked sceptical, and he grinned back at her. "I'm inexperienced. Completely different thing. And second, being inexperienced is not the same thing as being ignorant. You'd be amazed at the things you can find illustrated in medical books."

"So it's all theoretical," she teased.

He grabbed her around her waist and swung her back up onto the rock. She shrieked with surprise and pushed at his shoulders, but she also parted her knees as he stepped closer, so that he stood cradled between her thighs.

"A little respect, please. You might need some lessons yourself." He bent down to kiss her again, and she tilted her chin in anticipation. He smiled and dipped his lips to the crook of her elbow. "Here, for example." He glanced up and saw her looking at him in confusion. Perfect. He closed his eyes and gave the tender spot a swirl with the tip of his tongue and then nipped gently at the sensitive skin. She squirmed in his arms, and he felt a ridiculous surge of triumph.

"There's a lovely little bundle of nerves here that doesn't get nearly enough attention." Another nibble. "Your breasts get all the glory, but this spot"—another lingering kiss—"is for experts." He kissed his way lower, to the pulse at her inner wrist. He noted its unusually rapid tempo with interest before continuing to the sweet creases of her palm. He tasted each fingertip and each of the three unexpectedly intimate little deltas between her fingers.

He watched her as he went, eager to see what pleased her. Her eyes were half lidded, her focus entirely inward on her own responses and sensations. He was hard, uncomfortably so, but he tried to put that fact aside for now. He had a point to prove, and he refused to be distracted until he'd made it.

"I could touch you all over, like this," he murmured. "I want to touch you everywhere." He brushed his lips across her palm again, and she shivered. "The soles of your feet. Your ankles. The backs of your knees." He tucked her hand back against his shoulder and ran his hands lingeringly down the tops of her thighs. He reached the hem of her skirts and pulled them higher, inch by inch, until he could cup her knees in his palms. He grinned into the sensitive curve of her neck.

"You wore silk stockings to climb up a mountain?" He pressed a kiss to her neck, just below her jaw.

"Maybe I wear them all the time," she said breathlessly. "I like silk stockings."

"Hmm. I like them too. I like them very much." He slid his fingers a few inches higher, to the ribbons and lace of her garters. "And I like this frilly nonsense here," he whispered against her ear.

She seemed to be holding her breath, letting it out in little sighs with each move he made.

"Where else do you like to be touched, darling?" She responded wordlessly, reaching down to pull his hand higher under her bunched petticoats.

He dipped past the gauzy muslin of her pantalets, until he could brush his fingers through the delicate curls between her thighs. Her hand guiding him parted her slick folds—hesitantly at first, until she urged him on with a little whimper of pleasure.

She leaned towards him, clearly expecting him to pull her closer into his arms. Instead, he leaned forwards, slowly pushing her back until she lay on the sun-warmed stone. He kissed the tender little hollow at the base of her throat, skimmed down to the swell of her breasts, and on to the corseted valley of her stomach. She finally realized his intention and propped up on her elbows to try to catch his eye.

"Theo! You don't have to—"

"I want to. You can't possibly know how much I've thought about pleasuring you like this." She bit her lower lip in indecision, and it just made her look more adorable. "Please. If I'm terrible at it, just tell me and I'll put you back to rights." That earned him a little laugh, and she dropped her head back down. She bunched her skirts up in her fists, blocking his view of her face as he returned to his work.

He dropped kisses on the tops of her thighs as he pulled the little pantalets down to her knees. He brushed his lips across the sweet swell of her lower abdomen, pausing at the shining pale curls on her mons. He swept a single exploratory finger along her folds and thrilled as Ilsa gasped.

"Good?" he asked, and she made a low humming noise that he took for a yes.

Bolder now, he parted her folds and indulged himself in a long, slow lick. She tasted of salt and musk, not at all what he'd expected and yet somehow still exactly right. He'd read about this act, overheard snickering remarks between grown men and dirty jokes whispered between boys. None of that compared to the reality of this warm, glowing woman spread before him, waiting and eager for the pleasure he could give her.

He applied himself, he suspected, with no great skill or finesse. But Ilsa didn't tell him to stop or push him away. After a minute or two, he felt her fingers in his hair, subtly guiding lower, higher, deeper, as she chased her pleasure. He had a passing fear that he might disgrace himself and be in for an especially awkward walk back through town. Then Ilsa arched her back suddenly, her fingers fisting in his hair and in her skirts, and she shuddered under his mouth, cried out incoherently. He gave one final flick of his tongue before she shoved him away onto her thigh, laughing.

He tidied them both up as best he could with his handkerchief. Ilsa flipped her skirts back down over the lovely silk stockings.

"Oh! Your hair!" She giggled, and he reached up to investigate the damage. "You look like a cranky rooster." He patted his head, and there was, indeed, a distinctly roosterish quality to the ruff of pomaded hair left from Ilsa's clasping fingers. She slid down to her feet and attempted to undo the damage with her fingers; in the process, she bumped against the other lingering result of their sylvan interlude.

"I could take care of that for you, too," she murmured. "If you'd like."

It was tempting. Extremely, painfully tempting. But his appetite for risk seemed to have found its limit for the morning. "I'm enough of a wreck as it is. If you start plying your wiles on me now, I won't make it back to work alive."

She skimmed her fingers along the rigid outline. "Fair's fair, though." He groaned and snatched her wicked little hand away from danger.

She smiled as he lifted it to his lips and pressed a kiss to the inside of her wrist. "Later, then? I should have the test results ready to show you in a day or two."

Her smiled widened, crinkling the corners of her eyes. "I'd like that very much."

He held her hand until they reached the first sign of habitation, just where the dirt path turned to gravel. Theo had managed to recite the provincial capitals enough times to restore his own appearance to decency. There was an uncomfortable moment as their hands pulled apart, and he smiled sheepishly.

"I hate that I can't walk down the street with you on my arm."

She paused to twist and pin her tumbledown hair back under her hat and smiled at him reassuringly. "It's okay. This is only for a little while, right?"

"Right." At sixteen, he had loved her and failed miserably at keeping her by his side. But now things were right where they'd left off all those years ago. In fact, they were better. As soon as this business at the St. Alice was sorted out, he could court her properly. Publicly. He'd lost her once, and he'd be damned if he let anything come between them again. In fact, even if the whole business blew up in his face and he wound up disinherited, he'd find a way to support the two of them. It would be worth it to see the look on his father's face when Ilsa walked into that cavernous old mansion as his betrothed.

He pulled her close for one last kiss, just a playful peck on the lips. "I'll see you later this week, won't I?"

"Eight o'clock this Wednesday," she confirmed. "Same place as before."

"I'll leave the door propped. And if you're a very well-behaved young lady for the rest of the day, I might even let you sit on my lap again." She crossed her eyes at him and hurried off in the direction of the boardwalk. He stood and watched her until she was out of sight. When it seemed as if she'd put enough distance between them to avoid attracting unwelcome attention, he set off himself. His leg and hip ached now, with all the promise of worse to come, but he whistled cheerfully as he limped along.

The porter hailed him almost as soon as he entered the lobby.

"You look to be in fine feather today, sir. Have a pleasant walk?"

"Yes, a very pleasant walk," Theo replied. "In fact, it was quite probably the pleasantest walk of my life."

• • •

Ilsa took her time heading back to Wilson's. Partly because it was a beautiful day, and partly because she needed a chance to think.

What she'd told Theo when they'd parted ways had been true: this was only for a little while. She had no illusions about her place in his world, let alone in his future. Within a month or two, she would probably be out of his life. But she also couldn't deny that the spark they'd shared at sixteen was still there. If anything, it was stronger now that they were more mature. Now that she, at least, had a better idea of what she wanted and what a man could offer her. She'd had a fair few beaus over the years, and the intimacies she'd shared with them had been a pleasure and a comfort in the midst of life's hard work. What a shame that anyone had ruined such a lovely thing for Theo.

She stopped at the post office on her way down the boardwalk. She waited patiently as old Miss Eastman monopolized the counter to do something complicated involving a cheque. Had Miss Eastman ever had a sweetheart? Had anyone ever taken her for a hike and then kissed her silly among the pine trees? Had she ever thrown caution to the wind and spread her legs for her lover in the warm sunshine?

The clerk behind the counter cleared his throat loudly; it was Ilsa's turn at last, and she had been too busy daydreaming to notice.

"Sorry," she said. The clerk handed over a packet of mail wordlessly.

Ilsa flipped through the stack. Bills, inquiries for Wilson's Bathhouse, and one addressed to I. Pedersen. She had almost forgotten sending the letter to the broker. Her heart started to hammer again as she tore the envelope open.

Dear Mr. Pedersen:

Thank you for your inquiry. I would be happy to assist you in procuring merchandise for your new sundries business. Unfortunately, December is my busiest month because of orders for the Christmas season. I would, however, be happy to meet with you at any time between January 7 and 10.

I prefer to meet prospective clients in the Woodward's cafeteria, since a great many of our goods are stocked by this fine department store and you may get a sense of how they can best be marketed and displayed. If you find my terms amenable, we will sign any contracts in my offices. Depending on the eventual terms of your lease, this will set things in motion for an early March opening date.

I can also be of assistance in helping you locate a storefront and preparing a lease. If you are interested in that service, please do let me know, and I will have my colleague, Mr. John McPherson, join us. He is one of Vancouver's most able commercial real estate brokers, and I do business with him regularly. We advise out-of-town clients to plan a stay of about three days.

Please reply with an acceptable date and time at which we might meet, and I will look forward to making your acquaintance in person.

Yours sincerely,

Mr. Mortimer Hayley

Ilsa took a breath. She had expected that her first meeting with Mr. Hayley would be mostly social, but it looked like business in Vancouver moved rapidly. For the first time, she could actually picture herself walking among the gleaming rows of goods at Woodward's, visiting the food halls and the perfumery, being waited on and catered to. January was perfect, really. She needed time to put together a new dress—Mr. Hayley was going to discover that Mister Pedersen was actually a Miss, and she needed to be the most polished, businesslike Miss he'd ever seen. And she wanted to be around to help Jo with baby Sarah for at least the next few weeks. But her savings were in the bank, and her new life was waiting.

She folded the letter back into thirds, slipped it carefully back into its envelope, and set off for Wilson's with fresh determination in every step.

Chapter 13

The water samples from the uphill streams all tested negative for pathogens, as did the ones he'd gathered surreptitiously around the hotel. It was a disappointment, but he would test every pump and cistern in the whole damn town if he needed to. Still, the cause of the mystery illness would eventually reveal itself if he kept at it.

Unless the epidemic solved itself first. No one had been sick this week, which had put Morse in a considerably better mood and caused Dr. Greyson to crow at every opportunity about how the stomach flu always resolved on its own.

He had to be missing something. The knock at his door was a welcome distraction from the frustration of his laboratory notes.

"Coming," Theo called.

Jim Porter greeted him. "Letter's come for you, sir. Fancy stationery, so I thought I'd run it up to you directly. In case it's important."

"Thanks," he said cheerfully, tipping him double. He was a very good porter, after all, and Theo was feeling in general charity with the world.

He recognized the tight script on the letter's address immediately. *Mrs. Olivia Elizabeth Foster-Minden Whitacre.* His good mood evaporated like ether. Up here, it had been so easy to forget his mother. And that he'd have to see her for Christmas in only a few short weeks.

He could toss the letter into a drawer and try to forget about it, but he knew it was no use. Its existence would camp out in the back of his mind, wiping out every positive thought with its poison.

He stretched out on the bed and flipped the letter over in his hands, looking for clues as to her mood. The downstrokes were heavy: a bad sign. He imagined the angry flourish her gloved hands would have made as they wrote the final address. *Doctor Theodore Henry Albert Whitacre II.* The fact that she used his full name was another bad sign.

He carefully opened the envelope and began to read.

My Dearest Teddy,

I am so very much looking forward to your visit at Christmas. I have been planning the dinner menu with Cook for weeks, and it promises to be simply divine. We will be enjoying both a goose and a suckling pig this year, and, of course, all the merry trimmings (including a trifle and an almond blancmange for dessert). I have invited several fine couples to share our table. You will be delighted to hear that Emily Morrison and her family have agreed to attend. I have spoken to you about Emily Morrison before. She inherited a fine independence from her great aunt—Mrs. Dowling, on her father's side—and has the charitable heart required to overlook your limitations.

My dearest, I hope you appreciate how much Dr. Greyson looks out for you. He is such a dear man and thinks only of your happiness and what is best for you. That is why he has brought it to my attention that you have been seen in company unseemly for a man of your breeding and position.

Theodore, it strikes at my heart to know that even though you were raised to have a strong moral character, you continue to fraternize with women of the lower orders. I can only imagine that, with your sensitive nature, you feel some misplaced sense of pity for a woman who was formerly in the employ of our family. But I must insist that you remember that this person chose to forfeit any right to your charity through her own depraved and indecent behaviour. The passage of time can only have magnified her failings, and I trust that you will not allow yourself to be preyed upon a second time.

Mrs. Richard Deighton recently effused to me about how well you cared for her when she was laid low. How her feelings would have been outraged had she known that the hands who had ministered to her had been first been polluted by the touch of a "masseuse." How could she ever trust you, or your place of employment, again?

I expect that your contact with that woman will cease, and that there will be no need to continue this discussion when you return home. You will give Miss Morrison your utmost care and attention, and I will ensure that word of your indiscretion does not reach the Morrison family. Dr. Greyson has assured me of his confidence.

With all love,

Your Dearest Mama

Theo read the letter again. Secrets clearly didn't exist in small towns. And he somehow wasn't surprised that his mother had remembered Ilsa's name. Nobody held a grudge like Olivia Whitacre.

How much could Greyson know? No one had seen him with Ilsa, to his knowledge. Had he told Mr. Morse? No, the wily old fraud likely wanted a bargaining chip to hold over his head in case Theo challenged his authority again. One word to Morse, and Theo would be dismissed for moral turpitude or some such trumped-up nonsense.

He balled up the letter and threw it in the wastepaper basket. Then he retrieved it and ripped it into tiny pieces. How dare Greyson and his mother intrude on his personal life. How dare she force him up here and then try to bully away the one bit of happiness he'd been able to eke out of this backwater. How dare they treat Ilsa like a shameful secret, when she was worth a million Emily Morrisons.

He respected Ilsa. He had loved her. He was beginning to suspect that he still loved her all these years later. And yet ... he couldn't imagine Ilsa sitting in his mother's parlour, taking polite tea with the ladies she used to wait on. Would she have the patience to put up with the ridiculous expectations placed on women in that world, where every word and gesture was rigorously scheduled and rehearsed? Probably not, but then, he had never been happy in that world either. Maybe he was thinking too narrowly. She was clever and far better at navigating the unwritten rules of socializing than he would ever be.

She had never thrown his "limitations" in his face, and she hadn't belittled his ambitions to study in Paris. Why should he even want to drag her back into the airless parlours of Vancouver in the first place? If they moved to Europe together, no one would ever have to know her background. It could work. They could make it work.

If his mother thought that she could snap her fingers and watch him fall into line, she was sorely mistaken. She might prefer it if he moved back home forever and let people wait on him hand and foot, but that wasn't going to happen. He wasn't going back to being poor Little Teddy, not for anyone.

When he arrived in the dim, echoing basement spa on Wednesday night, Ilsa was sitting on the bench at the attendants' counter, waiting for him. He smiled to himself—he had fond memories of that particular bench.

"Did you know they don't even lock that door?" she asked. "Anyone could wander in and get up to no good." He strode over to her, cradled her face in his hands, and kissed her. She was startled but leaned into him, deepening the kiss. He threaded his fingers through her hair. God, he loved how she smelled, how her loose, pale curls brushed against his fingers. His mother was right. He didn't care a whit about Emily Morrison, or any other woman on earth. If that was a character flaw, he could live with it.

Finally, she pulled away, smiling. "What's all this about?" she asked.

He kissed her again, mostly to reassure himself. "It seems that Dr. Greyson has discovered that we've been ... ah, been together."

Ilsa froze, and her eyes widened. "What? What did he say, exactly?" She struggled to keep her voice at a whisper.

"I don't think he knows any of the details, thank God. Only that we've been meeting each other."

"But how did he find out?"

"No idea. People keep telling me it's impossible to keep a secret in this town. I guess I need to start believing them. At any rate, Greyson knows I've been meeting you, and he wrote to my mother. And now my mother has written to me. "

Ilsa closed her eyes for a moment and took a deep breath. "What does she want?"

"What she always wants. I am to stop being happy at once or she will drag me back to Vancouver by the scruff of my neck." She stood and wandered over to the little fountain where the bronze lady poured water endlessly from her uplifted jug.

"Why does Dr. Greyson even care?" she asked. "Would he fire you?"

"Possibly. Possibly not. Either way, the shame of it all will cause my mother to have hysterics and take to her bedroom for a month."

Ilsa huffed and sat down hard on the fountain's marble edge. "I don't see how it's any of her business what you do. You're a grown man."

He eased down to sit beside her and squeezed her hand. "You're right. It's not her business, and that's probably driving her insane right now. She couldn't stop me from leaving to go to school, so she needs to find some other way to keep me on the leash."

"You can't let her, Theo. You don't deserve that."

"I'm sure she thinks she's simply taking care of me. Doing me a favour. Making sure I come back home and stand around at cotillions until I find a girl exactly like her to be miserable with forever. God, I hate those dances."

She laughed. "So it's not Fraser Springs. You hate all dancing, everywhere."

Music began to drift down the stairs; for the first time since Theo had arrived, someone was actually playing the grand piano in the lobby. He didn't recognize the cheerful, ragtime number.

Ilsa clapped her hands with delight. "Oh, that's too perfect!" She stood up and held out her hands to him, palms down. "Dance with me."

"I don't know how. I've never learned any steps." She pulled him to his feet anyway.

"I worked in a dance hall, remember? I know all the steps to just about everything. I'll teach you." She gave a little twirl, flaring her skirts out around her ankles like a dervish. "Besides, it will give your dear mama a conniption when she finds out."

It was an appealing thought, but he still hung back. "I'll tread all over your feet."

"Ha! I've danced with much clumsier men than you."

"I honestly doubt it."

She ignored him and took his hands again, settling one on her waist. "Are you sober right now?"

"What? Of course."

"Then you're already ahead of the pack." She was grinning at him, clearly thrilled, and he couldn't help smiling back. He'd willingly court disaster as long as she enjoyed herself.

"Fine. But something simple, please?"

"How does the one-step sound?"

"Just one step in the one-step, I assume?" She nodded and moved closer. "I don't suppose they make them any simpler than that." Ilsa put her left hand on his shoulder, and he lifted her right hand in his. He'd at least seen this before, so he could get this far on his own. "Now what?"

"The important thing is to keep your feet moving. Start with your left foot and walk in place." He did as he was told, stiffly, feeling a bit like a wind-up toy soldier. "Now, rock side to side with each step. No, from the waist." They began to sway like trees in a brisk wind. "Yes, perfect. And now we simply walk around the room in a circle. You start off forwards, and I'll follow you."

They made it two steps before, as he'd feared, he tripped over her feet and nearly pushed them both sprawling onto the floor. But she simply leaned into him and laughed. "Don't stomp like an elephant. Shift your weight onto the balls of your feet, and walk that way." He tried it, and the next few steps felt much more natural. Ilsa really was an extraordinary dancer; he knew he should be leading, but she gently nudged him along when he hesitated, adjusted their course with a quick skip or a light-footed little pivot when he short-footed them or drew a step out too long.

Why had he avoided this for so long? The music's syncopation disguised his limp, and spinning around the room with Ilsa was intoxicating. Too soon, the anonymous piano player went silent, and they slowly drifted to a stop. She sighed happily and leaned into him, her cheek pressed against his shoulder. He rested his chin on top of her head and held her. For that moment, in the dark basement of a hotel in the middle of nowhere, Theo Whitacre felt like the most contented man in North America.

• • •

Ilsa swayed in Theo's arms, even though the music had stopped. She'd suggested the dancing as a distraction, a game to lighten the mood after a difficult conversation. She didn't like the hurt, the self-loathing she'd seen in his eyes as he'd talked about his mother and the bleak, lonely future that had been mapped out for him.

The thought of Theo—sweet, sentimental Theo—alone and untouched for all this time pulled at her heart. She released his hand and slipped her fingers through his dark hair, tipping his head back just enough to kiss his throat. Then his chin. And then his lips. He hummed with pleasure, and she deepened the kiss slowly, deliberately. Like the dancing, he should have taken the lead, pulling her along in his wake. But instead they found their own equilibrium, a rhythm of give and take that was only for them.

Eventually, he pulled away from the kiss, leaning his forehead gently against hers.

"Ilsa," he sighed. "Why the hell are you so sweet to me? I didn't do very well by you, all those years ago."

He traced the curve of her lip with his thumb, his palm cupping her cheek. The touch made her shiver with pleasure. Why did his tenderness fluster her so much more than his rudeness or his self-importance? This sweetness, this vulnerability, was all so lovely, and it was even lovelier because she knew it could never last.

"I suppose you're simply an easy person to forgive," she hedged.

"I'm not, though. I'm awkward and blunt and arrogant." He paused. "And inexperienced."

This was more familiar territory, and she caught at it without hesitation. She and Theo might not have a future, but they did have tonight. She could at least show him what intimacy should really be like. "There's a cure for that, you know. Don't you have a room here?"

He blinked. "I ... yes. I do."

"I didn't get a good look at it the last time I was here. Would you like to show me again?" She curled her hands around his shoulders. He had gone very still. If she was pushing too hard, or too far, a word from him—a look—and she would play the whole thing off as a joke.

Instead, he pulled her against him, hard. "Are you sure?" he rasped.

"Very sure. I've done this before." She waited a moment for that to sink in. "Is that going to be an issue?"

"Honestly? I'm glad at least one of us knows what they're doing."

"I thought you'd read all about it in your books." She teased him to cover her relief—he wasn't going to lash out at her or try to make her feel ashamed of her past.

"You were always better at the practical things," he reminded her with a little smile. And then there was nothing but the press of his body against hers, long and hard and lean, and the heat of his kiss. She let herself dissolve into the warmth of his lips and the satin tangle of their tongues. They kissed until she was aching for air, aching for . . .

"Not here," she gasped. "I want a room with a big bed and a lock on the door."

"I want that too," he agreed. His voice shook just a little. "I want you."

She kissed him, a little peck, and pulled back to take his hand. "Then lead the way."

She followed him up the carpeted stairs to the lobby and then across it to the grand stairway that led up to the rooms. They went slowly, to keep a careful watch for guests and staff, and to allow Theo to choose his footing carefully. Despite their snail's pace, her heart raced from the risk.

She was so focused on getting to Theo's room without being seen that it was almost a surprise when they actually arrived. He opened the door quietly and then tugged her in after him into the dark room. She heard Theo turn the lock and then felt his hands on her waist.

"Should we risk the light?" he murmured. "There's only the one, and it's bright as day."

"Electric lights are so unromantic. But I want to see you. Can you open the curtains?"

"Wait right here." She heard the *shush* of heavy drapery being pulled apart, and a pale shaft of light washed over Theo and across the bed. "I think the moon's full tonight. That's lucky."

"Very lucky," she agreed. She made her way to him, around the big four-poster bed that loomed huge in the room. She slipped back into his arms, suddenly feeling a buzz of nerves. This would be his first time. It would be her first time with him. She wanted it to be perfect, and she knew that nothing ever was. She sighed, and he stroked her hair.

"Second thoughts?" he asked. It was strangely reassuring to hear the waver in his voice.

"Never. I'm just thinking of how many buttons and buckles I'm going to have to undo before I can see you naked."

He grinned, his green eyes washed out to grey in the moonlight. "Then allow me." He slipped out of his coat, dropping it to the floor, quickly followed by his waistcoat. He loosened his tie and unbuttoned his collar one-handed as he toed out of his shoes and socks. Her mouth went a little dry as she watched the way his shoulders pulled at the crisp linen of his shirt. He might have a weak leg, but his physique more than made up for that in other areas. He wasn't bashful in stripping off above the waist—she'd see it all already, after all. But his fingers hovered over the buttons of his trousers, and she smiled a little at his hesitation.

"My turn," she whispered. She slid her hands along his waistband and then undid the rest of his buttons. He was hard for her, tenting the front of his underwear, and she swept her palm across his straining erection. He drew in a sharp breath, and she stepped back.

"I have buttons too, you know." Theo gave a wolfish grin. Despite some fumbling, together they stripped her down to her chemise in no time. Without the support of the corset, her breasts felt low and heavy until Theo cupped and gently hefted them in his palms. She leaned into his hands, and he sighed before pulling her down with him into the plush velvet bedspread. She wriggled out of the chemise, and he groaned softly, bending to kiss one pink nipple, circling and sucking.

He shifted to tend to her other aching breast, and she gasped as the cold air touched the wet traces of his kiss, hardening her nipple to the edge of pain. He kissed and nibbled his way back up to her lips, and they lay face to face, touching and caressing. The position was so familiar, and yet his body was so different from her memories. He was bigger, stronger ... hungrier. She pushed off his drawers, running her hands down his firm thighs before sweeping back up to palm the hot weight of his cock. He plunged his tongue deeply into her mouth in response, and she closed her fingers around him, gently gripping his hard length.

His hands roamed over her shoulders, down her back, along the tender creases at the tops of her thighs. She stroked him rhythmically, matching her movements to the pulse of their kiss, and soon he was thrusting helplessly into her hand.

"Stop," he gasped, breaking their wild kiss. "I can't. I'll— "

She released him, smoothing her hand down his flank. "Is this good?" she asked. "On your side?"

He nodded. "Will ... will it work for you, like this?"

She only smiled and lifted her upper leg up and over his hip— the position nestled his cock just were she wanted it. Judging by Theo's whimper of pleasure as he slid between her thighs, it was exactly where he wanted it as well. She rocked against him, the wet friction dragging a guttural moan from his lips. His hand left her breast and closed around the swell of her hip, pulling them together even more tightly without actually entering her. She moved against him again and again, wrapping her arms around his neck and kissing him deeply, hungrily, as she rode his shaft towards her own pleasure.

"What do you want, Theo?" she purred into his ear.

"Oh God. I want you. I want—"

"Do want to be inside me?"

"Please," he almost sobbed, incoherent with urgency.

"You have to say the words. I want to hear you say what you want." His breathing was all groans and whimpers, his hands gripping her bottom and the nape of her neck hard enough to leave marks.

"I want to be inside you. Now." She tilted away to slip her hand between their bodies, guiding him in. He was so achingly hard, slicked with her desire. And then he thrust home, filling her so deeply that she tipped her head back and cried out. The sudden pressure against her clitoris tumbled her over her own precipice, and she gasped as she shuddered apart around him. He pumped desperately—once, twice, three times—before he was locked in the shuddering grip of his own release.

They strained and undulated together, riding out the aftershocks of pleasure, until finally they were motionless except for the heave of their breathing. Distantly, Ilsa realized that Theo had somehow found the self-control to withdraw and spend against her thigh. She smiled to herself as she discretely used a corner of the sheet to tidy up. Of course Theo would think to take care of them, even now. Then a second, bittersweet realization: he didn't want to be tied down any more than she did.

Theo exhaled a deep, satisfied, gust of a sigh, and she smiled against the hollow of his shoulder. This was enough. This was more than enough, and she would enjoy it while it lasted. She stretched lazily, enjoying the slide of the silky-soft bedsheets against her skin, and then let Theo tuck her alongside his warm, lean body. She snuggled close, and he folded one arm behind his head and curled the other possessively around her shoulders. He looked, she thought, quite smug for someone who'd only had sex once.

She caressed the coarse, dark hair of his chest, wishing there were more light. She'd never really had a chance to enjoy the view of his front, but if it were anything like his back …

"Do you think anyone would come looking for us if we just stayed here for the next few days?" he asked.

"You could probably get away with it, but some of us have real jobs," she said with mock seriousness.

"I told you before, I'll hire you on as my nurse. Problem solved."

"I'd be a terrible nurse. I'd boss you around in front of your patients, and you'd end up dismissing me without a reference."

"I won't stand for any insubordination," he agreed. "And then there's the issue of propriety."

"Of what?"

"If you were my nurse, it would be entirely inappropriate for me to chase you around the examining rooms and kiss you in front of the patients." He pinched her bottom playfully, and she wriggled to slap his hand away. "No," he went on, laughing, "it wouldn't do at all. I suppose I'll just have to marry you. Then I can work you all day long without even having to pay you."

"That," she snipped, "is probably the most honest description of marriage I've ever heard."

"No, hear me out. We'll get married, and then of course, we'll have to go on a honeymoon for whole a year. Nobody has to work on their honeymoon. We'll pawn all the wedding gifts to pay people to bring us all our meals in bed. This is a brilliant plan."

"Brilliant," she agreed. "I'll still boss you around terribly, though."

And that was when he took her hand in his and stared straight into her eyes. "Marry me, Ilsa," he said, with complete sincerity. "Marry me, and you can do anything you like."

Chapter 14

Ilsa pulled back from him, putting a scant inch or so between their bodies that felt like a mile. "Wait. Are you being serious?"

"Why would I joke about something like that?" He shifted onto his side to face her.

"Theo, you can't."

"Can't what?"

"Seriously want to get married."

"Well, not this exact instant. But I thought …" he trailed off. "Being with you in Vancouver was the last time I was really happy. And now by some miracle, we've found each other again, and we still make each other happy. Why shouldn't we get married?"

"We can make each other happy," she assured him. "We just don't have to rush into anything."

"All right." He had to keep his cool. This could all be a misunderstanding; perhaps she truly didn't realize how serious he was. "How long would you have to wait for it to count as not rushing?"

"I don't know. I haven't thought about it. I didn't expect any of this."

"That's my point. Exactly. This is a gift, darling. We should take it while we have the chance."

She sighed. "What about your parents?"

"Hang my parents."

"No. If you want to be serious, let's be serious." He closed his eyes and rolled onto his back, so that only their arms were touching.

"Do you really want to talk about my mother? Here? Right now?"

"Yes. I do. Say we run off together tomorrow. Elope and show up on their doorstep married until death do us part."

"There would be a scene. We'd all survive."

"She would murder me with her bare hands. And then your father would cut you off without a penny for the rest of your life."

"I'd support us. Set up a practice."

"With what money? Do you have any idea what it would cost to set up an office? Not just the rent. You'd need fixtures, and the licensing, and all those bandages and knives and things."

"It would work out! I'm a doctor, not a ditchdigger. I could take out loans. The first few months would be hard, yes, but— "

"You have no idea what hard is like. None. I'm sorry, but you don't, and you wouldn't like it."

He took her hand and squeezed it. "I know I couldn't do it on my own. That's why I need you with me. You'd be my partner. Every doctor needs a good nurse."

"I don't want to be a nurse. I barely held myself together during Jo's labour, and I certainly couldn't do it for a dozen strangers a day. I told you what I wanted, and it's not nursing."

"You mean the little store?"

"Yes. The little store." He could feel her tensing in his arms.

"But you wouldn't have to do any of that if we were married," he reassured her. "I'd take care of you."

"That's sweet of you. I've been waiting ever so long for you to sweep in and rescue me from all my plans."

Theo sighed. Every time he tried to reassure her, it only seemed to drive her further away. This had seemed so simple in his head. Of course they would get married. Of course they would be together. He had never even considered anything else. "I didn't mean it as if you're helpless. I meant that I'll support you. If you want your own store, we'll get you a store. Let me help."

Ilsa was quiet for a long moment. "I want to open a store for myself. By myself." She reached out and touched his arm very gently. The gesture was so close to pity that it curdled his stomach. "I thought you had your own plans," she said softly.

"My plans all involved you," he managed. Of all the confessions he'd made to her, somehow this one felt the rawest. Little gusts of cold air swept under the windowsill, tracing icy patterns against the sweat drying on his skin and amplifying how very naked he suddenly felt.

"Oh. That's ... Theo, I'm flattered. I really am. But I've never seen myself getting married. Not to anyone."

He hoisted himself up onto his elbow. "So all of this. This was ... what for you? A fling?"

"I should get back to Wilson's."

She clearly wasn't interested in giving him an answer, which was, he supposed, answer enough. So he just watched her as she slid out of his bed and starting dressing. She kept stealing quick glances at him, as if waiting for him to speak, but both his brain and his mouth had dried to a husk. Somehow things had once again ended with him wordlessly watching her leave, just like when she'd been dragged from his bed all those years ago.

"Can I see you again before I leave for the holidays?" he finally asked.

"When do you go?" She came back to sit beside him, and that was familiar, too. He felt just as helpless and miserable and inadequate right now as he had when he'd been bedridden and the only thing Ilsa had wanted from him was a checkers game. He took her hand anyway, trying to make the motion seem affectionate and not desperate.

"In a week. Next Monday."

"I don't know. I want to. But with the baby everything's so ..." She waved her hand vaguely. "You'll be back soon though, right?"

"Not until after the new year. It's okay," he said, releasing her hand and drawing the covers up to his chest. "Have a merry Christmas if I don't see you before I go."

"You too, Theo." And she kissed him, an almost chaste goodbye of a kiss, and she was gone.

• • •

When Ilsa got back to Wilson's, the kitchen was empty. She closed the door with a bang, hoping that the noise would alert Jo to her presence and she'd come downstairs. She needed her friend right now.

Had she made a mistake? Not in sleeping with Theo; she was quite pleased about that part, actually. But now he wanted to marry her, and he clearly expected her to trot around behind him playing the role of long-suffering nurse and housewife for the rest of her life. She had not spent the past three years researching and saving to find herself taking orders from anyone. Not even from Theo.

If she'd met him again years from now, when her business was established, she would have considered marriage. Or if Theo were someone different, with a different family, maybe it would work. But marrying each other, right now, could go only one of two ways.

The worst-case scenario had been her first thought. Theo's father would disown him, and even if Theo got a practice up and running, it wouldn't flourish. Not with the weight of a scandal pushing down on it. He just didn't understand how things would be, the two of them alone against the world. He'd always had a safety net. He'd never felt the fear of not knowing if he'd have a place to sleep at the end of the month or how he'd afford to eat if the price of eggs went up. And he couldn't exactly get a job on a fishing boat or in a warehouse, so her shop would have to support them both. She'd seen men made bitter and resentful by far less.

The other picture wasn't as grim, at least not at first. His family might grudgingly acknowledge her, and he'd have access to their resources. Maybe they'd even be able to go to Europe so he could continue his education. He would enjoy his lucrative profession, and maybe she'd even have her "little store." His friends' wives would find her "seamstress hobby" just darling. They'd say how sweet Theo was for indulging her in it. But it would inevitably become a distraction from the duties of being a rich man's wife, a doctor's wife. She would find herself closing the shop early to attend a gala, then opening late to have some professor's wife over for tea. Her customers would drift away, and one morning she would wake up and all she would be was Mrs. Theodore Whitacre, Wife of Dr. Theodore Whitacre.

She needed an outside opinion. When Jo had been falling in love with Owen, she and Ilsa had had so many dawn conversations. But now ... she sighed. Her door banging had only woken the baby, who began crying. No, it wasn't a cry. It was a shriek that would drill its way into your ears no matter where you were in the house. The baby had somehow discovered a unique pitch designed for maximum suffering.

Ilsa would have to keep herself company and keep her own confidences. She trudged up the stairs, remembering how Jo had plopped herself down and refused to budge until Ilsa had told her the whole story about Theo. On the second landing, she stopped outside the Sterlings' bedroom door that, unusually, stood open. Jo was up, walking in circles with baby Sarah. Maybe she would come downstairs after the baby quieted and they would be able to talk. It didn't take long to feel silly standing outside of a married couple's bedroom door. Ilsa climbed the last few stairs to the third floor and her room.

Upstairs, she changed out of her wrinkled dress and hung it in the armoire. The baby's wailing cut through the floorboards. She squeezed her eyes shut in sympathy. But behind her closed eyelids, the images sprang unbidden: how she had moved her hands down Theo's naked body, how warm and quiet it had been with just the two of them snuggled in bed, how easily they still fell into conversation. Why did she have to like him so much? For the first time in a very long time, Ilsa wanted to cry. But she refused to do that. This house had reached its quota of crying for today.

Instead, she retrieved her hatbox from under the bed. She lit a candle and sat down at her small desk.

Dear Mr. Hayley:

Thank you for your prompt response. I am happy meet you on January 8 at noon in the Woodward's cafeteria. Please also arrange for Mr. McPherson to be in attendance, since I would be grateful for his expertise in the matter of commercial real estate.

Sincerely,

I. Pedersen

The act of writing the letter, of taking a next, decisive step towards independence, settled her. She would let matters cool down a bit with Theo, for both their sakes. They could see each other again, to assure him that there were no hurt feelings and no regrets, before he returned home for Christmas next week. Without encouraging him too much, though. Surely she could walk that line.

But then one day turned into two, and Sarah came down with a case of croup, and before Ilsa knew it, the week had flown by. She would have to meet him at the docks, publicly, to say good-bye now. It would be formal and awkward and people might talk, but she couldn't just let him leave without saying goodbye. She got up early to get ahead on her chores and carve out an hour or two, but then an argument flared between some patrons over breakfast, and she had to ask one of them to leave. The others sat in sullen silence, and it took all her focus to cheer everyone up. She hurried through the dishes and raced upstairs to put on her coat and her boots when she smelled smoke.

Something had gone wrong with the stove, and it was belching soot and greasy, black smoke. They had needed a new stove for ages, and with Nils nowhere to be found, she didn't trust anyone enough to fix this one. She shouted the girls and patrons into some kind of order, opened the windows and extinguished the stove with the sand in the fire bucket, but by then, the room was a sooty mess.

She was helping Annie through a coughing fit when she heard the distinctive three hoots of the SS *Minto* pulling away from the docks. She had missed Theo, and now he'd be gone for weeks and weeks. Maybe he'd never even come back at all.

It was probably the smoke that made her need to step outside into the chill before tears started rolling down her face. She took some big gulps of fresh air. No, this was for the best. What would she have said to him anyway? She couldn't give him the only answer he wanted. Maybe he wouldn't even have wanted to speak to her so publicly. Dr. Greyson already knew about their meetings. A dockside chat would only stoke the gossip flames. This was for the best, Ilsa told herself, staring at the dead and dying husks of this year's green beans and tomato plants. It was silly to be sad over something she couldn't change, when she had so much else that needed doing.

Chapter 15

After two months in the quiet of Fraser Springs, the Vancouver streets seemed like a pandemonium of noise and foul odours. Even the fresh dusting of snow did nothing to dampen the assault on Theo's senses. He stared out the carriage window as dogs barked and tram cars clanged and men argued in the streets. Did civilization really smell like dead fish and horse dung?

Finally, the carriage arrived in the porte cochere of the Whitacre mansion. It was one of the few structures not destroyed during the Great Fire, and its venerable brick facade and rows of trimmed hedges stood at odds with the more modern wooden edifices on the street. The stained-glass windows blazed with light, casting bright patterns onto the snow below.

The driver lugged Theo's baggage onto the wide front porch. Bottles of Restorative Vitality Water, which Dr. Greyson had insisted on sending to his mother, weighed down the bags. Why anyone would want to drink sulphuric hot springs water was beyond him. He'd seen the miners and loggers who bathed in the stuff. Who knew where it all drained to. He felt bad for the poor driver and overtipped him scandalously.

Theo took a deep breath and knocked. The butler opened the door immediately—he must have been hovering on the other side of it. "Welcome home, Master Whitacre."

"Good evening," Theo said. Instantly, he was whisked into the unchanging world of the Whitacres. Someone took his coat and spirited his bags off to parts unknown. He was escorted to his favourite easy chair in the living room, and a maid arrived with a steaming cup of drinking chocolate and a plate of bland digestive biscuits. The fire was already crackling at just the right temperature. He should have relaxed into the luxury, but it felt strangely foreign to him now: all these people scurrying around, quietly pushing him back into the worn grooves of routine.

It didn't take long for his mother to appear at the top of the staircase. "Theodore, my darling!" She enunciated the words as if she were performing the character of A Very Rich Woman in a stage play. Her corset was just as tight as ever, giving her voice a breathless quality, and her face has been powdered into an unnatural pallor.

"Hello, Mother." He stood to greet her.

"No, no, dear! Do not move an inch! I forbid it! You must be so terribly tired after your journey!" Her dramatic staircase entrance complete, she descended slowly, the train of her crepe evening dress slithering along behind her. He smelled her perfume long before she entered the parlour. Had she always been this theatrical, or had he simply been accustomed to it before?

Theo stood anyway and kissed both of her cheeks. "Good to see you, Mother."

She eyed him, frowning. "You are thin. Too thin. I knew I should have sent a chef up with you. Your father said it would be terribly insulting to the St. Alice Hotel, but really, how good can a backwater establishment be? I am sure you must be famished. Sit! No, I insist, Teddy. Sit and drink your chocolate!"

He sat, and his mother arranged herself on the settee across from him. "Martha! Martha! Fetch me my notebook." She eyed him again. "My darling, you are positively gaunt. I did warn you that doctoring would be too much for your constitution."

"I feel quite well, Mother," he said. "The hot springs are very restorative. Speaking of which, Dr. Greyson sent a gift along for you. A case of some special elixir he's been brewing at the St. Alice.

He says while you certainly don't need a fountain of youth, this is the next best thing."

"Oh that dear man! He really is too good to us." She raised her voice and snapped, "Martha! The notebook!" without bothering to turn her head. She sighed. "Since your departure, we had to replace Eloise, and the new one is not at all bright."

Martha, who was standing beside his mother with the notebook, did not react to this slight. His mother took the notebook and opened it. "Now, dear, I hate to trouble you after your long trip, but we have a busy social calendar. Martha, tell Max that Theodore's eveningwear will have to be sent out to the tailor. Really, you are so thin. Although your shoulders seem bigger. Like a deckhand." She wrinkled her nose. "Well, there is nothing at all that a little tailoring cannot fix."

She opened the book. Theo sipped his chocolate to suppress a sigh. At least talking about social plans was better than talking about the "lascivious behaviour" she'd referenced in her letter.

"Now," said his mother, "in advance of our Christmas dinner, you are to send Emily Morrison a nosegay. If you have any preferences, the florist needs to be informed by noon tomorrow. I have been told that she will wear green, so I think a lovely spray of winterberries, with perhaps something thrown in for fragrance, would suffice. Would you rather gardenias or white roses?"

"I don't know the first thing about flowers, Mother."

She gave a sharp huff. "I know you do not mean to upset me, dear, but men are positively lining up around the block for a chance to send Emily Morrison a nosegay. I suppose I can have the florist select for you, but what would you like to write on the note? I have worked so very hard to secure this match for you. And, really, there should be no objections this time."

Theo set down his cup. "Because?"

His mother's face went quite still under the layers of powder. "Because? Because you are a Whitacre, and any decent young woman would jump at the opportunity to make an alliance with this family," she said quickly. "Anyhow, the Morrisons are very good stock. He owns a shipping company, and dear Emily plays the flute beautifully. I shall just write it for you. 'Miss Emily, I do look forward to sharing the pleasure of your company during this festive season.' Is 'Ever yours,' too forward? No, of course not. She'll appreciate the display of sentiment."

His mother, for all her theatrics, was a terrible liar. "Mother."

"Yes, darling?"

"Has dear Emily landed herself in a spot of trouble that she needs to marry her way out of?"

"Theodore!" His mother's outrage had no heat to it. "How dare you speculate about such a nice young woman? What has gotten into you? Really, I think that horrid little village is turning you coarse. I begin to wonder if it is a good idea for you to even return."

So that was what this was all about: Theo leaving again for Fraser Springs. "If I'm to marry Emily Morrison, I should at least know the circumstances surrounding our courtship."

The elaborate dresses and makeup, the preening voice: his mother reminded him a little of Mrs. McSheen. Yes, she was wealthier and had better manners (and better hats), but they both had the same forced gaiety tinged with sadness and a little mania. His mother had always loomed so large in his life, but today he could see the effort that went into her persona. The hours she'd spent applying makeup just to greet her own son, the way that makeup settled into the wrinkles on her face and highlighted them instead of masking them, the corsets she reduced her way into, the exaggerated propriety that always seemed to be filling the void of his father's absence. She'd worn a formal gown to welcome her only child back home. For the first time, he felt almost sorry for her. But not sorry enough to marry dear Emily Morrison.

His mother sighed. "If you must know, yes. There was a small … fuss." Her bright voice returned. "But it's all for the best. Perfect, really, the way it will work out. A wife and a child, ready-made. That way, you do not have to bother with—" She made a vague gesture. "You know how you are. And no one could hope to marry into a better family than the Morrisons. Even if the circumstances are a trifle irregular."

Theo just stared at her. "My medical training is barely finished. I'm hardly in the position to take a wife, let alone a wife and child."

His mother waved that away too. "Your father and I have been very patient in that regard. We allowed you to go to medical school, and we even paid for it, plus we permitted you to muck about with Dr. Greyson. But you simply were not raised to work, my love. Look what it's done to you. Emily will handle all your social obligations beautifully, and you can always find a nice hospital board to chair. You can still keep up with the doctoring world with no effort at all that way." She dismissed the doctoring world as if it were simply another genteel hobby, like art collecting or horse breeding.

No one was ever going to expect anything of him but to occasionally serve as a living, breathing coat hanger for a well-tailored evening suit. He wouldn't even have to go to the effort of siring his own children, for Chrissakes. Let another man do that for him. Why not, when everything else around here was done by someone else?

"I can't commit to anything until after my term in Fraser Springs is complete."

At those words, his mother's eyes turned flinty, like a bird of prey spotting a potential meal. Theo had feared that look his entire life, because it usually meant something unpleasant was about to happen to him. "You will not be returning to Fraser Springs. Dr. Greyson and I have discussed it at length."

He wasn't playing that game anymore. He stood. She stood. For a moment, it seemed as if she might block the door. "It's been a long day of travel. I'm in no mood to argue with you right now. If you'll excuse me, I'll retire for the evening." The use of contractions alone would earn him a day of silent, disapproving fury. He didn't give her a chance to respond. "Good night, Mother."

Once upstairs, he stretched out on his childhood bed. His pajamas and toiletries had been already laid out for him, a glass of water waited on the bedside table, and a ceramic hot water jug was already wrapped in flannels under the covers. It was all delightfully comfortable, and he wanted nothing to do with any of it. It was going to be a very, very long two weeks.

• • •

Last year, Wilson's Bathhouse had treated staff to a Christmas feast, with roast pork and mulled cider and dancing. This year, instead of decking the halls with boughs of holly, the common room was draped with laundered diapers. In fact, Ilsa had forgotten that Christmas was approaching so quickly until a client had asked if Wilson's would be closing for the holidays.

Upstairs, infant wailing wrecked the quiet. Again. The poor thing had colic now, and she would scream herself purple. No amount of feeding, cuddling, or rocking would soothe her. Changeling, Ilsa muttered to herself, feeling unkind. To make matters worse, a snowstorm had rolled over Fraser Springs the day after Theo had left, and there had been flurries almost every day since. Nils was still nowhere to be found, so the tasks of shovelling and melting ice to get water had fallen to Ilsa as often as it had to Owen. Many of the girls had left days ago to be with their families.

The baby's screams grew louder. Ilsa trudged upstairs. In the bedroom, Jo was rocking baby Sarah. Both were crying.

"Aww," Ilsa said, taking the baby from Jo. "It's okay. You can take a break."

Before the baby, Ilsa had never seen Jo cry. Now, it was a daily occurrence.

"I just don't know what she wants," Jo sobbed. "She's not hungry. She doesn't need to be changed."

"That's because she doesn't know what she wants. It's hard being born, isn't it, Sarah?" The baby wailed. "Yes, I know. So hard. It's not easy being a baby." She reached over with her free hand and rubbed Jo's back. "You should take a nap. Sarah is going to make herself useful and help me with the dinner. And the laundry. It's Christmas tomorrow, so we might as well have something a little nice."

This made Jo cry even harder. "Oh God, it's Christmas Eve? We don't even have a tree. I didn't get the staff presents."

"No one around here needs presents. I've already asked Owen to work out the Christmas bonuses for everyone. We'll have a nice, relaxing day off tomorrow."

Jo sniffed. "Sarah doesn't even have a stocking."

Ilsa wanted to say that Sarah couldn't even focus on objects a few inches away from her face and certainly wouldn't care if she had a stocking. Instead she said, "We'll do something nice for Sarah's first Christmas. I promise."

Jo tried her best to smile. "I'm sorry. You shouldn't have to do all of this for me."

It was hard to hear her over the baby's wail. "Oh, it's all temporary. Pretty soon I'll be teaching Sarah how to fetch firewood and shell peas. Short-term pain for long-term free labour."

Jo finally managed a real, if weak, smile at that. "Well, you girls go have fun."

Perhaps it was the rhythm of folding towels or simply being swaddled with muslin to Ilsa's body, but Sarah finally fell asleep. Not wanting to disturb her, Ilsa continued with her inside chores. At least the snow had reduced the client load. Before long, the house had been swept, the pork was marinating, a stew was simmering for supper, the salve supply was replenished, the tables were wiped down, and she was thoroughly out of chores. Not wanting to risk putting down the baby and waking her up, Ilsa simply sat at the kitchen table and stared out at the falling snow.

Maybe the snow had delayed a letter from Theo. Mail didn't always get through when the weather got rough. She sighed, and the baby grunted in her sleep. She needed to stop fooling herself. Did she expect Theo to be her pen pal after she'd refused his proposal? Did she think they were just going back to being friends, dancing and taking long walks? Men were so fragile. At the slightest hint of rejection, they disappeared. Or worse.

Theo hadn't thought it through. He'd probably blurted out a proposal because that's what he thought a gentleman was required to do, not because he sincerely wanted to be her husband for the rest of their lives. The past few weeks had certainly not made the prospect of marriage and children seem any more appealing. In fact, right at this moment, domestic life looked like a particularly devious kind of torture. Even Jo, the strongest person Ilsa knew, had become a crying wreck.

If she'd said yes to Theo, if they'd skipped down to the justice of the peace and signed their papers two weeks ago, his parents would have disowned him by now, and then what? He'd be trying to set up a doctor's practice in a gossiping, judgmental little town like this one? Or in a big city, where you barely even saw your neighbours and nobody cared if you lived or died? With a baby like this one and an endless stream of dirty diapers and wailing screams she couldn't walk away from?

Maybe she just wasn't built for domesticity. Either way, it didn't matter. She had told him no, and that was that.

• • •

A week into his stay in Vancouver, Theo felt as if he had become a mannequin in a department store window. His mother kept prattling on about "when you are married to dear Emily" or "after dear Emily's baby arrives," and when he would correct her to say that he was not marrying dear Emily, she would ignore him. Day after day, visitors paraded through the front parlour, bringing gifts of fruit, nuts, wreaths, and poinsettias, all of which his mother would fawn over and then distribute to the staff. Tradesmen came to erect the Christmas tree and to assemble an elaborate structure of wreaths that hung like a chandelier above the dining room table. Soon, the house was stuffed with paper chains and candles, and the gigantic pine tree in the parlour bowed under the weight of so many glass baubles and gilded walnuts and strings of cranberries.

He had yet to see Father. He'd knocked at the door to his bedroom four times, and each time had been informed by a pinch-faced nurse that Mr. Whitacre was resting and was not to be disturbed under any circumstances.

Theo drifted. He went shopping for Christmas gifts, but the sight of his pale, bespectacled face laid over the bright storefront displays only depressed him. He bought presents for his parents that they would neither need or want, knowing that a failure to produce gifts for them on Christmas morning would lead to a bout of maternal sullenness that would last well into the new year. That task dutifully accomplished, he somehow wound up loitering in front of a jewellery store window.

The Whitacres had a personal jeweller who sometimes came to the house to deliver the set of rubies the firm kept secured for his mother. And, of course, to discreetly suggest future purchases in anticipation of a certain happy event. Theo humoured the charade but had never actually taken an interest in the baubles on offer. This year, though, he noticed a simple ring engraved with flowers and inlaid with little seed pearls. Ilsa would love a ring like that. She would find the gift extravagant, he knew. And besides, she didn't want to marry him. But if she did— perhaps she would prefer a sapphire, to match her eyes. She wouldn't want anything gaudy, just a small stone that glinted when held to the light. He sat for a half hour mentally designing a ring for a woman who did not want to be his wife, while his mother was probably putting some diamond monstrosity on reserve for Miss Emily Morrison.

Like the rest of the Christmas preparations, the plans for him to propose to Emily seemed to continue on without him. He tried to get his mother to listen, to convince her that this simply was not going to come off, but no one seemed to pay him any mind. His opinion was not required or requested.

He was reading a medical journal when his mother came into the room.

"Theodore, Mrs. DeCoupe was just by, and she has offered to let you and Emily take your friends to their summer cottage this summer! So generous of her," she cooed.

"I'm not marrying Emily," he said for the hundredth time that week. He didn't even look up from his journal.

His mother gave no sign of hearing him. "Perhaps you can invite the Browns and the Millikens. Edwina Milliken was married last summer, and they are such a lovely young couple."

"I'm not marrying Emily," he reiterated, his words dissolving into the air like smoke.

"I'm going to write to Emily and tell her. I know that when I was expecting, I did so like to have something to look forward to."

He set down the journal. "I need you to promise me that you aren't going to keep on with these plans. I have no intention of marrying that woman."

His mother gave a light sigh. "Oh, and Theo, would you be a dear and write to Dr. Greyson to request more bottles of his Restorative Vitality Water? I promised some to Mrs. DeMonte."

That was the only other topic of conversation that mattered in this household: Dr. Greyson's miraculous spring water. Wasn't it simply delicious? (Theo doubted that). Didn't it seem to be taking years off her face? (He very much doubted that). She was going to make Dr. Greyson rich, the way she was ordering it for her friends.

Did he need to shake her? Scream at her? It was Christmas Eve, so if he murdered her, the police probably wouldn't arrive until Boxing Day. He could be long gone by then.

As she was about to leave the room, his mother placed a rectangular piece of metal on the little side table by his chair. He picked it up: it was a silver cigar lighter, which had *To My Dearest* engraved on it.

Theo didn't smoke.

"I already wrote to Emily on your behalf thanking her for the thoughtful gift and telling her that the spark of youth in her eyes would put any lighter to shame. You should make a point to bring it out during dinner."

He wanted to use it to light the house on fire. At least that might get him out of this godforsaken Christmas dinner.

He was toying with the lighter, flicking it on and off, when the butler appeared with a stack of mail addressed to him and a letter opener. The first five envelopes contained Christmas letters: boasts disguised as holiday traditions. Theo skimmed over who had gotten married or promoted, who was getting his next degree, who had received an award for tending to the poor, sick, and dying. The last letter, however, was battered around the edges and bore a stamp he didn't recognize. He opened it.

Dear Dr. Whitacre,

I hope that you are having a festive holiday season and that this letter finds you well. I was supremely disappointed that you were not able to accept a position with us. As I told you previously, your insights into transmission vectors were the most promising of any of our applicants, and you have, of course, the additional gift of being familiar with the French language.

If you have not yet taken up another offer, I would still very much like to have you work with us here. This past summer has been a brutal one for cholera and typhoid, which has caused the government to take renewed interest in our research. We have received a very generous funding increase, and are now able to sponsor an additional fellowship. I am pleased to offer it to you. You will, of course, receive a monthly stipend for your living expenses. You need only to pay your ticket here.

Please inform me immediately of your decision, so that we may extend the offer to another physician if necessary. I do very much hope to hear an affirmative response.

Yours,

Dr. J. P. DuBois

Ilsa had once told him that going to Paris would be simpler for him than for other people, and, looking around the room, he realized that she was correct. Pawning Emily Morrison's lighter would probably pay his fare all on its own.

What was stopping him? Family honour? Family money? What good did either of those do if the string attached to them was marrying Emily Morrison?

And there was Ilsa. But he couldn't very well sulk around Fraser Springs, hoping she would change her mind. She had turned him down. She hadn't even spoken to him after that night. Besides, soon she'd been off in Vancouver with her store. Fraser Springs held nothing for either of them.

Before he lost his nerve, he wrote out a response. He would go to Paris. Well, first he would have to get through this miserable Christmas. And he would have to go back to Fraser Springs to retrieve his equipment and the rest of his belongings. But then it was off to Paris. He was going, and he didn't care if he had to smuggle himself out of this mausoleum in a rug to do so.

• • •

The parcel arrived for Ilsa on Christmas Eve, half hidden among all the other Christmas presents and cards. The girls were off with their families, and Jo and Owen's sleep deprivation meant they wouldn't have noticed if Jolly Old Saint Nick himself appeared in their parlour.

Her ticket on the SS *Minto* was booked. She had arranged a reservation at a modest traveller's inn, one that was supposedly safe. And now, the final piece had arrived: a Christmas gift to herself.

Ilsa hustled up to her room and closed the door behind her. She carefully untied the twine and peeled away the crisp, brown paper. The garment box smelled of lavender even before she opened it. Ilsa took a breath, then undid the ribbon that held the box closed. There, nestled among tissue paper, was the first brand-new dress she had ever owned. She'd made her own dresses and she'd altered hand-me-downs, but this dress had been created for her and no one else. It was pale green with darker green piping along the bodice and cuffs. Brass buttons marched in shining rows down the sleeves.

She lifted it up to admire the perfect stitching. She buried her face in the skirt: the supple fabric smelled of lavender and laundry starch.

She had dozens of chores to do, but she took her time trying it on. She re-twisted her hair into a tidy chignon, then turned at last to the mirror. The falling snow outside filled the room with a diffused, gauzy light, and she hardly recognized the woman who stood in front of her. She looked savvier, richer. Her posture was straighter. Even her figure—which she had been told over and over was immodest by its very nature—seemed elegant. She stood before the mirror refined and poised and utterly like someone who could handle herself in the world. She felt as if she had bought a new skin, not just a new dress.

This was why she wanted to open her shop: to give other women this feeling. She twirled a little, and then she gave the mirror her most severe expression. She was ready. The only thing left was to tell Jo.

After Christmas. She hung the dress beside her work costumes. They would all have a Christmas worth remembering, and then she would worry about goodbyes.

• • •

On Christmas Day, even his father was forced to the table to share in the expensive, high-stakes merriment. The old man had the posture of a baby who could not support its own neck; he sat hunched in a wicker wheelchair, shrouded in blankets and glaring at everyone. His brain was addled by dementia—and maybe a touch of syphilis—so he would repeatedly nod off and then wake with some inappropriate story.

Theo was dressed in white tie and tails, newly tailored. At precisely a quarter to six, the fabled Emily Morrison and her family arrived. Emily turned out to be a thin woman with brown hair, elaborately curled and piled atop her head in the latest fashion. It must have taken some poor hairdresser hours to accomplish. She wore the promised green dress and prominently displayed on her wrist a monstrous corsage, which was presumably the nosegay that had required so much of his personal attention.

She greeted Theo with a smile that did not extend to her eyes: a sign she wanted to marry him even less than he wanted to marry her. Too bad for dear Emily. He doubted that she had any more say in the matter than he did.

"It's a pleasure to meet you, Miss Morrison," Theo said, bowing stiffly.

Emily's eyes never left his cane. "Yes. A pleasure," she responded.

Their mothers fussed around them, making too-loud comments about the decor, the food, what a very merry Christmas they were all having, how very handsome the two young people looked together. They reminded Theo of a pair of seagulls squabbling over scraps on a beach. For half an hour, he sat beside Emily in the parlour in silence while the rest of the guests arrived and their mothers prattled on about what a perfect couple they made.

At the supper table, Emily was once again seated beside him. Theo sat across the table from mother, who shot him sharp looks.

"So. Emily. I hear you play the flute," he tried.

She nodded. "I do enjoy it." She had a thin, reedy voice. She didn't look at him.

"I would enjoy a chance to hear you play."

She smiled coolly. "I'm sure it can be arranged." Of course it could. Everything about their lives could be arranged.

The dinner lapsed into silence as Emily picked at her jellied eel.

Emily's father cleared his throat and tried to chivy the conversation along. "It must have been terribly lonely for you up North, with no civilized company."

Oh, to hell with it. No one was going to listen to what he said anyway. No one cared a whit about what Theo Whitacre wanted to do with his life. If he didn't want to go through with this farce of an engagement, he would have to set off a few fireworks.

"It was, at first," he said. "But as luck would have it, one of our former housemaids had moved to Fraser Springs, which was a very pleasant surprise." He made eye contact with his mother as he said it.

"You didn't tell me that," she said, an edge of steel undercutting her cheerful voice.

"Oh, yes," he said, still staring at his mother. "You remember Ilsa Pedersen. Blond girl, Swedish. Used to play checkers with me when I was bedridden."

His mother reddened under her makeup. "We had so many maids over the years, darling. You can't expect me to remember every one."

"I'm surprised you allowed him to fraternize with the help," sniffed Mr. Morrison.

"We certainly realized the folly of our inattentiveness." In lieu of the traditional serving bell, his mother had acquired jingle bells to give summoning the servants a festive touch. Martha arrived silently with the first plates of the next course.

His father, who had nodded off into his third tumbler of scotch, perked up. "Wait! That was that little tart you dragged out of his bedroom! The one with the nice tits."

"Harold!" his mother hissed.

Theo kept the same bland expression he would have worn had his father remarked on the unseasonably rainy weather. "That's the one, Father. It's a funny story, really. You see, we were both sixteen at the time, and— "

His mother stood abruptly. "No one wants to hear that story, Theodore." She swayed a little. Had she had too much to drink? That wasn't like his mother. Perhaps she had picked up bad habits to fill her time during his absence.

She opened her mouth to speak, but no sound came out. Her eyes focused somewhere in the middle distance, above their heads, and then she dashed headlong out of the room. The sound of vomiting followed immediately after. The dinner guests glanced uneasily at one another.

"I'll, uh, go check on her," Theo said. "Please help yourselves to the"—he glanced down at the plate Martha had just set in front of him—"the something suspended in aspic."

His mother had retreated upstairs to her bedroom. The servants looked extremely reluctant to follow. "Can someone go help her into bed?" Theo asked the hallway at large. Martha and another servant, whose name he'd never learned because his mother had never shouted it, sighed and disappeared upstairs. No one wanted to deal with his mother at the best of times, but most would rather fight a bear than tend to her when she was ill.

After taking a moment to steel himself, Theo climbed the stairs and tapped at his mother's door. Even from the other side, a horrible odour assaulted him. A familiar horrible odour, that he'd last encountered at …

He rushed into the kitchen and barged his way towards the cold storage. Only five bottles of Dr. Greyson's elixir remained out of an original forty. But he'd been home for a fortnight, and the incubation period of cholera was usually two or three days. Five at the most. Besides, he'd tested one of the bottles and it had been clean—practically sterile, in fact. So what was he missing?

He had the chef make the oral rehydration draught, then went upstairs to check on his mother. When he entered the bedroom, he was greeted once again by the same foul smell he'd grown so used to at the St. Alice Hotel.

"I'm sorry you've taken ill, Mother."

"You're not sorry," she moaned from under her duvet. "You probably poisoned me to avoid having to marry Emily. And after I worked so hard to give you a happy Christmas."

He ignored the accusation of attempted murder and felt his mother's forehead. "You don't have a fever. But dehydration will already be setting in and—"

"You're so ungrateful," his mother continued and then sat up suddenly to retch into the pail the servants had left next to her nightstand. "It's bad enough having a son who's an invalid and can't even give me a grandchild, but an ungrateful invalid? Sharper than a serpent's teeth are thankless children!" she misquoted dramatically. And then promptly vomited again into the pail that her ungrateful, serpent-toothed child held out for her.

Heaven alone knew what was happening downstairs in the dining room. Between his own admissions and his father's colourful details, he should be well and truly implicated in a shocking sex scandal by now. Or perhaps he would somehow manage to be both impotent and a sex fiend. And a poisoner to boot. He'd certainly picked up a lot of interesting habits in Fraser Springs.

"You need to rest," he told his groaning mother. "I'm having the kitchen bring you up a restorative I've been using very successfully to rehydrate patients. You should drink as much of it as possible."

His mother glared at him. She was so pale that the complexion powder looked orange. Her eye makeup smudged down her cheeks in sooty trails. "My only child, a poisoner. Poisoned his very own mother. You wanted a chance to play doctor in front of all my friends, was that it?"

Theo had mastered pushing down his anger, saying "Yes, Mother," speaking in a calm and respectful tone of voice. Not today. "I am a doctor, Mother," he said. "And even rich people get the flu. You're not special." He walked towards the door. "Besides, if I were going to poison you, I would use arsenic. It hurts more."

Downstairs, his father snored alone at the table. The Morrisons and the rest of the guests were nowhere to be found, leaving behind their untouched plates of braised ox hearts in aspic. Thank God for small blessings. Suddenly, Theo was famished. Martha appeared to clear the plates.

"Could you bring out the rest of my courses all at once? Since the chef has gone to so much trouble. The staff can tuck in to whatever's left in the kitchen."

"Is it fit to eat?" Martha asked.

"Yes. I'm fairly certain my mother got sick from too much of that Restorative Vitality Water."

"We'll throw it all out, then. Nasty smelling stuff."

"No, I'd like to test the bottles later. But please, enjoy the meal. You all deserve it. Oh, and Father's asleep, so perhaps you can send someone out to pop him back into bed."

And so, for two hours, Theo sat in silent solitude at a grand table that blazed with wreaths and candles. Salmon in a delicate pastry. Roast quail. Lamb and goose. Coffee and almond blancmange for dessert. All washed down with excellent wine and champagne. He could hear the sound from the kitchen of the servants laughing and chattering, and the occasional pop of a champagne cork. Well, at least someone was having a good time.

Outside, snow splattered against the window. Was it snowing in Fraser Springs? How was Ilsa celebrating? He imagined her in a setting like the dance: laughing and golden, surrounded by friends and admirers. Enjoying honest, hearty food and passing around cups of rum punch. She would be wearing that lovely green dress, with her hair up in a crown of braids. Maybe there would be dancing. Maybe there would be mistletoe.

Well, at least the dinner party was over. And the marriage to Emily Morrison was almost certainly off. He'd count those as Christmas miracles. He toasted himself in the mirror, finished his wine, and headed up to bed.

• • •

Christmas had been subdued this year, but Ilsa was glad to share it with Owen, Jo, Doc Stryker, and the handful of girls who had not gone home to their families. Still, a pall hung over the festivities. The Sterlings were drawn and exhausted, worn-out ghosts of their usual affectionate selves. Nils was still nowhere to be found. Although he often vanished for weeks at a time, he'd never missed a Christmas before. His absence made Owen—who was the closest thing Nils had to a best friend—especially jittery.

Ilsa had tried her best to bring a little merriment to the evening. That had to count for something. She'd embroidered Sarah's name on a tiny stocking and stuffed it with a small lace cap she had sewn out of some scraps. She'd decorated the table with pine boughs and candles, and Doc Stryker brought his accordion and played a few Christmas carols. She'd even rustled up enough eggs to make eggnog. Still, no one was in a very celebratory mood, and the party broke up early.

After she'd cleared the dishes, Ilsa went up to Jo's office. Owen had made a hash of the staff bonuses, and now it fell on Ilsa to untangle it. To her surprise, he was already sitting behind Jo's desk with a haphazard assortment of papers spread out in front of him.

"Just the lady I wanted to see," he said. "Her accounting system's got me baffled again."

"It's simple once you learn the general idea." Ilsa walked over to stand at his shoulder and ran her finger down the long rows of numbers in the ledger book. "See? There's the account for daily operations, then staff payroll, then the repairs fund, and then savings. You took the money out of payroll, but it should have come from the savings because it's a bonus."

"And that's why nothing's adding up now." Owen's publisher in Vancouver handled most of his royalties and Jo took care of their shared finances. "Am I right in thinking that we can move money back over from the savings to even it out?" Ilsa nodded. "So I rob Peter to pay Paul and then pray that things stop breaking for a while." He paused. "Actually, maybe there's more money in payroll than I think, since we haven't had to pay Nils." At his friend's name, he turned to look out of the office's window, as if expecting to see the big Dane trudging down the boardwalk.

"He'll be back soon," Ilsa said. "And I'm sure your math works out."

"I hope so." He rubbed his forehead. "Does that all make sense to you, with the accounts?"

"It makes perfect sense," Ilsa admitted to her surprise. She had come up here expecting to clean up Owen's mess, but he'd figured out the problem himself and was already putting it to rights.

"And I've made a start on scheduling some of the new clients. Does this look right?" Ilsa examined the schedule at Owen had made. He'd made allowances for seniority and time off, and even for the competitive squabbles that were sure to come up between a few of the girls. It was nearly flawless.

"I'd switch Annie and Elsie on the Thursday morning times, since Elsie doesn't get along with Mrs. Pennington, but other than that, it looks perfect. You're a natural."

He shrugged. "It's about time I started to pull my weight around here, eh?" Ilsa liked Owen, so it was uncomfortable to laugh at his joke when, secretly, she agreed. He was always writing or off somewhere talking politics or conservation, or tromping around the mountains with Nils, while Jo ran herself ragged keeping the bathhouse afloat.

"Well, thank you for stepping up and handling this," she said.

"It's not so much stepping up as sliding over. Sometimes I write the books and Jo takes care of everything. Sometimes my royalties keep us flush and she can take a break. Jo's ... having a rough few weeks, so it's my turn to carry the load. With your help, of course." He flashed the charming grin that had won him both Jo and the last election. "When she's feeling more like herself again, she'll probably tell me I've been doing everything all wrong and to get my nose out of her business."

Jo had always been a perfectionist. Ilsa hadn't really thought about the possibility that Jo might prefer it that Owen stayed well away from her account books. And his writing did pay a lot of the bills.

"You're a good team."

"We are now, I hope. I thought we'd drive each other insane when I first moved here, you know." He smiled, an inward-turning private little smile. "I'd probably make more money if I still lived in Vancouver, and her life would probably be easier if I could repair stoves, but being together is more important than anything else. We made it work."

Down the hall, the baby began crying again. Owen flinched. "Why don't you go walk Sarah for awhile?" Ilsa suggested. "I'll take care of the rest of this."

Owen attempted a smile and hauled himself to the office door. "I don't know what we'd do without you. Truly."

She was beginning to hate those words, as well meaning as they were. Lately, it felt as if she was all that was holding Wilson's Bathhouse together. She wasn't bitter about it: no one had asked her to take on all of these extra tasks. She had simply seen what needed doing and made sure it'd gotten done. If—when—she left, someone else would step up. Owen, perhaps, or one of the other girls. Maybe whoever Jo hired on to replace her.

The revelation should have been liberating, but instead it stung. She might not be as irreplaceable as she thought.

Chapter 16

Theo arrived back in Fraser Springs a week early, unable to stomach the tension in the big West End house any longer. His mother was making a grand show of giving him the silent treatment, and, every time he was within earshot, complaining loudly about his ingratitude to her gaggle of friends in the parlour. Even though she had recovered from her illness quickly and without any complications, she'd taken to sitting in his old wheelchair with a blanket across her lap. Martha pushed her around the house.

"And then he *poisoned* me. My own son! I pay a king's ransom for him to become a doctor, and how does he repay me? Not by healing the sick but by poisoning his own mother! And after I worked so hard to make him happy. You must see what I am working with. He doesn't go to parties. He refuses to take any care with his appearance. Still—*still*—his dear mother finds a perfect wife for him. And even that is not good enough for him. I think the fever addled his brain when he was a child. I really do."

Murmurs of encouragement came from her cronies.

"Oh, but you are such a devoted mother, Olivia. You simply cannot blame yourself."

"Some people are simply beyond help. They're born that way."

Their strategies for dealing with the various scandals of Christmas dinner seemed to have been ripped from the plot of an opera or a stage play. Theo should be committed to a mental institution. He should spend a night in jail to straighten him out, and then he should give an interview to a respectable newspaper declaring that he had been temporarily deranged by passion for dear Emily.

"Perhaps we should carry on with the Morrisons, providing they are still amenable," his mother suggested. "We might announce the engagement in the newspapers. Then we send Theodore off to Europe, but we put out that he's gone missing. Foul play is suspected. Emily gives birth—no one minds a baby born during an engagement—and we give the dear little thing our last name. Emily will have dignity and financial security, we will have a grandson, and Theodore can stay in Europe. Or return in a few years claiming some manner of amnesia. Do people still get amnesia?"

His mother would never believe that her sickness had been Dr. Greyson's fault. Or even that it had been a bout of the stomach flu. If he stuck around any longer, he was liable to end up chloroformed and dragged to the altar. At the first opportunity, he packed his bags and jumped ship while everyone in the household was out at Sunday services. On his way to the steamer docks, he had the cab take him to the jeweller's. It was a whim he chose not to examine too closely. It never hurt to be prepared, after all.

As he disembarked the paddlewheeler in Fraser Springs that evening, Theo realized that he wasn't even sure he still had a job at the St. Alice. His mother might easily have written Dr. Greyson. And who knew what Dr. Greyson might have told Morse. He wanted to see Ilsa again, but he wasn't sure that she'd welcome his abrupt re-appearance after so many weeks of silence. For lack of a better idea, he dragged his baggage through the snow to Doc Stryker's bar.

As he stepped inside, the patrons went silent. Then, to his consternation, they erupted in a cheer. Theo looked around to see what the celebration was about.

"Drink on the house for the fellow who delivered Jo's baby!" exclaimed Doc.

"Hey! Happy New Year, Dr. Chicken Leg!" a few of the old-timers cried.

It was flattering, but he wasn't entirely sure what to do with the attention. He gave a short wave and made a beeline for the bar. Doc smiled and slid a glass of beer in his direction.

He recognized the man waving at him from a crowded corner as Walter from the bathhouse. Theo made his way over and took a hastily vacated seat at a scarred wood table. The beer was strong and surprisingly good. He answered a few questions about his recent whereabouts with vague mentions of distant family, and then he settled back to listen as his tablemates drifted back to their earlier topic of conversation. They seemed to be talking about mining.

"I'm going back to logging," one of the more grizzled-looking men was saying. "I hate to give up working so close to town, but them new chemicals make me dizzy. At least in the woods you get fresh air."

"There's an active mine near here?" Theo asked.

Everyone at the table looked at him like he was daft. The man gestured. "Sure. East of town, right up the hill."

"What are they mining?"

"Cadmium, arsenic, lead, zinc, you name it," another man said. "Doesn't operate full time, though. Once a week, sometimes less. Seems they're still trying to figure out the right process. So we'll get eighteen hours of work one day, then nothing for a fortnight."

This set the men off into a new round of grumbling.

"I don't know what that Morse fellow is playing at. He goes on about how his fancy hotel has the purest, most high-falutin' spring water in the world, and then he goes and pours a bunch of garbage into it. He's a snake, that one."

"Wait. They dump the mine tailings into the springs?" A few of the men nodded.

Theo leaned forwards. "So if you were to drink the hot springs water after they dump the tailings …"

"Wouldn't drink that stink water on a good day. On one of the bad days, you'd be liable to grow a tail. Nobody's dumb enough for that. Just use a little common sense, that's all."

Everything slid into place. Theo had been looking for bacteria, so he hadn't done a chemical assay. And even if he had, it might not have helped. The water bottled on the days when the mine dumped its tailings would be adulterated at higher concentrations than the days when they didn't. So you either had to drink a lot of the water in a short period of time, as his mother had done, or get a bottle from a batch taken right after the tailings had been dumped. That explained why not everyone got sick. It explained why the illnesses happened in clusters. And it certainly explained why only patrons of the St. Alice were falling ill.

With any luck, he could get his gear from the office of the St. Alice and complete the assay without Dr. Greyson or Morse knowing.

Doc Stryker was happy to let him stash his baggage at the bar, and Theo headed out through the snow, picking his way along the dark boardwalk. The snow concealed sheets of ice; one slip and he could crack his skull.

When he finally arrived in the basement of the St. Alice, treatments were wrapping up. Only a few attendants remained, cleaning and replenishing the towels.

"Good evening," he greeted them.

"Good evening, Dr. Whitacre," they said in unison. A few faces betrayed surprise at his early return to the hotel, but they went back to their work immediately.

Theo strode as confidently as he could to the big storage room at the end of the row of the lockers where clients could keep their personal effects during their visit. He shut the door behind him and scanned the ceiling-high shelves of towels, soaps, liniments … There! Along the back wall were at least two dozen crates of Restorative Vitality Water. He retrieved three of the long green bottles, each from a different crate, and slipped out of the storage room and straight up the stairs. His luck held; he crossed the echoing lobby without encountering a soul. Even the ever-present concierge seemed to have temporarily abandoned his post near the foyer.

He shot the bolt on the door of his little office, set the bottles on the narrow workbench that served as his desk, and opened the mahogany case that contained his microscope. He worked quickly and methodically to lay out the rest of the equipment he'd need, trying not to clink glass together or set anything down too heavily. There wasn't any good reason for anyone to be hanging around this part of the hotel at this hour, but he didn't want to chance possible interruptions and awkward explanations.

Theo set up his Bunsen burner and lit it under the first flask of the decanted water. While it heated, he unpacked a ceramic mortar that was still in its original excelsior-packed shipping box. That would do nicely. When the water reached boiling, he added a small lozenge of zinc to the flask, then held the cold bowl up to the mouth of the flask to catch the smoke. It turned a silvery-black colour. Arsenic. He had his proof.

On his way to Mr. Morse's suite, Theo was drawn up short by the foul odour that was now so familiar. He stopped and looked down the hallway just as a door opened and Dr. Greyson came out. The man looked as if he'd aged ten years since Theo had left. He stopped to blot the sweat from his forehead and sighed. Another outbreak must be keeping him busy. It didn't seem possible, but perhaps Dr. Greyson's Christmas had been as bad as his own.

He was halfway to the stairs before he noticed Theo. "A belated merry Christmas, dear boy," he said in an exhausted imitation of joviality. "And congratulations on your engagement!"

Theo gave him a thin smile. "Happy New Year, sir. And I'm afraid I'm not engaged."

"Then I must have misread your mother's letter. We didn't expect to see you back so soon."

"When I discovered the source of the outbreak, I thought it best to return immediately."

A flush of irritability overlaid Greyson's exhaustion. "Well, well. The boy wonder thinks he's cracked the case. If you came all the way up here to rant about cholera again, you've wasted a trip."

"Is Mr. Morse in? He might be interested in my findings, at least."

"You are not to bother Mr. Morse. He has enough to do without your pestering him." But Theo was already on his way up the stairs. Dr. Greyson followed behind, spluttering objections. When Theo paused to knock on Morse's door, Greyson grabbed the handle and pushed his way in.

As the two squabbling doctors burst into the room, two men jerked their bent heads up from a map spread out on a table: Mr. Morse and Owen Sterling.

"Excuse me, gentlemen," Morse said sharply. "This is a private meeting."

Greyson tried to compose himself by smoothing his vest over his stomach. "My apologies for the abrupt entrance. Teddy here was intent on barging in with more of his laboratory nonsense."

Sterling straightened and held out his hand to Theo, who shook it. "I'm happy to listen to whatever nonsense Dr. Whitacre wants to tell us." Theo glanced over for confirmation to Morse, who nodded.

"I've identified the source of the outbreak. We need to act immediately."

Morse sighed. "Not this cholera nonsense again."

Sterling looked startled but waited for Theo to go on.

"It's not cholera. But it's something just as dangerous." Morse tried to object, but Theo ploughed on. "And I can prove it. I performed a Marsh test just now on a sample of your Restorative Vitality Water. You see that silver-black substance in the cup?" He handed the little ceramic bowl to Morse, who glanced down and handed it off to Sterling. "That's a positive test for arsenic."

"Poppycock!" Greyson said. "We boil that water."

"Boiling doesn't get rid of heavy metals. Mr. Morse, do you know what's in the tailings from your mine?"

Theo watched Morse's face as he put the pieces together. "Damn it," he muttered. He slammed a hand on his desk, causing the papers and ink bottles on it to jump. "Damn it, damn it, damn it."

Theo turned to Sterling. "Those tailings get into the hot springs. Water bottled on the days that the tailings are dumped will contain arsenic, lead, mercury, cadmium—"

"Enough," Morse said. "You've made your point."

"We are profoundly lucky that no one died."

"I drink that water myself!" Greyson seemed to have regained his powers of speech. "It's perfectly safe."

"You told me you'd tested it," Morse said in a voice that sent a little chill down Theo's back. It was the same alarmingly calm delivery that his mother sometimes used before she lost her temper spectacularly.

Morse and Greyson began talking over one another. Sterling held his hands up for silence.

"Everybody wait a damn minute! You were selling the hot springs water for drinking? That stuff tastes like turpentine even before you start putting arsenic in it."

"It's medicinal," Greyson insisted. "No one expects medicine to taste pleasant."

"We need to immediately recall all the water," Theo said. "We need to tell people that— "

Mr. Morse, having regained his composure, cut him short with a wave of his hand. "Yes. Right. Very good, Dr. Whitacre. We'll remove the water quietly. The influenza epidemic will remain an influenza epidemic, and the water will be bottled from a different source."

"But that's not good enough," Theo said. "Some guests probably took bottles home with them. They need to be warned!"

Sterling and Morse exchanged meaningful glances. "What?" asked Theo.

"Sit down," Sterling said. He looked to Morse. "Why don't you tell him?"

Morse got up and went to the sideboard, where he poured four drinks. He passed them to each man without a word, and Theo took a polite sip of the burning liquid. Finally, Morse sat down in the remaining chair and stared contemplatively into his glass. "The St. Alice hasn't been able to cover its expenses this past year. It barely broke even the year before that. I had hoped the revenue from the new mine would provide something of a buffer for the finances. But it's been nothing but a money pit. And add in a slow season and this 'flu' business?" He took a long swallow and closed his eyes for a moment. "Mr. Sterling and I were trying to come to an agreement that would save the St. Alice, and with it, your jobs."

No one in the room spoke. All of this pretentious opulence was nothing but a web of illusions and debt.

"It's a difficult situation," Sterling said quietly. "With the timber and the mines petering out, tourist dollars are the real lifeblood of Fraser Springs. And with the St. Alice on the edge already, any damage to its reputation could tip the whole town under."

"But you've been poisoning people!" Theo exclaimed. "You can't just sweep it all under a rug."

"We will remove the water that's already been bottled," Morse repeated. "Perhaps we could replace it with that rehydration mixture Dr. Whitacre's been prescribing."

"That's just sugar, water and salt. You can't make money off that." Theo's hands were shaking. He had just revealed that the hotel had been poisoning its own guests, and the result was … a shrug? A new marketing strategy? They were more interested in the reputation of the St. Alice than the well-being of dozens, if not hundreds, of guests who had been exposed to toxins and heavy metals.

Greyson slumped in his chair. He stared down into his glass and said nothing.

"I took an oath to do no harm, and part of that oath is being honest with my patients," Theo said.

Sterling considered this. "You're a very good doctor. You may well have saved the lives of my wife and my daughter. But, with all due respect, you have the privilege of doing the right thing no matter the cost and then walking away. The rest of us can't do that. If the St. Alice closes, you'll be no worse for wear. But the rest of us have to think of the town and the people who rely on it."

So that was the way it would be. Theo was just a spoiled little moralizer who couldn't possibly understand the priorities of serious business. Well, if covering up a mass poisoning was what real businessmen did, he wanted no part of it. He stood.

"I'd like to tender my resignation, then." He set the ceramic bowl purposefully on Morse's desk. "If you need me, I'll be with the guest puking his guts up in room 219."

He left without waiting for a response, feeling braver and more terrified than he'd ever felt in his life.

Chapter 17

Everyone else had gone to bed hours ago, but sleep eluded Ilsa. Now was a good a time as any to un-deck the halls. Usually the tree remained up well into January, but she didn't imagine that anyone wanted to be reminded of this year's pathetic Christmas. Her conversation with Owen nagged at her. Jo and Owen had such different backgrounds and ambitions, but they had worked it out. Then again, the Sterlings didn't have to contend with the likes of Theo's mother.

She carefully unwound the garlands and put them back in their box for next Christmas. She probably wouldn't be around when these garlands were taken out again. The thought made her a little sad, and a little excited.

She heard footsteps on the stairs; maybe Annie was sneaking out to see that logger she'd been stepping out with lately. Ilsa turned to tweak her nose about it, but it was Jo on the landing.

"Hey. Is everything okay?"

"Do you hear that?" Jo asked.

Ilsa listened. She didn't hear anything. "No?"

"Silence." Jo grinned. "Sarah is usually wailing by this point, so I woke up. Then I noticed Owen still wasn't back from his meeting, and I heard someone rustling around down here. I figured it probably wasn't a burglar."

"Because there's nothing here worth stealing. Unless he's after my secret stash of chocolate."

Jo gasped in mock horror. "Ilsa Pedersen, have you been holding out on me?"

"Follow me, and don't you dare tell another soul."

A few minutes later, they both were in the kitchen sipping hot chocolate in contented, companionable silence.

"So what are you doing up?" Jo finally asked.

"Couldn't sleep."

"And you couldn't sleep because?"

Ilsa shrugged. "Maybe it's too quiet in here. This is the longest Sarah has slept since she was born."

"I might be lost in Babyland, but that doesn't distract me from everything. Something's been going on with you lately."

"I just have a lot on my mind, that's all."

"Such as?"

"You're like a hound on a trail, aren't you?"

"Nothing gets between a meddler and her meddling." She touched Ilsa's shoulder. "I know I've been distracted. But you can tell me if something's wrong. I'm sorry I haven't been around much to talk about it."

Ilsa took another sip of her cooling chocolate, swallowing hard past the sudden lump in her throat. Why did talking to Jo suddenly make her want to cry? "No, I'm fine. Well, I will be fine. I'm on my way to fine. I only …" She looked away. "I guess I got too close to Theo again. And … well, you know how it goes. It was good. But then he wanted to marry me, and of course I said no."

"Why 'of course'?"

"I don't need a husband, that's all. I'm fine on my own. And he didn't think it through, That's the real problem. He just did what he thought was right. Then he'd be poor and he'd never get to Europe, and then where would we be? And if even if he wasn't poor, he wouldn't understand." Ilsa knew that she wasn't making sense, but the tumble of words felt so good.

Jo tried hard to follow the plot of this particular story. "Not needing a husband and not wanting to get married are two different things, you know."

"I just don't think I have the patience for it all. Being a wife and a mother and keeping house and doing what someone else wants all the time. I have plans of my own." Ilsa took a deep breath. It was now or never. "I want to open a store," she blurted out. "In Vancouver. I've been planning and saving and I even have a meeting with a broker next week." She risked a glance at her friend, and Jo was smiling.

"That's wonderful. You should have told me ages ago, but it's still wonderful. I bet you'll be a millionaire by next Christmas." Ilsa was suddenly bashful in the face of Jo's enthusiasm. Why hadn't she told her earlier? Why hadn't she trusted Jo to be happy for her? "Did you tell Theo any of this?"

She shrugged. "He said he would understand if it was important to me. But I want to have a real business, like you do. Not a hobby. I don't want to watch my dream swallowed up by his."

She had recited variations of that little speech to herself a hundred times since that last night with Theo. Jo was staring thoughtfully out the window.

"I completely understand wanting to go at it alone, prove yourself, and all that. And if all your doctor really wants is to dress you up in pretty outfits and plop you in a parlour to serve tea forever, I'd be the first to tell you to chase him out of your life with a stick." She reached over to take Ilsa's hand. "But there's something to be said for having a partner when you set out on a big adventure. Sometimes you just can't do everything all on your own. Sometimes … sometimes you need somebody to help you carry the load for bit."

The lump in Ilsa's throat had returned worse than before. Maybe Theo could do that for her. She hadn't even given him the chance to try, and who knew if she'd ever find anyone like him again? Who knew if she'd ever even be able to fall in love with anyone else?

Oh God. She loved him, and she'd told him he didn't matter to her and that she didn't need him, and now he was gone.

"Oh, no. Oh please, don't cry," said Jo. "This is the first day in three weeks that I haven't cried. Don't make me start. I was trying to make you feel better, I swear!"

"What if I'm making a mistake?" Ilsa asked. "It's hard enough imagining not waking up in Fraser Springs, not talking with you over coffee."

Jo squeezed Ilsa's hand. "Well, I'm not saying I want you to run off right this instant, either. Lord knows I would keep you here forever if I could. But you shouldn't grow old and grey in this place just because you might make a mistake."

Ilsa wiped at her eyes with her free hand. "Well. You're the boss."

Their hug was interrupted by Owen walking into the kitchen. His normally cheerful expression seemed tight and pinched. "It's quiet in here. And why is everybody crying?"

"We're just happy." Jo gave him a kiss on the cheek when he leaned down. "A certain little miss has decided that sleeping isn't so bad."

"Well, that's the best news I've heard all day." Owen gave a wan smile. He hung his scarf and hat on a peg and went rummaging in the icebox. "God, I'd murder someone for a piece of pie."

"There's apple left," Jo said. "Meeting with Morse didn't go well?"

Owen fished out the pie, snatched a fork from the drying rack, and collapsed onto one of the battered kitchen chairs without bothering to plate anything. "That's an understatement. Sometimes Morse seems like a genius and sometimes ..." He speared an enormous hunk of pie straight out of the tin and wolfed it down as if he hadn't eaten in days. "Did you know that Dr.

Greyson was bottling the hot springs water for drinking? Selling it as some sort of miracle cure. And wait, it gets better. They were bottling it on days when Morse's damned mine dumped tailings into the hot springs. That's what was making everyone at the hotel sick. Arsenic. Thank God Dr. Whitacre worked it all out before anybody died."

Ilsa sat up a little straighter. "Theo's here?"

Owen nodded. "Took the boat back the minute he figured it out, apparently."

Someone knocked on the door. Owen looked annoyed and Jo looked puzzled, but Ilsa knew exactly who would be foolish enough to be bothering people at almost eleven o'clock at night. She rushed to open the door.

Sure enough, a slim young man wearing a perfectly tailored coat waited on the front porch. His spectacles fogged with condensation, and he took them off and tucked them in his coat pocket.

"I wasn't sure anyone would be awake," Theo said. "But I was walking. And I saw the light."

"No. We're all awake. I mean, I'm awake. And Jo's here."

She turned around to see if Jo had followed her from the kitchen, but her friend was already herding Owen and his half-eaten pie up the stairs. "Hello, Dr. Whitacre," Jo said cheerfully. "Don't mind us. And don't let all the warm air out, Ilsa. Good night!" And then they were standing, alone, in the front room of Wilson's.

Theo stepped farther in and pulled the door closed behind him. "Can I get you anything to drink?" she asked, because one had to start somewhere.

"No, I ..." It was probably because of the cold, but Theo's cheeks blazed with colour, and his green eyes seemed unusually bright. "Thank you. Could we sit?" Ilsa nodded and dropped down into one of the two armchairs, and Theo took the other.

"You're, um, back early."

Theo shrugged. "I made the most of my time. I thwarted an engagement, got accused of attempted murder—my mother is not currently speaking to me, you'll be sad to hear—discovered the source of an outbreak of arsenic poisoning, and quit my job."

Ilsa didn't know where to start with all of that, so she went with the simplest thing first. "You quit your job? At the hotel?"

"Effective immediately. Morse is probably having my belongings tossed out in the snow as we speak."

"Oh, Theo. Why?"

"It's a long story, and I promise I'll explain it all in a minute. But I had to tell you something while I've still got my courage up." Theo rummaged around in his pockets for moment, then gave up with a huff and took both of her hands in his. "I know you told me you don't need a husband. You certainly don't need me. I've always known that.

"And right now, I can't promise you anything. I don't have a job. I'm probably disinherited already. But I do know, without a single doubt, that I love you. And I want to be with you. I've spent weeks and weeks trying to convince myself to want anything else, and it's never once worked. Every second I spent in Vancouver would have been a million times better if you had been beside me."

There must be something wrong with her throat again—it was getting strangely difficult to breathe.

"And I know you don't need me," he went on in a rush, "But I think that we can make each others' lives better. I don't want to tie you down. I want to drink champagne at the opening of your store, and I want to go back to school, and we don't even have to be married if you don't want to, as long as we can be together. Maybe we can go to Europe and move to a different city every week. Or maybe you'll decide you want to have a dozen babies. I don't know. I really don't. But I'd like to find out. With you."

He reached into his pockets again. "Damn it. I'm going to do this properly, I swear." He pulled his hand from the breast pocket of his coat. "Here." He held up a thin silver ring. Even in the dim light, it gleamed.

"I know you said I didn't think it through before, but I had. I'd been thinking it through for six years. If I asked you to marry me again, is there even a chance you would say yes?"

"Yes." Her mouth answered the question before her brain caught up.

"If you don't want to hear it, I understand. But I need to ask, and …" Theo blinked. "Sorry. Did you say yes?"

"Yes," she repeated. Her hands were shaking.

Theo looked down at the ring and up at her. "I hadn't really prepared for a yes," he admitted. "What finger does this even go on?"

Ilsa laughed and took the ring from him. Up close, it was delicately engraved with flowers, and a chip of sapphire glinted in the centre of each one. It was the most beautiful, perfect thing she'd ever seen in her life. She slipped it onto the third finger of her left hand. "Perfect fit."

"I feel like maybe this is the part where we kiss," he whispered. And so they did. His hands were freezing as he pulled her over into his lap.

After a while, when they had both caught their breath, Ilsa noticed that it had started snowing again, in flurries of big fat flakes that almost rattled the window. "You can't go outside in this weather," she pointed out. "We'd better get you upstairs." She stood—her legs were surprisingly wobbly—and Theo grinned at her when she swayed and caught her balance on the back of his chair. She grabbed his hand and pulled him towards the stairs.

He reached for his cane. "That's a completely scandalous suggestion, and I'm only agreeing to endanger your reputation because it will break your heart if I freeze to death outside of the St. Alice."

She'd forgotten that he probably couldn't go back to the St. Alice. "You're lucky I said yes."

Theo looked at her with that scholarly concentration that she loved so much. "I am," he whispered. "I really am."

EPILOGUE

The Vancouver World, Social Pages, June 17 1914, Evening Edition, A12

by Miss Imogen Thornbush

In a big city like Vancouver, a society gal can develop a terrible case of what the French call *déjà vu*. The same faces and the same jokes at every party, and a dear friend of this author once remarked that if she had to eat even one more bite of aspic, she'd turn into jelly and roll away down the street. The gossip, too, can get sadly stale around the edges. All you dainty darlings are so well behaved that you don't give us nearly enough to write about!

So it with great pleasure that I report to you that last night, our social scene was shaken up in the most invigorating manner. And where did this grand revitalization take place, you may ask? Not a soiree or a fundraiser or a dinner party, but at a funeral luncheon!

Attentive readers may recall the rather confusing scandal surrounding Dr. Theodore Whitacre some few years ago. The Whitacre name needs, of course, no introduction, but its handsome young scion has always been a bit of a cipher. To say that he was a reluctant participant in the social whirl is to put it mildly, and then he disappeared as if in a puff of smoke. (Some say he went into hiding on the Continent after poisoning an enemy, but we don't like to spread rumours.) It seems that Dr. Whitacre is rapidly becoming the Sherlock Holmes of the medical world, and only the passing of his father could fetch the prodigal son home. What's more, he has resurfaced with a most charming European wife on his arm.

Darlings, I can only say that the lovely new Mrs. Whitacre is a breath of fresh air in our musty drawing rooms. I have it on the best authority that she has studied in some of the finest fashion houses of Paris, and I can personally confirm that she has a simply uncanny eye for cut and color. Devoted readers of this column will be familiar with my tragic quest to wear pastels, which have always been at war with my complexion. No more! Mrs. Whitacre took one look at me and declared that I would look a treat in mint green. When I visited my dressmaker this morning, she draped me in mint green silk, and had dear Mrs. Whitacre been at my side, I would have fallen on my knees in gratitude.

What's next for the lively Whitacres? (Whoever would have thought one would use the term "lively" to describe a Whitacre! The dowager Mrs. Whitacre gave her new in-law a rather frosty reception, but I suppose no woman of a certain age likes being shown up, especially not on the occasion of her husband's funeral.)

Dr. Whitacre has been engaged to bring his diagnostic expertise to St. Paul's Hospital, where he will make a welcome addition to their esteemed ranks.

A little bird tells me that Mrs. Whitacre will be available to design custom gowns for her closest friends. Even more exciting, she will be opening a *boutique* near Woodward's to provide all the bits and bobs a stylish gal might need to update last year's gowns for this year's styles. Mrs. Whitacre assures me that these little touches are at the very heart of what makes French women the envy of the fashionable world.

So welcome to the Whitacres! Saying *bonjour* to a little Parisian glamour is exactly what our fair berg needs. Whatever Mrs. Whitacre is designing, I will be the first in line to buy.

About the Author

Laine Ferndale teaches literature and writing to pay for a fairly serious chai latte habit. She lives with her husband and her adorably needy cat.

Find Laine Ferndale on Facebook and on Twitter @laineferndale.

Printed in the United States
By Bookmasters